Selfless Love

By

Natasha Hughes Smith

The Reflections Series

Cover design by Faith Riggs

Published by Talking Stories with Natasha

Email: authornatasha@yahoo.com.

Copyright 2023 Natasha Hughes Smith

Paperback ISBN 979-8988977001

For the last few years, Shannon had been living vicariously through her best friend, Vivian Johnston-Barrington, who had married a millionaire and the love of her life, Vincent Barrington. Shannon had settled on the belief that she must not deserve the happiness that Vivian had found and she definitely must not deserve that type of man. Successful men were elusive to Shannon and when she did happen to date one, he shared the same narcissistic personality as the poor ones that crossed her path, but times ten. Subsequently, she would stop focusing on dating; instead, she would just enjoy attending grand affairs with her bestie, traveling the world with her and being the best godmother to Vivian's son, little Bernie.

Shannon contemplated the last few years as she unpacked the last box from her move. She had just purchased a large home in the Jefferson-Chalmers neighborhood in the Canal District of Detroit, Michigan. Her new home was a huge red brick American-style Foursquare home with an attached garage. It was easily 4,000 square feet with a semi-enclosed porch and a large enclosed balcony off the master bedroom. It sat on the Canal District which was affectionately called the Venice of Detroit providing those homes with backyard access to the Detroit River and Lake Saint Clair. Although she didn't own a boat, that would be the next item she saved up to buy; purchasing that home had already set her back and the deposit ate up most of her discretionary savings.

She could smell the fresh pot of chili simmering on the stovetop; she wasn't the best cook in the world when it came to non-soul food dishes, but she wanted to serve something homemade to her friends. She had invited Vivian and Gloria over to see her new home and she had promised to cook for them. But if they were smart, they probably would nibble on something before coming over, thought Shannon, as she walked to the kitchen to check on the dish. She had to admit that it indeed smelled delicious; maybe she had outdone herself this time. She stirred the pot and then tasted the chili.

"Ok, girl! Not bad!", laughed Shannon as she turned off the stovetop.

She eyed the kitchen clock and realized that her prompt friends would be there any minute and she needed to make sure that everything was ready. She gave a quick once over to be sure her place was kid-friendly; she didn't want any mishaps for her little Bernie. Vivian was going to leave him with his grandparents, but she had insisted on seeing him. Just then, she heard the doorbell and she used the app on her ever-present phone to speak to her guests. She noticed that it was indeed Vivian and Gloria on her front porch.

"Just a minute, ladies!", Shannon announced as she rushed to open the door for her friends. "Hello, sweethearts. Come on in! Especially this one!", exclaimed Shannon as she took Bernie from Vivian's arms.

"Hey there, girlie! Your home is gorgeous!", Gloria complimented as she entered.

"I agree. I just love the older homes now.", cosigned Vivian as she entered and began looking at the ceiling.

"I just bet you do, that Barrington Estate will make anyone fall in love with woodwork. Maybe that's the real reason I selected this beauty.", confessed Shannon.

Shannon's home was an interior designer's dream; the previous owners had maintained the antique features that gave life to that architectural design but paired it with modern updates. There were wooden beams framing the ceiling and door trim coupled with a wide wooden staircase that captured the attention of guests as the focal point at entry. To either side of the small foyer were rooms. To the left was the formal dining room that led to the massive kitchen and to the right was an enormous living room that spanned back to the rear of the home. There it merged with the family room which was off the breakfast eating area that sat adjacent to the kitchen.

Shannon beckoned for the ladies to step into the foyer as she closed the door. She put Bernie on his feet and he immediately noticed the toys she had waiting for him in the living room.

"Go play sweetheart.", Shannon said gently, "He makes me want another one."

"God no! Not with my brother!", insisted Vivian.

"Say that!", agreed Gloria hating to speak ill of Joe.

"Well, there's no need to worry. Joe got a vasectomy years ago. It was probably a blessing in disguise.", concluded Shannon.

"Yes, Lord. Thank you, Jesus!", Gloria shouted as she waved her hand in praise.

"Stop it, girl!", laughed Shannon as she playfully hit Gloria's raised hand.

"Wait a minute! When has he ever worked a job that offered health insurance, but knowing him he probably got it done in someone's basement.", laughed Gloria.

Vivian joined in with Gloria until they noticed that Shannon wasn't laughing with them.

"I added him to my health insurance for a while as my live-together-partner.", Shannon said in a near whisper out of embarrassment.

"Live-together-partner? You guys have never lived together!", expressed a shocked and bewildered Vivian.

"On paper we did.", sighed Shannon as she tried to hide her face in her hands.

"What else have you lied about doing … on paper? I hope he's not getting your 401K!", fumed Gloria as if Shannon were her child.

"I'm dumb about him, but not plain dumb.", Shannon defended herself.

"Child, the jury is still out on that one!", Gloria said as she shook her head in disappointment.

Vivian tried to make light of the situation as she could see the discussion could go way left and they could end up bashing the pitiful love story of Shannon and Joe. It was worth bashing, but she just wanted to forget that it ever existed.

"If we keep talking about my brother or his junk, I won't be able to eat that delicious chili I smell.", Vivian said with sisterly disgust and frustration with her best friend.

Shannon was all too happy to comply, especially since everything she was saying about him, made her look even more foolish than she felt about her past actions.

"Ok, I promise. No more talk of Joe Johnston Jr.", vowed Shannon, "Come on ladies. Let me give you a quick tour of the main level."

"Great!", Vivian delighted.

"I know I'm about to sound old-fashioned, but …", Gloria started.

"It's okay, you always do.", added Shannon with a giggle.

"Ha, ha, ha. But seriously, why did you make this huge purchase on your own? Why not do it with a husband?", Gloria inquired.

"You sound just like my grandparents. You guys got to understand that there is no guarantee that I will ever get married. Look at how old Nicole is now. She's 19 and it hasn't happened yet.

I can't put my life, goals and dreams on hold anymore. Everyone isn't as lucky as Vivian.", confessed Shannon.

The sadness in Shannon's eyes didn't go unnoticed; Vivian hated that Shannon felt unseen by quality men. She tried to explain to Shannon that she shut them out in every way imaginable. Shannon's body language and words completely stopped them in their tracks. Vivian had witnessed it and noticed those same good men were afraid to approach Shannon.

"Well, if you keep yourself open to possibilities, you never know what could happen.", suggested Vivian as she took Shannon's hand.

"Yes, preach!", agreed Gloria as she took Shannon's other hand.

"What? I *am* open.", Shannon defended as she guided the two through her home by the hand.

"Prove it!", Vivian insisted.

"Ok, how?", Shannon accepted the challenge.

Gloria listened attentively to the plan as Vivian laid out her agenda.

"I was just talking to Vincent the other day about his good friend who's single. He's handsome, tall and a managing partner at his family's law firm. He comes from a wealthy family that has been rich as long as the Barringtons.", Vivian smiled as she delivered his credentials.

"Ooh, tell me more. Is he a blonde or redhead?", Shannon asked with piqued interest.

"He has model good looks, caramel skin and hazel eyes.", began Vivian.

"Huh?", questioned a confused Shannon.

"He's African-American. His name is Raymond Brown II.", beamed Vivian.

"He has my vote!", Gloria chimed in and clapped her hands in excitement.

"Not mine.", informed Shannon, "Let's eat. You can see the rest of the place later."

"See, that's what we're talking about! She just threw up the closed sign!", concluded Gloria as she shook her head in disappointment.

"She sure did.", agreed Vivian speaking as if Shannon wasn't a part of the conversation.

"You both know I prefer to date white guys. Black men are not into me. I've tried.", Shannon explained as she pulled away from Vivian.

"God knows, every relationship you've had with a white guy hasn't been successful. I don't see you giving up on *them*.", Gloria declared.

"Exactly, my brother being prime example number one.", mumbled Vivian as she held up her index finger.

"I thought you didn't want to discuss him anymore.", Shannon threw her head back in frustration, "I don't know if I want to meet this Raymond guy or not. I don't have time for another disappointment.", whined Shannon as she shuffled her feet as she walked to the cabinet for bowls.

"Vivian, tell me, what is his heart like? Did he hang with Vincent's old crew you used to tell me about?", inquired Gloria as if asking for herself.

"Oh, no. Raymond never did and thank goodness that Vincent let his old friends go. Vincent realized he had outgrown them, so he reconnected with Raymond and Giovanni, old childhood acquaintances. Both guys are great fun, loyal and caring.", explained Vivian as she walked to the refrigerator to check for beverages.

"Good!", sighed Gloria.

"Well, give me Giovanni then! Tell me about him.", complained Shannon.

"No, he's the youngest and not ready to settle down. He's Giovanni Bianchi and a young playboy like his father. Trust me on this!", Vivian warned her friend.

"The old mob boss' son?", questioned Gloria.

"Yes, but his father went legitimate back in the late 70s, so Giovanni runs those businesses from what I heard. That family has major bank also!", informed Vivian.

"Yeah, dirty money.", concluded Gloria.

"Isn't it all dirty money when you get to the level of the Barringtons and possibly even the Browns.", Shannon interjected.

Vivian looked uneasy after the comment and Gloria shrugged her shoulders contemplating the truth of the statement.

"Well, I'm sure that boy can dip his foot right back into murky waters if he wanted. I'm sure he still has connections to the mob. You need to go to church and meet a real *good fella*.", fussed Gloria.

"You know that might be a great idea.", agreed Vivian.

"Really, Vivian did you go to church with Gloria to meet a *good fella*?", Shannon asked sarcastically.

"No, I was looking for a wealthy man.", Vivian disclosed.

"Exactly and I'm looking for a white one. Neither of which is there! Besides, I want to have sex; so, we can count the church guys *completely* out! Ok!", Shannon dismissed the idea.

"I forgot that you like bad boys.", Vivian teased her best friend.

"You two are ridiculous and liking a bad boy is even *more* ridiculous!", Gloria chastised.

"No, I do not! I like good men too, but they just aren't drawn to me like the bad boys.", contemplated Shannon.

"Again, prove it. Let's go back to my original suggestion, Raymond. There's a fundraiser coming up for the children's hospital; my husband and I can introduce you two. It can be like a first date but you'll have Vincent and me there as a buffer.", suggested Vivian as she poured a glass of soda pop.

"That sounds really good. Pour me a glass of pop too. Thanks.", Gloria said as she pushed her glass across the island to Vivian.

"Gloria, are you the one being set up?", Shannon teased as she looked uncertain, "I still don't know how I feel about this."

"Just try something new. If it doesn't work out, I won't ever try to hook you up again.", begged Vivian.

"Please try it!", Gloria persisted.

"Ok, ok, ok!", Shannon said emphasizing with her hands by holding them up as if surrendering. "If it turns out to be a disaster, I'm not going to let you forget it!", Shannon swore her vengeance.

"Yes! Believe me, you won't be disappointed!", squealed Vivian as she put down Gloria's glass to hug and kiss Shannon on the cheek.

"Now, I probably need to go shopping to buy a nice outfit.", sighed Shannon then she covered her face with her hands.

"Ooh, a shopping trip. When is the fundraiser?", asked Gloria.

"Yeah, when?", inquired Shannon.

"This coming Friday.", Vivian said as she grimaced with an eye closed.

"I have less than a week! We need to go shopping today or tomorrow and Gloria will have to skip church!", exclaimed Shannon.

"I am not skipping out on the Lord; He hasn't done that to me. So, you girls can have fun without me.", informed Gloria.

"Yeah, it would be better to go tomorrow so I can leave little Bernie at home.", agreed Vivian.

"Ok, so I can meet you at the Somerset Collection and you can help me find the perfect outfit or dress.", suggested Shannon.

"You look stunning in dresses; so, I think you should wear one. In fact, it'll be my treat!", recommended Vivian.

"Vivian, girl, you don't have to do that!", insisted Shannon.

"You're right, but I want to. You need to nab this man!", laughed Vivian.

Vivian was exhausted by the countless loser tales that Shannon had shared over the years; now that she had leveled up so should her best friend.

"You do so much for others, let someone do something nice for you for once.", Gloria insisted as she reached for Shannon's hand.

"I agree!", exclaimed Vivian as she placed Shannon's other hand beneath her chin and begged with her eyes.

"Ok, I'll let you spoil me this *one* time.", Shannon conceded.

"Yes!", shouted Vivian as she hugged Shannon, "And the next time we go there, you'll have Raymond's credit cards!"

Shannon and Vivian shouted with laughter with Gloria ready to chastise them.

"Ok, my two little gold diggers!", laughed Gloria then she thought about her own love life, "Wait a minute! Does he have a young uncle?"

The ladies were shouting and laughing so loudly that little Bernie came running to see what he was missing out on.

"What you doing Mommy?", said little Bernie as he walked around the island to see what was going on. Once he saw there was nothing exciting going on he shook his head and blurted, "No fun."

He ran back to his toys which were far more entertaining than what he saw happening in the kitchen. The ladies couldn't control their laughter as they watched his little legs dash from the kitchen.

"My delicious chili is getting cold. You better eat my food! I slaved hours over this chili. Here!", Shannon playfully fussed as she piled a heaping scoop of chili in the bowl and handed it to Vivian.

"Girl, that is too much food!", complained Vivian.

"The way you and Vincent go at it, you'll be pregnant again soon! You'll need this nutrition.", laughed Shannon as she shoved the bowl into Vivian's hands.

"Don't give me that much, I'm way past the baby-making years!", laughed Gloria, "But you hook me up with Raymond's rich uncle, I and the Lord *will* work something out. Just call me Sarah, honey."

Again, the ladies laughed so much that they couldn't see past their tears and Shannon could barely breathe. It was the first time in a while that Shannon was allowing herself to be excited about a prospect, but she didn't want to get her hopes up too high.

Chapter 2

Raymond became less enthused each day which drew closer to the fundraiser and now it was a day away. He normally would be ecstatic about the event; he loved the reporters, cameras and socialites. As the committee chairman, he was extremely proud of his work; but he had promised his best friend, Vincent, that he would allow him and his wife to set him up on a blind date. He wasn't sure that they even knew what he really liked; there were times when he wasn't even sure himself. He tried dating whoever was in season; when light-skinned girls were in, he tried that. When big butts and hips became popular, he tried that too and was shut down at every turn by every curvy brown dime piece that he approached. He finally found his niche when he started dating white girls.

Raymond felt they were easier to please and had less attitude, and they were basically more palatable to his mother and grandmother. He liked them well enough, but over the years he felt something was missing. When he needed to vent his emotions over some of the discriminatory actions of the day, the ladies couldn't relate and quickly dismissed his emotions. How could he marry someone who couldn't empathize with his deepest hurt and emotions? He yearned for a woman who could understand that he was Black first and rich second. Vincent and Vivian reassured him that Shannon was someone special; that she had a deep sensibility and heart as well as being extremely intelligent. When they told him she was African -American, he cringed.

How could he be so powerful in business and in life and be so afraid of meeting Shannon, he thought as he stood looking out his expansive view atop the beautiful Penobscot building in downtown Detroit. It was named after a Native American tribe from Maine. It was designed in the art deco style of 1905 and stood 100 feet tall; it was a brilliant piece of art and there he was rich, handsome, successful, connected and afraid of a woman he didn't even know. Before he could dive headfirst into a sea of self-pity, the intercom buzzed.

"Sir.", Roberta greeted her boss.

"Yes, Roberta. What do you need?", Raymond inquired.

"Mr. Barrington is on the line for you. Should I transfer the call?", asked Roberta.

"Yes of course.", replied Raymond; damn, he thought, he's going to ask me about the upcoming date.

"Ray! How are you? How are you feeling about tomorrow?", Vincent asked eager to hear Raymond's excitement.

Here we go, thought Raymond.

"I'm good now, but I don't know how I'll feel tomorrow. How are you?", asked Raymond hoping to redirect the conversation.

"Forget how I'm doing! Why aren't you feeling good? You're not thinking about backing out, are you?", Vincent voiced concern.

"You know … I don't … it doesn't end well with Black girls. I hate hearing myself say it, but it's true.", explained Raymond.

"Well, forget about every other Black woman you have ever dated, any woman for that matter because Shannon is something special.", informed Vincent.

"Really, I've heard that before.", Raymond said doubting the validity of Vincent's accolades.

"Have I ever tried to hook you up before?", Vincent inquired then answered as Raymond opened his mouth to respond. "No, I try to mind my own business so people know to mind theirs. So, you can trust me on this.", Vincent reassured his best friend.

15

"If *you* say so. I won't back out, just so you know the Browns have never sired any cowards.", Raymond announced proudly.

"Good to know. See you tomorrow.", laughed Vincent.

"Okay, bye.", sighed Raymond after proclaiming a false bravado.

He decided he would put on a brave face and meet the infamous Shannon Washington despite his many reservations.

"Shannon Washington, I'm not afraid of you.", Raymond paused as he pondered her name; it hit him that she would have the same hyphenated name as his proud, glamorous and formidable grandmother if they married. "Why the fuck am I thinking about if we get married? God, please don't let her be like my grandmother.", he said as he rested his face in his hands.

Shannon had not been on her A-game that week. She spent all week tempted to call Vivian to cancel the date. She started the week excited and then with each passing day she became jaded and negative about Raymond Brown. What type of dorky name is Raymond Brown, she thought. She heard her phone vibrate on her work desk and she looked down sensing already who it was and sure enough, it was Vivian.

"Hey, girlie, what's up?", asked Shannon knowing it would be about the fundraiser.

"Hey. Are you all set for tomorrow evening?", Vivian questioned.

"Yeah, but some of us do still have jobs.", Shannon deflected.

"Like that's ever stopped you from doing stuff for yourself during the day. Did you forget that I know you?", laughed Vivian.

"Well, to be honest, I'm thinking about canceling. I don't have time to be disappointed.", Shannon insisted.

"You don't have any problem with it any other time.", laughed Vivian as she thought of Shannon's past boyfriends. "Besides, you won't be! This is a really good one! My sweetheart wouldn't be friends with him otherwise.", Vivian persuaded.

"Well, Vincent has become quite discerning since he became a new man.", Shannon rationalized out loud.

"Okay, that settles it then! I want to treat you to a day at the spa tomorrow before the event. Please take the day off.", Vivian pleaded.

"I'm surprised you waited until the last minute to ask me.", Shannon said surprised by Vivian's lack of planning.

"Well, you have Vincent to thank for that. It was his idea. He assumed I had set up a spa day for us and when I said no, he said I needed to get on it. So, here I am, getting on it.", Vivian giggled.

"Okay, Vincent! Whatever you did to change him, I need to use on Joe.", laughed Shannon.

"Not funny. We are not wasting time talking about my loser brother anymore. He is out! Done! Never to be discussed again!", Vivian fussed loudly.

"Okay, calm down! You are right in my ear! I'll try not to think of the one who shall not be named.", Shannon acquiesced.

"Sorry about that; you know how I get about my brother. Anyway, I'll send a driver to pick you up in the morning around 10 am. We'll go to the spa and the stylist for hair and make-up. Sound good?", Vivian offered.

"Yeah, sounds like an awesome plan.", Shannon approved the gesture.

"Great! See you in the morning. Bye.", squealed Vivian.

"Okay, bye!", exclaimed Shannon as anticipation returned.

How could she not be excited about the event with her best friend bubbling with excitement? It really would be great if they both had extremely successful and rich husbands. To think, they would be best friends married to best friends. Subsequently, Shannon would be truly able to relate to the new lifestyle that Vivian had obtained. They could take turns sending drivers to pick each other up or treating each other to spa days and vacations. Shannon leaned back in her office chair as she daydreamed forgetting she was in her small cubicle until she bumped into the flimsy wall almost knocking it over.

"Shit!", fumed Shannon as she readjusted the flimsy wall unit. No more cubicles for me when I land Mr. Rich, thought Shannon, as she repositioned the wall.

Friday started with a blur, Shannon mindlessly did the spa and hair day with Vivian. She was so nervous that she was in a daze the entire time and couldn't retell the morning's events to a soul, not even to save her own life. The evening arrived much quicker than anticipated. She nervously handed her car over to the valet attendant as she smoothed down her dress to make an entrance. Oddly, she felt that the event would change her life forever; one would think that would be exciting, but instead, she was petrified.

Shannon sneaked into the facility and managed to dodge Vivian and Vincent whom she saw enter the ballroom. She went the opposite way to avoid them a little while longer and ducked inside the ladies' restroom just outside the elegant ballroom of the Colony Club. There, she eyed her reflection in the mirror. Vivian had outdone herself when she recommended that dress to Shannon; it was stunning and she had to admit she made it even more so.

The dress was an orange one-shoulder maxi dress with a peek-a-boo crystal bodice and a high split and a side bow. The bodice was attention-grabbing so she opted to wear large rhinestone tear-drop earrings instead of a necklace. She wore a short pixie hairstyle; her soft black curls framed her heart-shaped face perfectly to highlight her pouty copper lips and her dramatic cat-eye as it shimmered with matching eyeshadow. The dress accentuated her large breast, tiny waist and full hips; and the shoes, oh the shoes, she thought. Her shoes were three-inch Stiletto heels dipped in copper-hued crystals like her bodice making her normal five-foot-eight-inch frame almost six feet. She had the perfect curvy hourglass figure that drew more attention than Shannon realized.

Raymond took notice like most of the men that watched her airy footsteps as she entered the restroom. He was tempted to wait for her to exit so that he could speak and perhaps introduce himself, but the more he thought about it that seemed borderline stalker-like behavior. So, he entered the ballroom to search for Vincent and Vivian. After entering, he spotted them and he was about to approach them when he caught a glimpse of the curvy dark-chocolate beauty entering the ballroom from the hall. He was hesitant to approach for a number of reasons, what if Shannon spotted him and secondly, the beauty was African American? Her pouty lips shouted attitude, but those curves beckoned him to come near.

"What the hell.", whispered Raymond as he confidently decided to approach the beauty.

Shannon nervously eyed the crowd to see where Vincent and Vivian were, but she was distracted by the sexy caramel-skinned hunk that was approaching her. He had curly hair that she imagined running her slender fingers through as she gently dragged her long nails along his scalp. Perhaps she should talk with this sexy devil instead of being bored by Raymond Brown. No sexy man could ever be named Raymond, thought Shannon, as she smiled at the approaching tall eye candy.

Raymond wore a three-piece black tuxedo; the vest had midnight blue trim along the v-fold on the vest. The midnight blue buttons on it were stitched at a diagonal cut giving it a contemporary vibe. He paired the tailor-made suit with a midnight checkered blue tie, matching cuff links and patent-leather loafers with antiqued gold bit hardware across the vamp of the shoe. Just as he had spotted her, she had become mesmerized by him. Raymond noticed that she had been scanning the crowd as he began to approach; he hoped she wasn't looking for her date or worse, her husband.

"Hello. You look absolutely delectable. I hope you aren't looking for someone?", Raymond inquired but praying to God above that she was not.

Shannon blushed at his compliment and straightforward approach; there was no doubt that he was interested. She liked and appreciated his approach.

"Thank you. Just my best friend. And you?", informed Shannon.

There was no way this well-put-together man was single, thought Shannon as she eyed the room to see if a woman was ready to spring into attack mode.

Raymond smiled coyly glad that she had noticed him as well. "The same as you. I invited my best friend and his wife; I had been looking for them.", explained Raymond.

Cynicism crept in like an old unwanted friend causing Shannon to look him up and down while she waited for the ball to drop. He was perfect she thought, what's the catch? Raymond stood proudly as she examined him from head to toe. Raymond surmised there was no doubt in his mind that he was handsome and she obviously thought he was fly.

"What do you think of my event? I'm the committee leader and I spearhead this event yearly", Raymond asked the knockout beauty hoping to impress her.

And there it was, he's arrogant; I knew something had to be wrong with him, thought Shannon.

"It's like most. I attend events like this often.", Shannon informed as she glanced pretending not to be impressed although she actually was.

"I thought we did a pretty good job.", Raymond chuckled embarrassedly.

He started to think it was a mistake approaching her and that he should have waited to be introduced to his date. Perhaps she likes talking about herself, he thought.

"Tell me about yourself. What do you do for a living?", he asked, hoping to relax her.

So, now he's looking for a sugar momma? I am not the one boo, I am *NOT* the one, she thought.

"I'm an IT consultant and engineer.", Shannon provided as she started searching the crowd again for Vivian.

It was quite clear that she was bored with him and the conversation was done, but Raymond didn't want to give up. He figured he'd have her attention once he informed her what he did for a living.

"I'm the Managing ...", Raymond stopped abruptly when she interrupted him.

"I see my friend.", Shannon informed rudely and she looked over his shoulder to wave frantically at Vivian to be rescued.

She quickly darted past Raymond as she rushed to Vivian's side. He was stunned by her behavior and frozen in place; he didn't even turn around to see where or to whom she was rushing. He had never been so embarrassed in public before. He needed to find a drink to calm him or he wouldn't be in the right mindset to even meet Shannon. If he didn't find a libation right away, he was going to take out his frustration with the elusively rude beauty on Shannon.

Raymond quickly flagged down a waiter who was dispersing champagne; he gulped it down like water and quickly reached for another when he heard his name. He saw his other best friend approaching him.

"Ray!", Giovanni greeted him with their signature cool handshake, "Are you excited about this blind date Vincent has planned for you?"

"Hell no! Then I made things worse by approaching a gorgeous lady. I haven't seen a woman that pretty since finding pictures of my grandmother from back in the day.", expressed a frustrated Raymond.

"Ok, being strung out on your grandmother, is a little sick.", teased Giovanni.

"Admiring my grandmother's beauty is not sick.", insisted Raymond.

"Whatever, lighten up. So, what happened? I guess you fucked it up in some way. Did the two ladies meet?", inquired Giovanni eager for a good laugh.

"No, they didn't thank goodness. This chick really got under my skin.", explained Raymond still whirling from their encounter.

"Ok, tell me about this chick you met.", Giovanni pried.

"This chick had curves in all the right places, you know? Her dress was sexy as hell; she looked sophisticated and elegant, but when we talked, she was rude as hell and she lost interest really quickly.", Raymond said between gulps of his drink.

"Maybe you'll have better luck with the hook-up.", suggested Giovanni as he sipped his much stiffer drink.

"Yeah.", Raymond said without much hope or enthusiasm.

Giovanni found it hilarious and couldn't wait to see how this blind date looked; as far as he was concerned, any woman who needed to be hooked up wasn't worth the hook-up.

"Raymond!", exclaimed Vincent as he approached his pals when he really wanted to say slow down on the booze, "Are you ready?"

"Yeah, if she's nicer than the sexy chick I just tried to holler at.", explained Raymond as he stared at his empty glass in frustration.

Despite being embarrassed by the mystery woman, he still couldn't get over how beautiful she was. He was even ready to vent about it to his best friend. He was about to tell Vincent about the sexy curvy vixen when Vincent brought his attention to Vivian.

"Here's your date now, coming with Vivian.", Vincent announced.

Raymond turned to see that said rude vixen was approaching along with Vivian.

"Damn!", whispered Raymond.

Damn, thought a stunned Shannon; she and Raymond both looked annoyed and frustrated. Vivian noticed the expressions on their faces and didn't understand why they would be so openly rude; however, Giovanni and Vincent had a pretty good idea. Giovanni didn't bother to hold in his amusement and began laughing as he sipped his drink waiting for the show to begin.

"Hello, guys. Raymond I'd like to introduce you to my best friend, Shannon Washington. Shannon, this is Raymond Brown II,

Vincent's best friend.", Vivian excitedly introduced the pair hoping she could soon rectify their expressions.

"We met earlier; however, we didn't introduce ourselves. I've just been referring to her as the rude woman I just met.", Raymond partially confessed.

Giovanni choked on his drink then he mumbled, "You mean rude curvy sexy chick."

Raymond cut him a quick glare to stop him from saying another word.

"I'm rude? You were the one bragging about yourself!", insisted Shannon then she whispered to Vivian, "Not impressed."

Vincent couldn't make out what Shannon had whispered to Vivian, but her expression screamed disinterest and perhaps some foul language. But even Ray Charles could see that Vincent and Vivian had their hands full if they wanted a relationship between their best friends to work out. Vivian and Vincent made eye contact and their eyes spoke a thousand words to each other.

"I'm sure Raymond wasn't bragging.", laughed Vivian hoping to convince Raymond that Shannon was teasing. "Raymond did you tell Shannon that you sit on the planning committee for this event.", asked Vivian.

Raymond attempted to speak, but Shannon interjected a response on his behalf.

"He sure did. I guess you have a lot of free time on your hands. I guess your firm does not have much work nowadays.", answered Shannon as if someone had asked her.

Vivian pinched Shannon and whispered, "What the hell are you doing?"

Don't start that shit, thought Vivian as she stared flabbergasted at her friend.

"As I tried to tell you, I am the Managing Partner at my family's law firm. I make my own schedule and my time is my own.", informed Raymond annoyed that he couldn't explain it to her before.

"Shannon has such a sarcastic sense of humor!", lied Vincent with an uneasy chuckle.

He eyed Vivian to convey that she needed to snatch Shannon away and get her straight. Vivian acknowledged her husband with her eyes and excused Shannon and herself.

"Gentlemen, please excuse Shannon and me. I need her assistance with my dress. I don't know what's wrong with my back zipper.", lied Vivian as she manhandled her friend's hand and practically dragged her off to the ladies' room.

The pair forced fake smiles on their faces as they dashed out of the ballroom, but Vivian couldn't contain herself until they reached the restroom.

"Shannon, what in the hell! I told you Raymond comes from a very wealthy family. What was up with that attitude? Do you think I'd lie and set you up with a working stiff? This man comes from old money; I already told you that his family has been rich as long as the Barringtons! Did you forget?", fumed Vivian in a mock whisper.

Shannon was embarrassed by her own behavior; she was acting like she didn't trust that her friend had the best intentions at heart. However, if she were honest with herself, the problem was that her absent father had taught her not to trust men who looked like him.

"I don't know what got into me. I guess something hit a trigger.", confessed Shannon.

"You *are* the trigger. You are always self-sabotaging. Please don't do that this time!", begged Vivian as she gripped both of Shannon's hands and held them to her heart.

Shannon noticed that Vivian was close to tears and it caused all their heartfelt moments since high school to come flooding back. Shannon could feel her own tears begin to bubble to the surface; there had been so many times when she cried in Vivian's arms. Vivian was there every single time Joe crushed her heart under his feet. Shannon wondered if maybe Raymond was different and could be that special someone. There was no denying that she was extremely attracted to him, more than she had been to any man; to be honest, it frightened her to her very core.

"I promise I won't be rude to him anymore. I won't embarrass you and Vincent.", vowed Shannon as she hugged Vivian tightly.

Vivian smiled delightedly as she wiped away her tears and the two entered the ballroom hand-in-hand. Raymond noticed the return of the two ladies as they smiled as if the bombshell hadn't been rude as hell before leaving. Let's see which Shannon has returned, thought Raymond, the sweet and lovable one that Vincent and Vivian can't stop bragging about or the bitch that he met earlier.

"Raymond … I apologize for my reactions earlier. It has been a heck of a week leading up to this event. I'm not myself.", Shannon fibbed.

"No worries, I guess … I do understand that jobs can be very stressful.", lied Raymond.

He loved his career and what was stressful for some, energized him to accomplish his best work. He noticed a glimpse of an annoyed expression on Shannon's face that quickly disappeared. She hated for anyone to speak of her work as a job;

she considered it a career and her talent, far from that of a menial job.

"Yes.", Shannon faked agreement.

Vincent, like Vivian, realized things were very awkward and decided he would suggest heading to their table. Giovanni was all too eager to follow silently as directed with a Cheshire cat smile all the way. Vincent stayed back as he reached for Vivian's hand.

"I hope you had a good talk with her. I've never seen her act like that before.", expressed a concerned Vincent.

"She gets that way when she's scared, my poor sweet thing.", Vivian confided as she tapped his hand to reassure him that it wouldn't last.

Vincent bestowed a doubtful look at his wife as they followed their friends to their assigned seats. The pair saw Shannon playing nice as she allowed Raymond to assist her with her chair. The married couple sighed an audible relief that maybe the night wouldn't be a bust after all.

Shannon was determined to push through her doubts about Raymond Brown and try to get to know him for the sake of her friends. Besides, he was the best catch she had ever been introduced to and she definitely hadn't dated anyone on his level.

As the night progressed, Shannon reverted back to that fearful schoolgirl as she sat listening to his intellectual conversation. He was so attentive and had seemingly forgiven her rude outburst from earlier. She sat doe-eyed and for most of their conversation, her mind was swirling with thoughts of her past, her fears and a glimmer of hope for the future. If someone quizzed her on their discussion, she surely would fail.

"I'm working with a task force to address some of the changes in laws that have resulted in protecting business owners at the expense of injured customers.", Raymond continued his discussion.

Raymond noticed her child-like eyes, gone was the defensive stare; she looked innocent, scared and in awe of him. He realized at that moment she was a complicated woman and it would require great skill to unlock the pieces of the puzzle that was presented to him. Fortunately for them both, he felt he was *man* enough to unlock the treasure that sat beside him. His countenance softened and he wanted to be the protector and defender that he saw she needed him to be. The protector who honored her heart, her body and her talents; someone who truly saw her value and cherished it.

"Again, I am truly sorry for how we got off on the wrong foot. I would love an opportunity to make it up to you so you can see I know how to treat a woman.", Raymond boldly confessed.

"That would be nice!", Shannon said coyly although inwardly saying she would give it a shot for Vivian's sake.

"May I have your number?", asked Raymond.

As Shannon provided her number, Raymond made a silent vow that he would be the man that she could depend on and could lay her vulnerability before him trusting him to protect and shield it.

Chapter 3

Shannon was still on a rollercoaster ride from the fundraiser; as her thoughts relived the events of that night, her emotions went from embarrassed to thrilled and then hopeful. Despite her almost blowing the whole thing to hell, Raymond surprisingly had wanted to exchange numbers. He had already called her a couple of times and it was just Wednesday. He certainly wasn't like her usual guys; those guys didn't have time to talk unless they were checking for sex. Shannon found it so strange to actually have mature conversations with a suiter; it was a whole new world, she thought as she swirled in her office chair. It was indeed unfamiliar territory.

The buzzing phone on her desk brought her focus back to the reality at hand; she noticed that it was Vivian, who probably more than likely wanted an update.

"Hey, Vivian.", Shannon greeted.

"You sound happy. So that means things must be good between you and Raymond and headed in the right direction.", Vivian proclaimed.

"Actually yes … surprisingly yes.", giggled Shannon.

"I'm so happy for the two of you!", exclaimed Vivian as she continued, "So, are you two going out this weekend?"

"Yeah, we do have plans.", Shannon said shyly.

"Girl, if you don't spill it! Where are you going?", giggled Vivian.

"He suggested we do something casual like have drinks Friday night. So, girl, I was thinking he was going to ask me out to a local bar downtown or in Royal Oak. No, this man wants to take

29

me to The Whitney. There's a bar there called the Ghost Bar, I think.", chatted Shannon.

"Oh, yes; it's an exclusive bar, Vincent and I have been there many times together. Vincent also takes potential clients there for drinks as well.", Vivian educated her friend.

"Oh, wow! So, I guess I do need to dress up?", asked Shannon.

"Nothing formal, but you should look sexy and not like you just punched out on the work clock. Girl, this is a whole new game! Make sure you video call me after you dress. I need to make sure you have the right look.", insisted Vivian.

Shannon felt like they were in high school when Vivian helped the shy girl change up her wardrobe and not look so frumpy. She thought she was beyond that type of help, but she had to admit that in the past she was always better dressed than her dates by simply showing up in her work attire. They never wore anything fancier than jeans, a tee shirt or a hoodie. Dating a professional man, a man from elite society was indeed a game changer. She would have to change her entire approach to dating.

"Well, I guess I do need your help once more.", Shannon reluctantly shared.

"Yes, you do, in so many ways! You really do.", laughed Vivian.

"What? How many times are you going to say that?", Shannon questioned her friend's laughter as she giggled waiting for a response.

"All jokes aside, I'm serious. You sabotage anything good. I'm not going to let you do that this time!", fussed Vivian.

"Ok, Gloria. I thought I was talking to Vivian.", laughed Shannon.

"That's okay, I'll be Gloria since she's not on the phone. She's looked out for me for years and now it's my turn to look out for you.", insisted Vivian, then added, "You know ... I shouldn't wait until Friday to look at your outfit. Gloria and I should come over tonight and help you pick something out."

"You and Gloria? When has Gloria ever been a fashion queen?", laughed Shannon.

"We need her there for moral support.", Vivian snickered then added, "What do you say? I can have a traveling chef come to prepare a meal while we rummage through your wardrobe."

"You make it sound like we'll be rummaging through trash.", complained Shannon.

"Well ... some of your fashions should be pitched right into it.", laughed Vivian.

"You've got jokes.", laughed Shannon.

"I'm just saying.", giggled Vivian, "If everything goes well, you'll be moving in different circles that require a different look. And the old wardrobe will have to be pitched!"

"Ok, I'm about tired of you ragging me. So, just call Gloria to see if she can come by. I get off at four o'clock so you guys can come around five.", informed Shannon.

Shannon smiled at the thought of how enjoyable it would be to discuss Raymond, fashions and her possible future.

"Ok, it's a plan then. I'm sure Gloria is free and if she isn't, she'd be willing to drop everything to help you out. See you then.", exclaimed Vivian before disconnecting.

"Thanks, see you.", Shannon expressed.

As soon as Shannon disconnected the call, her old fears began to come to the surface disguised as excuses. She thought of all the effort required to date Raymond, the clothes, the events and the expectations of her as a woman. She hadn't been used to doing much to please her boyfriends, but maybe that was just one of the many problems with dating the men of her past. They didn't require much of her and she, of them.

Shannon rushed home after work without stopping anywhere; she had fought the negative voice in her head all day that told her all the effort would end up being a waste of time. It was like she had a devil and an angel on her shoulders all day. Vivian's voice was her angel reminding her that she deserved the love of a quality man and then there was her own voice, that of the devil, telling her it would be just one more disappointment in the long line of love affairs that broke her heart.

The short time home before her guests arrived flew by with her figuratively fighting the devil on her shoulder or within her depending on the view. She heard the door camera indicate a visitor, so she checked her phone to see that it was the chef. Wonderful, she thought, just leave it to Vivian to supply the best money could buy.

"Ms. Washington, I'm Jessie. Vivian hired me to cook for you and your guests.", the chef introduced himself.

"Oh, yes. Come in please.", Shannon greeted him then closed the door, "Let me show you to the kitchen and where the dishes, pots and pans are located."

"There's no need for your cookware, I brought everything I'll need to prepare extra items. I prepared most of it prior to coming.", explained Jessie.

"Okay, good. Right this way then and I'll show you where I keep the dining ware.", said a surprised Shannon.

As soon as she got the chef situated, she heard the bell ring again. She took a deep breath and then rushed to the front door. Although she was looking forward to the evening, she was uneasy about the fuss that would be made over her wardrobe. She again was fighting her own demons that were trying to convince her that *she* wasn't good enough for a Raymond/Vincent type and it all would be a waste of time.

"Hey, girlie! You're ready?", greeted Vivian.

Shannon wanted to say no, but before she uttered the negative words, Gloria chimed in.

"Yes, our girl is! She is going to snag this good man! In Jesus' name!", Gloria spouted as she hugged Shannon.

"Well come on in ladies. The chef is already here and getting things set up for us. So, what do you want to do first?", asked Shannon as she closed the door behind them.

"I think we should eat first because I know I will need at least two glasses of wine to deal with your wardrobe issues. I'll be drunk if I drink on an empty stomach.", laughed Vivian.

"I agree we should eat first, although I don't plan on drinking. I just don't want to be 'hangry' because then everything will look ugly to me.", laughed Gloria.

"Ok, that settles it. We'll eat first.", laughed Shannon as she teased, "The Lord knows I don't want to be bothered with a drunk Vivian and a rude Gloria. Neither would be cute."

The ladies shared a hearty laugh and joked about Gloria fussing over Shannon's fashions with a tipsy Vivian co-signing every complaint as Shannon led the ladies to the kitchen. The chef had everything displayed so professionally as he had pulled out Shannon's unused expensive ornate plates. He had placed them on decorative serving stands that he had set on the counters.

Shannon loved beautiful things even if she never used them. She had been waiting for the day when she could display them as a showpiece. Now as a new homeowner, it was the perfect time to do so. She had forgotten how beautiful the set of China was; it reminded her of herself. Other women would always tell her how beautiful and talented she was, but quality men seemed blind to it and she sat unappreciated just like the beautiful China she had purchased long ago. As the ladies sat around the island, Gloria and Vivian got a better view of the China dining ware.

"Child! Where did you get this beautiful China? Did you just purchase it?", Gloria complimented as her eyes beamed with appreciation.

"Oh, wow! This set is gorgeous!", added Vivian as she picked up a plate.

"I've had the set for years! I never use it. I was just thinking that I had forgotten how pretty it is. It was a huge splurge.", confessed Shannon.

"Well, this will be something you can pack up and take to the Washington-Brown Manor.", giggled Vivian with Gloria smiling in agreement.

"Yes!", chimed in Gloria as she gave Vivian a high-five.

"So, you're renaming the house after me already?", laughed Shannon.

"That's the actual name.", beamed Vivian to her shocked friends as their faces questioned her words. "His grandmother was a Washington and she hyphenated her name to Washington-Brown."

"Oh, God, could we be related?", questioned a scared Shannon.

"No! You're not getting out of this date. There is no way you are related to them. The Washingtons are from the East Coast and so light they all could have passed for White.", laughed Vivian.

Shannon looked at her deep chocolate hands as she spoke, "Hell no, my black ass is definitely not related."

The ladies squealed as they continued laughing over dinner. Gloria had become even more curious about the infamous Raymond Brown.

"You know I am a sucker for a curly-haired brother. Does he have loose curls or tight curls?", Gloria queried.

Suddenly something came alive in Shannon's eyes, a light that neither of her friends had ever seen before. Gloria later realized that the light was hope.

"Yes, he has soft black curly hair, loose enough to run my fingers through it and the clearest smoothest caramel skin I've ever seen. He's tall and very handsome; like model good looks that you would see only in Hollywood.", Shannon gushed.

Vivian smiled and nodded at Gloria as Shannon went on and on about her beau. After speaking incessantly about Raymond, Shannon took a breath and blushed.

"I'm sorry about going on and on about Ray, but I've never experienced an educated man being interested. I hung onto his every word like a little girl infatuated with her teacher. Just think I almost blew it.", sighed Shannon.

"Don't you worry, you'll have another chance.", teased Gloria.

"She better not screw this up.", Vivian said sternly as she slid her empty plate away, "Speaking of, we better tackle this wardrobe."

"Very funny. You and Gloria are becoming quite the comedians.", Shannon said sarcastically as she reached over to tickle Vivian under her arm. "I wonder if Raymond is just as worried about what he will wear to our date Friday night."

Vivian's laughter interrupted anything else Shannon might have wanted to say.

"Did you not *see your man* at the fundraiser? Gloria, let me tell you he's an impeccable dresser. He has to be with friends like Vincent and Giovanni. Have you seen *my man*?", laughed Vivian.

Gloria and Shannon nodded as if to say she had a valid point; Vincent was an eye-catcher for sure and now had the personality to match. It's funny what true love can do when you finally open yourself up to it, thought Shannon.

"Honey, don't you worry about Raymond. Just focus on *your* outfit. I'm ready to see what you're working with.", informed Gloria.

Oh boy, here we go, thought Shannon.

"Ok, let's do it. I pulled a couple of things out that I was considering and you ladies can tell me what you think.", suggested Shannon.

"Or let you know if we need to scrap the whole look.", giggled Vivian. "I want you to wow him every time you go out just like you did the first time you met!"

"Yes, girl. This is the one; the man sent by God! I feel it! Thank you, Lord.", Gloria exclaimed as she praised the Lord by waving her hand.

"No pressure ladies.", pleaded Shannon who needed to feel light and airy so her fears wouldn't take hold.

"It's nothing but pressure, this might be your one shot at true happiness. We don't have time for anything less.", concluded Vivian as she took her best friend by the elbow to hurry her up the stairs.

The ladies walked up the restored wooden staircase for the first time. During their last visit, Shannon didn't give a complete tour since Vivian had side-tracked her plans with talks of Raymond and the fundraiser. The ladies noticed that Shannon had placed a few photos of her daughter and grandparents along the short wall along the stairs. The photos were a pleasant reminder of why she had worked so hard over the years. She wanted to make her grandparents proud and never regret the day they sacrificed their lives to raise another child. She only hoped that Nicole would inherit her best attributes of hard work and dedication to education from her and not how to choose loser after loser. It was not surprising to Shannon that Nicole rarely dated after seeing the example she had set, but maybe that would all change.

"I absolutely love the vintage integrity of your house.", voiced Gloria as she admired the upstairs.

"Thanks, I really adore it as well. Just wait till you see my bedroom. I have an enclosed balcony off my bedroom that I use for a sitting area.", Shannon boasted proudly.

The ladies passed the main bathroom in the hall and approached Shannon's master bedroom suite that sat on the rear side of the house. It was elegantly decorated in soft mauves and greys. As they entered, the balcony was a focal point directly in front of them. Shannon decided that she wanted her bedroom décor to be comfy yet sophisticated and although her balcony was enclosed, she selected an outdoor loveseat and chair set. The pair was made using a thick cherry wood base with chunky legs to match the wooden window trim of the enclosure. The pale grey cushions were thick and square completely outlining the frame of the loveseat and chair with the side cushions serving as armrests. Smaller pillows in shades of pink and mauve were tossed along the length of the loveseat and chair and a matching ottoman served as a coffee table.

"Ladies, this is my haven.", Shannon said as she directed them inside the balcony, "I just love the view of the canal and watching the boats pass by."

"You should be very proud of yourself Shannon. Your place is gorgeous and I know great design when I see it.", praised Gloria.

"Yes, the DIY channels have taught you well, Gloria.", laughed Vivian.

"Oh, yes I am a couch expert for sure!", laughed Gloria.

"I'm ready to see these clothes.", Vivian playfully fussed.

"All right, I guess I can't put it off any longer.", laughed Shannon as she led them to her walk-in closet.

The ladies walked past Shannon's bed to the closet; it was a plush king-sized bed with a thick vertical channel tufted wingback headboard and footboard. It was a beautiful muted mauve and Shannon had placed a deep rich grey duvet atop with numerous pillows of different shades and sizes of lilac, mauve, grey and cream. It sat between two windows with dramatic cream drapes that cascaded down from the ceiling to the floor. There were touches of polished chrome throughout the bedroom from the geometric chandelier to the drawer pulls on the nightstands. The floor mirror was a traditional beveled silver full-length mirror that added a timeless look to her contemporary flared-designed retreat. The intricate designs of filigree embodied that of France and old money.

As Vivian eyed her friend's taste, she realized there was a part of Shannon that had been hidden from her. She had no idea that Shannon liked such refinement; all her old apartments had been filled with hand-me-downs from her grandparents and even from Vivian when she moved from place to place. Vivian thought that it seemed as if Shannon never cared about such things and that she only wanted essential things not caring about the style just the practicality of it all. Hello, Mrs. Washington-Brown indeed, thought a wide-eyed Vivian. Shannon noticed the shocked expression of her best friend.

"You know, I've worked so hard over the years and I figured it's time to finally surround myself with things of comfort and beauty. I should be able to see the fruit of all my hard labor. I deserve it.", Shannon said almost doubting her latter words.

"And you do deserve this and so much more. I've been telling you that for years now.", Vivian said as she reached for her sister-friend.

"I love you girl!", Shannon said through tears as she hugged her friend who was more of a sister as she had no siblings.

"Yikes! Please don't start that crying; you'll have me boohooing in a minute!", laughed Gloria as she wiped her eyes.

"Gloria is right. We're acting like we're getting me dressed for a wedding or something.", laughed Shannon as she wiped her own tears away.

In the walk-in closet, there was a cream island dresser in the middle surrounded by shelves filled with clothes, shoes and purses. Vivian was ecstatic to see that Shannon hadn't left an empty shelf or space on the rack. She rushed over to shuffle through the rack and noticed that Shannon hadn't thrown any clothes away in years; many outfits were outdated and ones she remembered seeing Shannon wear a decade ago. It was meticulously organized but full of old things, and then she spotted a group of clothes with price tags on them.

"Wait a damn minute!", Vivian fussed as she held up a beautiful blouse.

Shannon and Gloria stopped discussing the island dresser to see what the fuss was about.

"What's wrong?", questioned Shannon as she quickly took the blouse from Vivian's hand to eye it.

"You haven't worn any of the clothes that I've bought for you. That's what's wrong!", Vivian scolded.

"Really? How many things?", questioned Gloria as she approached.

"This whole damn section!", Vivian pointed to the clothes, "Freaking unbelievable!"

Gloria was shocked that Shannon hadn't worn the stylish pieces.

"I haven't had a need to wear them. They are much too fancy for work and sadly too dressy for my usual dates.", Shannon embarrassedly admitted.

"This blouse would be perfect for your date with Raymond. I just hope it hasn't dry-rotted.", exclaimed Gloria as she shook her head in disappointment.

"Exactly!", fumed Vivian as she held the item up to Shannon.

"Give me that! Forget dry-rot, I hope I can still fit it!", Shannon said as she twirled the blouse to examine it.

"Try it on, that's the one for sure and you can pair it with some dress slacks.", suggested Vivian.

Vivian reached for yet another gift left unworn, the slacks she had paired with it as a gift. Shannon hesitantly started walking to her attached bath to slip on the blouse, but Vivian stopped her in her tracks.

"Where are you going? If you don't try this stuff on right here! We both have seen your goodies before.", announced a confused Vivian.

"Sure have. More than I've seen a man's, lately anyway.", laughed Gloria along with Vivian.

"And I've seen that body since high school, bone-thin, pregnant, chubby and now curvy. I've seen all iterations of it.", laughed Vivian.

Shannon laughed as she began to remove her blouse to try on the one her friends were insisting that she wear. It was a teal green V-neck wrap sateen blouse that would accentuate her small waist and full hips. She slipped it on and peered at herself in the full-length mirror in the closet that matched the one near her bed.

"I like it. It really suits my skin tone.", smiled Shannon at her reflection.

"It's not quite right. Let me fix it.", expressed Vivian.

Gloria and Shannon shared a confused expression as the blouse was perfect. Vivian approached Shannon and took her by the shoulders so they could stand face head-on, then she pushed the V-neck open to reveal more cleavage.

"Now, it's perfect! You've got to give Raymond something to think about that night.", laughed Vivian.

"Girl!", laughed Shannon, "Hand those pants to me. I guess you want me to look like a slut."

"No, I want you to look seductively sexy and alluring like you did the night of the fundraiser. You have too many assets to go unused.", teased Vivian as she handed the dress slacks to Shannon.

Gloria nodded silently as she watched the pair fuss like teens. Then, Shannon examined the taupe wide-legged dress trousers; she had never bought a pair of pants with a lining before. She slipped off her pants and swapped them for the more elegant pair. She loved the feel of the lining on her skin as she slipped it on; it felt expensive and soft. She couldn't help but smile even before she got a glimpse of the look.

"Oh yes!", squeaked Vivian as she nudged Shannon to the mirror.

"Absolutely beautiful!", chimed in Gloria then she spotted a pair of taupe ankle strap sandals, "Try these with it!"

"Oh! I forgot I had these. I bought these shoes because I loved the thick chunky three-inch heel. I figured it would be easier for me to wear.", Shannon beamed as she buckled the ankle strap.

While Gloria handed Shannon the shoes, Vivian had been looking through Shannon's costume jewelry for something to make the look pop even more. She spotted a gold-tone necklace that looked like it was four; she thought it would drop alluringly over Shannon's cleavage to draw even more of Raymond's attention.

"Put this on!", insisted Vivian.

"I bought her that one year for Christmas! I had forgotten about it since I've never seen her wear it.", laughed Gloria.

Shannon glided the 36-inch four-string infinity chain over her head. It laid exactly how Vivian hoped it would; it laid upon Shannon's full bosom. The contrast between Shannon's dark rich mocha skin and the gold was eye-catching.

"You are stunning! He's going to be more in awe of you after your next date!", giggled Gloria with Vivian bouncing and giggling along with her.

Shannon was mesmerized by her look; although the clothes and jewelry were not new, they presented and represented the change that she felt was on the horizon. Little did she know, she was not the only one still feeling the effects of their encounter.

Raymond would not have guessed that Vincent and Vivian's setup for a blind date would have taken a positive turn. Especially not after their first encounter, but he had enjoyed the phone conversations he and Shannon had experienced since the fundraiser. He didn't let Vincent know, but he had been looking forward to their next date all week. As he sat at the bar waiting for her arrival, he became just a little nervous that she might revert back into the bitch that he had first encountered. He was about to sip his drink when he spotted her enter the bar; she was just as stunning as the first time they met. She was nothing short of style and sophistication. She was everything his family would welcome and the perfect picture of what a wife should be for a man of his station. The men couldn't stop looking at her in admiration and desire; the women, sprinkled throughout, glanced at her with eyes of envy. Yet, he noticed that she wasn't fazed by any of it if she even noticed their reactions at all; she only had eyes for him.

Shannon entered the bar dreading that she might have a hard time finding him; she didn't know what to expect as far as the size of the establishment or the crowd, but there he was and she was instantly drawn to Raymond's penetrating stare. His hazel eyes pulled her near and ever closer to him. She wanted to get lost in his eyes and listen to him discuss his business deals and law. She felt that dating an intellectual was sexy as hell and frightening all at once.

Raymond was smooth as silk as he sat casually at the bar, yet his confidence oozed across the crowd like a magnet drawing stares and attention from anyone in his proximity. He wore a skinny-cut blue pinstriped blazer with an open white shirt matched with dark navy straight-legged jeans. The jeans hugged his thick muscular thighs and long legs resting atop black laced leather oxfords. His silver cuff links made his stainless-steel chronograph Shinola black leather band watch pop even more. It was no doubt to anyone with sight that he was a man of wealth, position and confidence.

Shannon beamed as she approached him and Raymond stood to greet her. His smile was slightly smirky then he parted his full lips to speak, but paused before doing so. She couldn't resist staring at them and imagining them kissing her cleavage as he slowly moved up her throat to her mouth. She swallowed as if that would clear her head and bring her thoughts back to reality.

"Shannon?", questioned Raymond wondering why she was not responding.

Shannon blushed as she realized he must have spoken and she had been standing there like a love-struck teenager. She cleared her throat to pretend that was the reason for her silence.

"Sorry about that. I had a little tickle in my throat. Hi Raymond. This is a really nice bar.", Shannon expressed hoping to make up for her fumble.

"Yes, it is. I love the décor and I don't have to be worried about the wrong crowd coming here and ruining everything. You know what I mean?", admitted Raymond.

"Unfortunately, I do. That's most of the places my other dates take me.", laughed Shannon.

She immediately regretted disclosing too much too soon to Raymond as she noticed his puzzled expression, but that happened on nearly every bar date she had. And it usually was her date, acting the fool and causing a scene. Ok, Shannon, don't talk about past boyfriends; keep it cute, sassy and sexy, she reminded herself when she stopped talking.

"Well, you won't have that issue with me if I can prevent it.", promised Raymond as he took her hand to guide her to the seat next to his. "Have a seat and let me get you a drink.", Raymond suggested as he pulled out the bar stool for her, "Bartender!", Raymond called to the attendant.

"Yes, what would you like Ma'am?", asked the young bartender.

Shannon was not much of a drinker at all so she decided to order her faithful standby.

"I'll take a glass of Sangria. Thank you.", Shannon offered her order.

"Boss, would you like another glass of whiskey on the rocks?", the bartender asked his frequent guest.

"Yes, thank you.", offered Raymond.

"Anytime Boss.", acknowledged the young man.

Shannon was impressed that the bartender seemed to hold Raymond in high regard. Whenever a bartender saw Joe coming, he threatened to call the police if he got out of hand. What a difference; literally night and day, thought Shannon.

"So, how was your meeting with old man Barrington?", she asked remembering that was on his agenda for the week.

Raymond had forgotten that he had mentioned that, guess she wasn't the only one providing too much information, he thought.

"Oh, it was fine. He wanted to sure up some things to make sure little Bernie has a solid trust fund. He is quite the doting grandfather. However, I think it was mainly an excuse for him to share stories of my grandfather with me. He admired my grandfather tremendously.", confessed Raymond.

"Really? I had no idea …", paused Shannon as she sipped her drink with a surprised expression.

"What? That the Barringtons had Black friends.", laughed Raymond, "Yes, my grandfather, Vincent's grandfather and Giovanni's dad were the closest of friends. They knew each other's dirty little secrets, I'm sure."

"I always assumed that the Barrington family was just another entitled rich and out-of-touch white family.", admitted Shannon.

"Well, I'm not saying they're not.", chuckled Raymond, "They only allow other wealthy families in their mix. The only color they see is green. My family fits the bill; we've been wealthy well over one-hundred-fifty years."

At that moment, Shannon felt inadequate, insignificant and not worthy of his attention. She sipped her drink once more to steady her nerves and just as quickly she remembered her best friend. If Vivian could fit into that world, why couldn't she? Raymond noticed that his words had made her feel uncomfortable and that was the last thing he wanted. To lessen her uneasiness, he thought he would ask about something that would put her at ease.

"Tell me, how did you and Vivian meet?", Raymond inquired.

"Well,", smiled Shannon, "I was new to Vivian's neighborhood high school. She didn't attend that school, but her slightly older brother, Joe, did. She happened to attend a basketball game. I was a player under my grandfather who was the head coach. She noticed that I didn't really socialize with my teammates or anyone after the game. She approached me to congratulate me on our win and we hit it off instantly.", Shannon reminisced.

"You've been close that long? That's a long time to be friends with someone.", voiced Raymond.

"I thought you and Vincent had been friends just as long.", informed Shannon.

"No, not at all. Vincent was a snob as a kid and even worse as a teen; he was into the fast crowd. He annoyed the hell out of me. We were no more than acquaintances back then, even well into our adulthood. We only got to know each other and got close after he proposed to Vivian. Her acceptance of his proposal really changed his life.", Raymond provided.

"They truly have a whirlwind love story.", admitted Shannon.

"Yes, they do. But when a man truly loves a woman, he'll turn his world upside down to win her over.", smiled Raymond,

"Next thing you know, he's spending hours at the mall, carrying her purse around and missing football games.", laughed Raymond.

"Not the purse.", laughed Shannon as she imagined Joe carrying hers.

For so many years, she had hoped he would change; but that was a lost cause and a dream that probably wasn't worth dreaming. Especially not when she had a man like Raymond Brown II sitting beside her.

"I can't imagine you carrying a purse.", laughed Shannon.

"Well, I've done some uncharacteristic things in the past.", sighed Raymond, regretting the comment as he sipped his drink hoping she wouldn't want to discuss it more.

"So, you've been in love before.", teased Shannon as she imagined him being a lovesick puppy chasing after some lucky woman.

"Well, a one-sided love affair is just a fantasy someone wise said.", laughed Raymond as he thought of Veronica.

Shannon could see that his whole demeanor had changed, she could tell that the love interest that he had spoken of had really done a number on him.

"Sorry, I didn't mean to bring up past relationships.", she admitted.

Way to go, Shannon, she thought sarcastically.

"No worries. It's okay. It was my ex-fiancée, Veronica. I was more in love with her than she was with me. I lost myself for a while trying to be the man, she wanted me to be. I'm a Black man first, a rich one second, but she couldn't understand that as a white woman.", confessed Raymond.

He hoped he hadn't said too much; he knew bringing up an ex could be the kiss of death with a new love interest. But it was his truth and if he and Shannon expected to develop something, didn't they need to know each other's pain or struggles, he contemplated.

Shannon studied the countenance of this successful, well-put-together and handsome man; she realized pain doesn't discriminate and that they had things in common. She wasn't the only one with a history of dating outside her race unsuccessfully. However, she had never experienced *that* issue concerning race. Her exes accepted her for what she was, a well-educated and successful woman with a nice bank account she added as she realized they all had their hands out for money in one way or another. It would be nice to allow someone else to take the lead financially for a change, she thought as she exhaled.

"Well with me, Raymond, you can be you. And I'd like to get to know exactly who you are.", Shannon uttered seductively.

For the first time, she realized there was so much depth to this man and he had a vulnerability she had never seen a boyfriend or lover express. It was strangely endearing and sexy that a man of his stature could reveal himself in such an emotionally bare way. He wasn't pretentious as so many of the Black men who expressed any interest in her were and he wasn't raw and feral as the white ones that she had dated. Consequently, she was a fish out of water; she had been reminding herself too much of that, she thought.

Their evening at the bar flowed well after they let their guards down, relaxed and discussed their interests. Surprisingly, the time jetted by without either of them being aware. There was an easiness to their connection even when a shy reserve crept in preventing either from spilling their entire soul at once.

"I would love to take you to Andiamo tomorrow night.", informed Raymond.

"That would be nice...", Shannon began.

As Raymond stared into her deep brown eyes, he realized he had an unusual desire to spoil her, wine and dine her; his previous reservations about her had dissipated leaving behind a pure curiosity about the curvy bombshell. They were lost in each other and their conversation; the time together was a non-stop stream of discussions until Raymond received a call.

"Excuse me, I must take this call.", explained Raymond as he stood to walk away.

"No problem.", indicated Shannon.

Raymond was very concerned that his grandmother was calling at that time of day. He along with the family was worried about her failing health. She had started to experience more traumatic episodes of dementia by forgetting people and places; she even confused relatives.

"Is something wrong?", he asked.

"Yes, darling it is. Why haven't you come home by now my love? It's not like you to keep me waiting.", asked a worried Eleanor.

Oh, God, thought Raymond, he had hoped that one time she confused him for his grandfather was a fluke and would never happen again, but there she was calling him to come home.

"Grandmother, it's your grandson Raymond. I'm not Grandfather.", he explained.

"You're not?", questioned a confused Eleanor who was close to tears, "Oh God, where is my husband? I don't remember his number."

"Grandmother, where is the nurse?", Raymond questioned as his concern grew for his near frantic grandmother.

Raymond didn't want to remind her that her husband had died months ago; it crushed his heart to think of her reaction. She would be experiencing the loss all over again. He could hear the nurse enter the room to soothe his grandmother. The nurse took the cell phone from Eleanor; she was surprised that Eleanor remembered how to use it. Then she noticed that it was Eleanor's grandson whom Eleanor had called.

"Mr. Brown, sir, I'm sorry. I'll attend to the Misses and calm her down. I assure you she will be fine.", the nurse apologized.

"Thank you, I appreciate that.", Raymond voiced his gratitude.

"Good night, Sir.", the nurse concluded.

Raymond had been gone awhile causing Shannon to wonder what was happening. Her mind thought of a thousand reasons why, but there was one that pounded in her thoughts and triggered her. She was lost in her thoughts until the bartender approached the counter and left a receipt. Instantly a wave of nervousness washed over her expression as she reached for it.

"Miss, is something wrong?", questioned the concerned bartender.

Shannon's lower lip began to quiver as she looked toward the direction Raymond had walked then she looked down at the check. The bartender knew exactly what her fear was.

"Boss has already settled the account. He'll return; you've got a good one there.", informed the bartender as he pointed to her approaching date.

Raymond's light-hearted mood instantly changed as he approached the bar. Every negative thought that Shannon had ever imagined seemed to leach onto her making her fear that this would be the one and only date they shared. He pulled out the chair and sighed as he lifted the last drop of the remaining whiskey to his lips. Raymond noticed Shannon's concern and hated that he was bringing his family drama to their date.

"I'm turning into almost the worst date ever.", Raymond said as he feigned a chuckle, "My whole vibe has changed. Sorry about that. That call was from my grandmother. She called me thinking she was calling her late husband. That was the second time that her dementia had her thinking I was him. The fear and panic in her voice were heart-wrenching. I can't imagine the panic that she must have felt thinking something had happened to him. She loved him so much, but she never publicly expressed it, but when he died ... I think it drained the life from her causing dementia to set in.", Raymond unloaded his worry and grief upon Shannon.

She reached for his hand to provide comfort as she knew all too well what he was experiencing. Her grandmother was also facing some health challenges of her own.

"It's torture to see the people we love deteriorate before our eyes when they used to be so strong and vibrant. I'm going through the same thing with my grandmother.", confided Shannon as she wiped away tears with her napkin, "My grandmother uses a walker from time to time now when her arthritis is intolerable. She's fearful that one day, she might need a wheelchair. I know it's a lot different because her mind is still sharp, but she feels helpless at times."

"I probably should take a rain check on tomorrow's date. Instead of going tomorrow, can we go next Saturday evening?", asked Raymond as guilt set in about his grandmother, "I should really check on my grandmother tomorrow."

"I completely understand and yes it's a date.", Shannon confirmed as she thought there was no way she would stand in the way of family devotion.

The pair simply gazed at one another in silence as if communicating telepathically; it was a surreal moment for the two and they knew a connection had been forged. Where it would take them, they didn't have a clue.

Chapter 4

Raymond made the short drive north on Woodward Avenue from his luxury condo in Birmingham to Vincent's mansion in Bloomfield Hills. Vincent had suggested that the three amigos hang out at his home for drinks and cards. Vincent never hosted anything during the work week, being the workaholic that he had become in the last few years. Subsequently, Raymond knew it was just a method of getting the details about his date with Shannon, but he'd play along with it since they were more like brothers than friends.

As Raymond pulled up the long drive to the Barrington Estate and up to the cobble-stone circular drive, he speculated about the hundreds of deals that the powerful Barrington men had made over the centuries that they had reigned one of the elite families of Michigan. The secrets that those walls must hold would be legendary and fit for any big screen; only the closest of friends like his grandfather and the Bianchi men shared those secrets, thought Raymond as he parked his convertible Bentley Continental GTC Mulliner. The car was a perfect match for a sophisticated urban powerbroker like Raymond; its grey exterior was almost matte with twenty-two-inch black sports wheels. The interior was black with a deep red that was almost burgundy with black leather seats trimmed in that same red almost like a racing stripe. As he exited his car, he noticed that in true form, Giovanni was late. After he closed the car door, he heard a loud bass booming closer.

Raymond turned toward the drive and noticed that it was Giovanni in his brand-new Bugatti Chiron. It was silver and navy blue with a matching interior. Raymond shook his head with laughter as Giovanni revved the sports car around the circular driveway in front of the mansion. Giovanni matched Raymond's laughter as he hopped from his vehicle.

"Man, you know you are just like your old man! Flashy as fuck!", laughed Raymond as the pair took the other's hand in an embrace.

"That's what we do! Shit, I learned from the best. He had all the hotties wanting a piece and I do too. You see me.", laughed Gio as he stepped back with his arms outstretched as if providing a better view for Raymond. "And you sound like your grandfather, always wanting to downplay your own flyness."

Raymond shook his head as he laughed at Giovanni's antics.

"Bro, they would be proud of us for damn sure.", confirmed Raymond as they continued to laugh as they approached the entrance.

Before either could announce their presence by ringing the doorbell, Copeland opened the door.

"Good evening gentleman. The young master Barrington is waiting for you in the game room.", informed Copeland

Copeland smiled as he reminisced about how their father and grandfathers used to hang out here when he was a child running the halls with John Barrington. It's funny how time can bring about a change, thought Copeland, who at one point thought Vincent wouldn't live to see mid-life.

The guys continued talking and laughing as they entered the game room. Vincent turned from the bar hoping that he hadn't missed out on any of Giovanni's tall tales.

"What did I miss?", asked Vincent then sipped his Vodka.

"Nothing, but the usual flashy as fuck Giovanni. Did you know he has a brand-new Bugatti Chiron now?", asked Raymond as he headed over to the bar.

"Fuck no! But you're one to talk with your new Bentley.", Vincent laughed as he pointed at Raymond for emphasis. "Giovanni, you just bought a Corvette Convertible Stingray C8R last year which made me buy one last month. Where does all this money come from?", Vincent teased as the trio shared a boisterous laugh.

Vincent enjoyed teasing Giovanni about his family's mafia roots knowing full well that Giovanni inherited many legitimate holdings from his father.

"Don't start that shit!", laughed Gio as he poured a drink. "Enough talk about me. I want to know about the date Raymond had with Shannon last Friday and what happened before you left her place Saturday morning. Did she beg you to stay?", questioned Giovanni thirsty for a drink and a good sex story.

Raymond hesitated as he choked on a sip of Vodka.

"My man? Spill it what happened?", inquired Vincent as he walked to the card table to set it up for a game.

Giovanni walked over to Raymond and pretended to need a closer look to search his face for answers.

"Fuck. Did she walk out on you? Damn!", laughed Gio as he threw his hand up at Raymond in disappointment.

"No, we had a good date, but you know it's been a while since I've been out with a sister. So, I was a little rusty...", Raymond started to explain.

"Ah, shit! You were a *little* rusty?", interjected a laughing Gio.

"Let him finish.", insisted Vincent with a smirk awaiting the good details he hoped would follow.

Giovanni walked over to the card table to set up the cards for a game.

"Yeah, it was nice … it was strangely familiar … like it felt like home.", Raymond attempted to put his feelings into words.

"It felt like home? Boring!", laughed Gio as he shuffled the cards as Raymond reluctantly sat at the card table.

"Every date shouldn't consist of endless bottles of alcohol and sex.", Vincent informed Gio as he struggled to hold in his laughter.

"It was great okay … at least until I got a call from my grandmother.", informed Raymond.

"Your nanna? What did she want?", asked a confused Gio.

"She thought I was my grandfather; she called worried and asking why I hadn't come home yet.", Raymond informed his friends, "She became hysterical when I explained that I wasn't him."

"Did you end the date?", asked Vincent as he dealt their hands.

"The fuck he didn't!", scolded Giovanni.

"No, I didn't, but I did cancel the plans we had just made to see each other the next day.", explained Raymond.

"What the fuck!", exclaimed Giovanni as he slammed his cards on the table.

"Man, I needed to check on my grandmother instead.", explained Raymond.

Vincent was the only one who seemed to understand Raymond's concern as he nodded his agreement.

"Bullshit! There was nothing you could do to help your nanna, so why not go on the date? That's why you pay the nurses, the fuck!", fussed Gio as he sipped his drink.

"I haven't called her nanna since I was a teen.", said Raymond as his annoyance with Gio grew, "So, if your mother, Vittoria, called you in distress, you'd say fuck her I'm getting my freak on?", demanded Raymond.

Vincent decided to interject so that the conversation wouldn't get heated as he knew Gio would kill for his mother. Gio was just as protective and crazy for his mother as his father had been all those years ago when they first met.

"Is that really the reason you didn't take her out the next day?", Vincent asked hoping that his pal was not self-sabotaging.

Giovanni nodded and pointed at Vincent in agreement that he likely had discovered the real reason.

"Naw man, I am really concerned for my grandmother … maybe … who knows… maybe I didn't want to take a chance that things wouldn't go well with a date back-to-back like that. But we are going out this weekend, though.", Raymond confirmed.

"Okay, that sounds good. I really think the two of you could have something special.", explained Vincent.

"I agree and be ready to get your dick wet. Make sure you have some condoms.", encouraged Giovanni.

"What the fuck? You act like I don't know my way around a pussy, the fuck!", complained Raymond.

"Well, not a black one. Her body is hot and begging for a good fuck. You need to be ready, stallion. That's all I'm saying.", Gio explained his reason for overstepping.

"I think our man has it under control.", laughed Vincent, "At least he does with the ladies. Cards? That's another story."

"Fuck.", sighed Raymond as he lost yet another hand.

"I wonder what it was like when our grandfathers played cards with your father, Gio.", pondered Vincent.

56

"It's funny how history repeats itself, they were closer than brothers and here we are, the same.", acknowledged Giovanni.

"Yeah, it's eerie; they were so close that they died within months of each other.", added Raymond.

"Shit yeah, it is. So, don't you bastards start checking out! I'm too young to throw in the towel.", laughed Gio.

"To friendship.", Vincent toasted.

"Friendship!", Raymond and Giovanni said together.

The trio held up their glasses to toast their brotherhood as they envisioned what their elders had done countless times in the past.

Shannon had looked at her ringing cell phone countless times that day as her best friend desperately tried to reach her. She just wasn't in the mood to discuss her love life; since she was home from a long day's work, she only wanted to prepare dinner and relax. She knew her date with Raymond went well, but there was a constant nagging voice in her own mind telling her differently. It said, "Maybe his grandmother really isn't sickly. He could have told you that, to end the date without hurting your feelings. He's slow dissing you before he ghosts you."

Shannon tortured herself every day since the date like a mad woman, happy and hopeful one minute then the next conjuring up every reason in the book that the relationship would fail. After all, that is what she was accustomed to, one failed relationship after another. She couldn't stand hearing Vivian's ringtone any longer so she reluctantly answered the phone.

"Hello.", Shannon greeted rather harshly.

"Is that any way to greet your best friend?", questioned Vivian who was just grateful that Shannon had answered.

"Girl, you've been blowing up my phone all day. I could barely focus on my work.", scolded Shannon.

"Yeah, right! When has anything ever stopped you from doing whatever it is you want to do?", laughed Vivian, "Now give me an update. You've been silent since your date."

"I'm surprised you didn't get any updates from Vincent. He didn't check in with Raymond?", Shannon queried, not really wanting to know the answer.

"I'm sure he did check with Raymond, but I'm checking with you. So, what's up? You haven't said not even one word about the date!", exclaimed Vivian.

"It was good.", Shannon said hesitantly.

"Good? That's all you've got; the woman who lives to talk about a man?", Vivian reminded Shannon of her usual antics.

"You know how I get in my own head. I thought it was good then I started thinking about the lies he could be telling me… I don't know…", sighed Shannon as she gathered her pots and pans to cook.

"Okay. Stop clanking the pots and pans and talk to me for a minute. Why are you thinking he's a liar?", Vivian said very curious to hear her friend's twisted logic.

"He ended the date a little abruptly and canceled our plans for the next night because his grandmother has dementia.", Shannon explained.

"Well, she does … did something happen?", asked Vivian.

Shannon was embarrassed to discuss the details now that Vivian had verified that his grandmother truly had health problems.

"His grandmother called him panicking about her dead husband … Damn it. I sound like a crazy person.", grunted Shannon.

"Yes, you do. You need to relax and stop expecting Ray to let you down just like the rest have. His grandmother means everything to him, just like yours does to you.", Vivian added to ease her friend's fears, "In fact, he told Vincent that you remind him of her."

"Really?", laughed Shannon, "So his grandmother is crazy too?"

"Yeah, a little from what I hear.", giggled Vivian, "I hear she was a little eccentric in her day. Just like you are a little quirky at times."

"Our date was so different from any I've had. You know he even got a little emotional.", Shannon commented.

"So. What's wrong with that?", Vivian curiously waited for a response.

"I'm not used to guys being soft. Are you sure he's not on the DL?", Shannon asked thinking she had discovered the truth that would shelve the budding relationship.

"Oh, my God! Really? So, if a man isn't rough, tatted up and stiffing you with the check, you aren't happy. That's some seriously sick shit.", fumed Vivian, "Let me get Gloria on the three-way."

"No!", shouted Shannon, but it was too late and Vivian had already clicked over to add the call.

"Hey, ladies. So, what's up? I'm trying to finish up cooking my dinner.", Gloria responded as she reached for a skillet.

"Shannon called Raymond soft and questioned his sexuality because he was concerned for his elderly grandmother.", fussed Vivian.

Shannon and Vivian heard the heavy skillet land clumsily on the stovetop.

"No, the hell she didn't! Forgive me Lord.", shouted Gloria in disbelief at her friend and her own use of a cuss word.

"I only said that because he was close to tears. I've never seen a man do that on a date.", complained Shannon.

"I don't know what to do with you. I used to say that about Vivian before Vincent got his act together. Whatever he did, I need you to do the same because you definitely need some 'act right'!", laughed Gloria.

"We need to convince her not to go in expecting this to fail.", begged Vivian.

"Lord knows you have held on to far worse men than this *filthy* rich Raymond.", fussed Gloria as she poured her cooking oil into the pan, "Need I remind you that he is a millionaire!"

"Hello!", chimed Vivian.

"Look, I'm not cutting him off. Raymond and I are going out this weekend. So, you both can relax with the pressure.", Shannon acquiesced.

"You better and don't mess this up!", Vivian insisted.

"I've got to go, I have another call trying to come through.", Shannon provided; she was glad for an excuse to vacate the conversation.

"Right on time Raymond!", giggled a hopeful Gloria.

"Bye!", Shannon quickly said before switching over. It would be nice to talk to him, she thought, "Hello!"

"Hey, baby. How's my girl?", Joe said in his raspy voice brought on from years of smoking almost a pack of cigarettes a day.

"Oh, Joe. I was hoping you were someone else. I'm doing fine.", Shannon confessed.

She was reminded of something Gloria always said when Joe was around, "The devil always shows up right when good things are about to happen for us. He seeks to steal, kill and destroy our happiness."

"You've been on my mind lately. I've just been remembering how good you taste, baby. Why don't I come through?", Joe informed.

"I'm not feeling that. I told you I'm through with booty calls. If you want me, we need to be in a committed relationship. For once, can you just call me for a real conversation? For starters, can you ask about our daughter? Do you remember her and the child support you owe?", Shannon scolded the deadbeat dad.

"Shannon, you know I pay when I can. In fact, my luck is turning around; I'm about to start a new job next week.", bragged Joe hoping to convince her that things would be different.

"Really?", doubted Shannon.

"Anyway ... I know how Nicole is. I called her yesterday. She didn't tell you that we talked?", Joe defended.

"I talk to her every single day while she's away on campus and she didn't mention not one word about you.", Shannon contested his rendition of the story.

"Well, you know how she is, but I didn't call you to talk about her though. I want to focus on us. You know when we get together, we get real nasty and I miss that.", Joe reminded her hoping to experience it again.

That was the last thing of which Shannon wanted to be reminded; she didn't know if his lovemaking was really that good or if it was just because he was her first. Time and time again, her body betrayed her causing her to allow him back into her life once again. She had vowed after their last breakup she was through with their boomerang relationship. She decided she ought to be blunt and end the conversation quickly.

"Joe, I'm dating someone else now. A really good catch, he's a friend of Vincent.", Shannon informed Joe.

"He sounds like a bore. I guess I'll have to convince you that what we have can't be matched.", bragged Joe.

"Did you tell that to Rita?", demanded Shannon, "You know what, don't even bother answering that. I need to finish cooking. Bye!", Shannon snapped then hung up on Joe before he could respond.

Shannon knew she sounded jealous and if she was honest, she was. Rita was a bitch that rubbed their relationship in her face every time Joe brought her to a family function. Rita fit in snuggly with Joe's mother and sisters, Carol and Jessica. Shannon never felt truly accepted by them, but Vivian had to remind her that neither was she. Shannon and Vivian were career-driven women to whom the Johnston clan couldn't relate. Shannon longed for acceptance and to create a strong family of her own, but instead, she had a fractured one with a daughter who couldn't stand to talk, hear or even look at her father.

As Shannon stirred her dish in the pot, she began to regret telling Joe that she was dating someone. What if it didn't work out. That would just be another thing he could hold over her head to convince her to get back with him. Darn it, she thought, why does her mind think of every possible negative situation that exists? When would she realize that if that's what she expects then that's what she'll get?

Despite Shannon's rollercoaster of emotions, the work week ended quickly for the budding pair. Raymond had considered the advice of his friends and decided to make some changes to their venue. He was thankful that Shannon didn't seem annoyed or make a fuss about the change of plans. He felt that she deserved some serious effort on his part as he had invited her to the Ghost Bar because that was his usual hangout; but on this date, he desired to show her that he truly had her in mind every step of the planning. Shannon also had a different perspective as well; she would have a positive attitude and go with the expectation of getting to know him fully.

Raymond left clear instructions with the live-in nurse that he didn't want any interruptions unless it was an emergency; he didn't want to hear from his grandmother or anyone else for that matter, not that night. He didn't want Shannon to feel that she came second to anyone and he would do whatever was in his control to ensure that. So, instead of them driving separately, he decided to have a limo service pick them up. He had planned it well; he selected their premier date package which included a bottle of Dom Perignon Brut Champagne and appetizers.

Raymond consulted a florist for a bouquet and had been very insistent concerning the pairing of colors for the roses. He requested the florist to pair a dozen white and a dozen pink roses together to create a splendid bouquet with red ferns and baby's breath. The white roses represented a new beginning for their budding relationship and the pink, sweetness and admiration; the red fern represented the passion he felt laid beneath the surface of their relationship. He allowed the florist free reign to design the other flower arrangements that were placed in the limo. Growing up his Uncles Bernard and Ricky, as he called them, always talked romantic gibberish about the colors of roses. At least that's how he thought of it as a teen, but as a man, he appreciated having those talks.

Raymond decided that he would change the venue to the Detroit Club which was more fitting to impress or make amends to a love interest. He wanted to make her feel like a princess and there was no better place than the Detroit Club. He, his father and grandfather as well as the same generations of the Barringtons and Bianchis had been members. The Barrington influence ran deep at the club; Vincent's great-great-grandfather had been one of the founding members of the club back in 1882. Consequently, Raymond was very familiar with it and he knew there was no way Shannon wouldn't feel pampered that night.

Shannon was ecstatic that she was going to see Raymond and dine at the Detroit Club. She had never heard of it before being invited so, she researched it online and discovered that it was an establishment for the rich elite of the city. It was a gem hidden in plain sight of the average working stiff. She decided it was time to cut tags off another fabulous piece that she had been holding onto for no apparent good reason. If Vivian and Gloria knew she had yet another outfit with a tag on it that had been tucked away in her closet, she wouldn't hear the end of their scolding.

She pulled the mauve two-piece from her closet; it was a long flare-legged pair of pants with a top with a high round collar, flared sleeves with an elastic band wrist and a stylish drawstring on the left to create a partially scrunched bodice. The blouse would showcase her small waist and full bosom; she was sure it would catch Raymond's eye. It had little need for jewelry, but she decided to pair it with a thick 24-inch Byzantine silver-tone necklace that would sit just atop her breasts. She had a pair of matching hoop earrings and a thick fashion watch that was also silver-tone.

She sashayed by her shelved shoes and remembered the perfect pair to accompany her outfit; it was a three-inch heel open-toe ankle boot in a tawny brown with a buckle fastened to fit securely around her slender ankles. She reached for the pair and removed them from the box; they might not have had a tag but from the look of the sole, she hadn't worn them.

Shannon stared at her reflection in the mirror; the soft curls of her pixie hairstyle, extended eyelashes and soft makeup were perfect and completed her look. She retrieved her small ornate white and pink glass crystal embellished clutch purse from her dressing table and exited her closet just as she heard her phone ringing inside her clutch. She peeked inside to see that the call was from Joe.

"I do not have time for the bullshit", she said to the ringing phone.

Joe was surprised that his call went to voicemail; even when Shannon was furious with him, she always answered his calls. He decided to uncharacteristically leave a voicemail message.

"Hey, baby. I was checking to see if you wanted to go out and celebrate. I just landed a good job and wanted to take you out on the town. Hit me back.", Joe expressed excitedly, although his voice belied his true feelings.

He was slightly embarrassed that she hadn't answered. He contemplated what was up with her and why she had changed. He decided he would check with his sister to find out what was really going on with Shannon.

Shannon took a deep breath; she was determined to focus on Ray and not allow old dogs to disrupt her excitement. She needed to vow to leave Joe in the past and move forward with Ray. As she walked downstairs to await Raymond, her stomach jumped with excitement; it was a freshness that she hadn't experienced in a very long time. If the truth were told, she hadn't been picked up for a date in ages, usually, she was the one picking up *her* dates. The promise of a relationship with a man she connected with emotionally and who was also financially secure was strange yet oddly felt like home. She hoped she wasn't alone in that sea of wonderous feelings; she hoped she would spot Raymond floating by.

Shannon heard the familiar sound of her alert system notifying her that a vehicle had pulled in front of her home. She thought, right on time; another thing to which she wasn't accustomed. She was curious to see what type of sports car he drove; she was sure whatever it was it wasn't a run-of-the-mill everyone has one type of car. She opened the door to spot Raymond, handsome as ever, exiting a Bentley limousine to greet her with a bouquet of flowers in hand. She was stunned by his thoughtfulness; she was ashamed to admit that at her age, she had never received a bouquet of flowers from a man.

She was close to tears; tears of joy and regret that she had wasted so many years on men who didn't even try to value her worth. She dabbed her eyes quickly and composed herself in anticipation of receiving the stunning roses from Raymond. She didn't know what was more impressive, the roses or the excitement in his eyes. Indeed, he was in the sea alongside her and she was beyond. That was the only word for how she felt at that moment, beyond.

Raymond, like Shannon, had felt his excitement for their date rise as the day approached; he hadn't been that hopeful about a woman, especially a Black woman, since college. Just as he had taken extra care in preparing everything for their date, he put that same effort into selecting his attire. He chose a semi-formal look that he hoped would complement Shannon; his pants were a taupe skinny cotton/spandex blend with a cream modern stretch bomber suit jacket with a soft knit slim fit turtleneck sweater. Nothing better could complete his look than his Shinola watch and his cream wing-tipped Cole Haan oxfords.

He wanted to play it cool and strut knowing he was fine, but as he exited the limo, he couldn't contain his desire for her. He was mesmerized by her stunning effortless beauty and to think for months, he had turned down Vincent's suggestion to date her. What a fool he would have been if he hadn't changed his mind, he thought. His words were stuck momentarily as he allowed his eyes to succumb to worshipping her beauty and his smile to pay homage to it.

"Raymond! Hello!", greeted Shannon with girl-like excitement.

"Shannon, you look amazing!", Raymond complimented as he leaned in to kiss her on the cheek.

She wanted desperately to turn her head quickly so they would kiss on the lips, but she decided against being so forward. She always complained that men only dated her for her body and sex, yet she was ready to serve herself up on her porch for every neighbor to see in the evening light.

"I have a little something for you", smiled Raymond as he handed her the bouquet.

"Thank you. These flowers smell so good.", Shannon acknowledged.

However, she thought what was truly amazing was all that he had done as she fully took sight of the limousine. And he thinks this is a little something, oh my what does he think is something *big*, she thought.

"Shall we?", asked Raymond as he reached for her hand.

"Yes, let me lock up first.", she said bubbling with excitement.

Raymond placed his arm around her waist and escorted her to the limo while the driver held the door open for the pair. Shannon stared awestruck as she entered the limo to find more flowers awaiting her and a bottle of Champagne. She'd only had Champagne once and it was divine and she was sure it wasn't top shelf as she assumed this one to be.

Raymond noticed that she was staring at the flowers as if she had never seen flowers before. He thought it was adorable, yet it was sad to him as well as he assumed that a woman as beautiful as she had never experienced beauty being showered upon her. Shannon's facial muscles were getting tired from her constant smiling and she began to feel embarrassed so she thought it might be good to talk instead.

"How was your work week?", she asked nervously.

"It was very productive. I was able to secure a client I'd been wooing for months. Everything changed after I met you. I guess you are my good luck piece.", laughed Raymond.

"Me? Don't blame that on me, 'cause if something goes wrong with the deal, I don't want to be blamed for that too.", laughed Shannon.

"It's funny. I didn't change up my tactic or verbiage with the guy. For some reason, during our last conversation, he just agreed.", Raymond expressed with a puzzled expression.

However, the more he pondered it he realized that something *had* changed. He didn't want to admit to her that the thought of her and the hope of a relationship relaxed him. He had been extremely tense in the months leading up to meeting her. He had been dealing with his recent breakup with his fiancée, his grandmother's failing health and trying to head a law empire.

"Enough about me. How about yours?", asked Ray hoping to gain a glimpse of her world.

"Not as exciting as yours I am sure, but I did decide to throw my hat in for a promotion. I've been a workhorse for so long, maybe it's time for me to try my hand at leadership as a Regional Director of Engineering and Development.", confessed Shannon.

"That sounds great. I have no doubt you have what it takes.", encouraged Raymond.

"Thanks. I feel like it's finally my time … you know?", Shannon admitted.

Raymond nodded in agreement; her sentiment mirrored what he had been feeling. Hope had been elusive to both in different ways, but now it felt like they were on the cusp of something wonderful. Shannon quickly changed topics not wanting him to know that he was the root cause of her feelings changing from disillusioned to hopeful.

"Did you hire someone to design these bouquets?", asked Shannon then immediately regretted such a silly question.

"We have a family florist that we use. I simply told her the flowers I wanted to use for your bouquet and she arranged them, but I did give her free rein on everything else.", Raymond admitted proudly.

"You've got to be kidding me. You selected these flowers and colors.", stated Shannon as she looked at the bouquet in her arms and waited for a punchline.

"I kid you not. I learned from two of the most knowledgeable men I know, my uncles Bernard and Ricky. They loved to talk about pleasing the loves of their lives by showering them with gifts and flowers.", laughed Raymond, "Growing up, I hated it, but now as a grown man I appreciate those memories and their wisdom."

"Vincent's grandfather, that Bernard?", inquired Shannon shocked to know he was that close to the powerful family.

"Oh, yeah. They were more than friends to my grandfather, they were like brothers.", Raymond smiled.

He began sharing childhood stories about his time with the elderly statesmen and she adored the joy she saw dancing in his eyes. She craved that closeness that he experienced growing up; he had so many role models looking out for him and mentoring him. She envied that as all she had were her maternal grandparents who raised her. She was surprised that he talked so lovingly about everyone, but his parents. Maybe he was like her and didn't have a connection.

"What about your parents? Were they involved in your life?", Shannon asked curious to hear that story.

"Oh yes, but my father was career-driven so to speak, until my grandfather realized my father did not have a knack for law or business; then my parents became jet setters. So, I spent more time with my grandparents. I really didn't start to get closer to my parents until I became an adult. I had to forgive them for being absent so much. We still don't have a great relationship though, but at least I try.", Raymond provided.

"Wow, I know all about absent parents for sure. I'm not as big of a person as you, though. I'm not sure I'll ever forgive them for abandoning me.", Shannon confessed close to tears.

Raymond saw that their conversation was once again heading to a serious and perhaps depressing topic and he wanted it to be light, but he was so thankful that they both felt that they could discuss anything with each other.

"Shannon, I'm not stronger than anyone else, I just realize that It's true that forgiveness is for us. I couldn't hold onto that anger and resentment any longer; it was killing me. It's okay to let go and to forgive.", Raymond whispered as he took her hand and kissed it.

He wanted to kiss away all of her childhood pain, but he knew that only she alone could release it. Shannon received his tenderness and inhaled deeply as she took in the richness that was him; from his cologne to the beautiful array of flowers that was just a sample of the love she sensed he had to give. She wanted to be vulnerable and not the stereotype of a strong Black woman. She didn't want to be strong all the time; it was exhausting, for once she wanted to relax and let her man comfort her and take control. Surprisingly, she did exactly that. She surrendered and allowed her body to lay in his embrace.

Raymond held her close to his heart and they didn't talk for the duration of the ride to the Detroit Club. It was in no way a normal second date for either of them, but despite that, it felt right and good. As he inhaled the fragrance from her pixie curls, he could imagine them creating a life together, even a little one playing in the yard with Shannon ever watchful to ensure little Ray didn't hurt himself. He smiled as his face lay atop her curls.

The ride seemed to stop almost as soon as it had begun; the driver announced that they had arrived at their destination. Neither wanted to loosen their embrace, but the night was young and there would be more time for that. Shannon stared out the window; she had never seen the Detroit Club or even heard of it before Raymond invited her. It was housed in a four-story brick and stone Romanesque Revival building. The driver opened the door so that the two could exit the limo. The couple began their walk toward the entry; it was tucked away by an unusual recessed archway that was only noticeable because a cloth canopy was added to create a stylish covering for the stairs that led up to the archway.

Raymond took her hand to assist her as she exited the limo. She felt like a movie star; the only missing pieces were the red carpet and the paparazzi waiting to snap pictures. Raymond escorted her up the stairs and into the luxurious club to be greeted by the club director.

"Good evening Mr. Brown. We've been expecting you. I've assigned waitstaff to attend to you and your guest. Please see me directly if you experience any concerns. Just one moment sir and I'll make sure everything is ready.", informed the director proudly.

If this is the treatment given to all, sign me up, thought Shannon.

"Do they treat all members this good?', questioned Shannon.

"No, just long-standing generational members like myself, the Barringtons and Bianchis.", Raymond reported with pride.

It was like she was living her very own fairy tale. She now saw a glimpse of the life Vivian now lived. These families were basically Michigan royalty, to say the least.

"Right this way sir.", instructed the director.

Shannon was absolutely flabbergasted at the special treatment and respect Raymond garnered from everyone. As they passed other staff members, they nodded to acknowledge his presence. She didn't feel worthy and had begun to fumble with her clothing until she heard him whisper.

"You can't improve perfection.", Raymond reassured her then winked.

Her self-consciousness faded with the gentle reassuring words and his eyes confirmed that he meant what he said. She noticed how proud and confident he was as he glided her to their reserved table that sat near the oversized fireplace. The warmth radiating from it was just enough to warm the room on a cool spring evening. The director attempted to assist her with her chair, but Raymond held up his hand to stop him. So that Raymond alone would be the only one to assist her.

The ambiance of the room shouted old money; the fireplace was ornate with a dark beautifully rich stained mantelpiece. The chandeliers were styled like old-world candelabras and there were matching ones placed as a centerpiece on every table. The tall draped windows were surrounded by rich wood paneling with exquisite wallpaper lining the wall from the top of the paneling and up to the dome ceiling. She tried to take it all in, but after the director sat them at their table another server approached to direct her attention elsewhere.

"Good evening, Mr. Brown and guest. What may I get you to drink?", inquired the waiter.

"I think I'd like a glass of your finest Merlot. That should pair well with the ribeye I'll have later; I feel like that tonight. Shannon, what about you?", suggested Raymond.

What about me, thought Shannon, I have no clue what to pair with what.

"What goes well with lamb?", she asked the server.

"I would definitely suggest, a glass of Cabernet Sauvignon.", supplied the waiter.

"Yes, please.", Shannon responded hesitantly.

"Make that top shelf as well. Thank you.", Raymond instructed as he handed the drink menus to the waiter.

"Yes, sir, of course.", the waiter informed as he accepted the menus.

"I hope you are enjoying yourself.", asked Raymond.

Are you freaking kidding me, she thought, "Yes, it's been an unforgettable night so far.", she admitted.

Raymond smiled; it was invigorating to take a woman out who appreciated his efforts and didn't complain about this or that and ask why he didn't do whatever they felt he should have. Vincent, you definitely knew what you were talking about; she's a good woman, thought Ray.

The dining room was filled with the most delicious aromas as the staff delivered the finest cuisines to their guests. Shannon hadn't tasted lamb that good, well if ever; she ate slowly to savor each morsel. Raymond beamed as she took each bite; he didn't think she realized that she closed her eyes as she chewed each piece. He found it irresistible and it seemed to make him appreciate his own meal that much more. As they talked, laughed and ate his eyes were fixated on her beautiful pouty lips. He wanted nothing more than to taste and devour them. He regretted not reserving a hotel room at the club; he could have easily taken her there and eaten her as his dessert. Yet, that would have been too presumptuous and he didn't want to offend her.

Raymond would have been surprised that Shannon shared that same sentiment. She was ready; it had been a year or so since she had been sexually intimate with a man. In fact, the fireplace looked quite inviting to Shannon; she could imagine their bodies entwined and kissing passionately in front of the warm flames. She blushed at the thought.

"A dollar bill for your thoughts. It looks like they're worth more than a penny.", laughed Raymond.

"Oh yeah, they are.", blushed Shannon, "You'll have to wait and see."

If things went well for them, she had some delicious plans for his sexy body. She pictured his muscles rippling as he disrobed; she couldn't wait. She had to sip some wine to help her refocus, but perhaps it was the wine that was causing her intensified sexual thoughts. The wine brought down her guard and she began contemplating what could possibly make a man born with everything be driven or have a purpose.

"You have the world at your fingertips. How do you maintain your drive? Most people dream of a day when they can get what you have. Then they would stop working and just leave everything behind.", asked Shannon.

"Like everyone else, I want to be recognized for my own talents and gifts; not just my family's name and reputation. But there is the ever-present family legacy. You know, not wanting to let my ancestors down who endured discrimination not just from whites but from Blacks as well. They weren't white enough to fit into white society and not black enough to be accepted by their own. I guess that's why many bi-racial blacks of that time created their own communities. So here I am taking on huge cases and making an even greater name for my family but more importantly for myself.", smiled Raymond.

"I get that …", she admitted then paused.

She was glad to know that it wasn't money that was the driving force; if it had been she would not be able to relate to him. She had seen so many people so busy chasing money that they couldn't see the happiness surrounding them and they were miserable.

"I guess I do it for my ancestors too in a way. I worked so hard in high school and college for my grandparents. I wanted them to know that the time, love and resources they provided to me were not in vain. They had been let down once already by my mother. I couldn't break their hearts all over again.", Shannon confessed.

She only opened up about her past trauma to Vivian and Gloria; she never told a man this much ever. If they knew anything it was from observation more than word of mouth. Raymond wanted to ask how so but thought it best to save that question for another time, but she continued by providing him further insight.

"I didn't want to hear my grandfather add up the tally of the money he invested in me. I heard enough about the clothes he bought me in high school. I darn sure didn't want to hear it about college tuition. So, I had to make good use of my degree.", reminisced Shannon with a giggle.

"Exactly! I let my baby sister, Crystal, take all the heat.", laughed Raymond.

"You feel me!", laughed Shannon, "But see I'm the only child of an only child, so I have to avoid the smoke at all costs." Shannon took on a more serious expression, "Now I do it for my daughter.", explained Shannon.

"Tell me about her. You don't speak about her much.",
expressed Raymond.

He had never dated a woman with a child before so he was
thankful that Shannon's daughter was a young adult. He wasn't
sure he was interested in being a stepfather to a child.

"I've been very protective of her over the years as I dated,
but she reminds me often that she's an adult now.", smiled
Shannon, "She's my heart and I want to be a good role model for
her, but I know I've dropped the ball in some ways. I want her to
be confident and self-reliant, everything I wasn't at her age."

"From what I've heard, she has many reasons to be proud
to call you, mother.", Raymond ascertained.

"Thank you, but by no means has it been easy.", Shannon
blushed.

"I'd love to meet her sometime. Do you think she'll like
me?", questioned Raymond as his smile hypnotized Shannon.

"She's a tough one to impress, but I'm betting on you.",
giggled Shannon.

Raymond winked at Shannon in confirmation that he was
up to the challenge. Little did he know that he was by far the only
one so far that would meet Nicole's requirements for her mother.
Nicole could spot and sniff out a loser a mile away and would set
off all the warning signals for her mother. The waiter approached
the laughing couple to check on them.

"We're all set.", informed Raymond to the waiter.

"No rush, sir. Take your time.", insisted the waiter as he
left the tab behind.

Raymond discreetly moved large dollar bills from his wallet
and placed them inside the sleeve. Shannon wanted desperately
to see the amount of the bill. It took every ounce of control for her

not to do what was customary for her and look. This truly was a new occurrence for her and she regretted not getting more advice from Vivian. She didn't want either of her alter egos, the broke-girl tendencies or the boss bitch to jack things up for her; neither of which would serve her well with Raymond.

Raymond stood to assist Shannon from the chair; he found it so amusing that she stared at the closed restaurant check sleeve. He wondered what she would do if she had seen the amount. As he pulled the chair back and she stood, her full buttocks rubbed against his hand. He couldn't wait for the day when its roundness would fill his hands. He quickly took her by the waist to steady her stance. The accidental touch to her rear sent chills racing up her spine; when he purposefully touched her waist, it sent tingles to her hidden gem and almost left her breathless.

Oh my God, she thought as she in turn placed her arm around his waist. She blushed all the way to the limo, just like a young woman who had received her first kiss. During the ride back to her home, the conversation was very natural, light and spontaneous. They both enjoyed the newness of the relationship and the ease at which they communicated. Unknowingly, they both had the same hopes for the night's end. Shannon hoped that he would accept an invite inside; it had been ages since she invited a man to her place and he would be the first to see her new home. Even Joe hadn't seen that!

As the limo pulled in front of her home, Shannon felt her heart skip a beat and her stomach flutter with anticipation. Raymond walked her to her front door as the gentleman she expected him to be, but she wasn't ready for the night to end. She decided it was time to be bold and set proper decorum aside.

"Would you like to come in for a drink?", Shannon asked as she turned the key to unlock her door not wanting to face him as she asked the question.

"That sounds chill.", expressed Raymond, but a drink was the furthest from his mind.

Although he accepted her offer, she was still grateful that he couldn't see the giant grin on her face. She didn't want to seem desperate or too eager for a man's touch. Lord knows it's been a while, she thought.

"Well, this is my new home.", she indicated after flicking the light switch and motioning for him to enter.

Raymond scanned the entrance and the living area to his right; he was impressed with her sense of style. As they entered the living room, he thought it was minimalist and very sophisticated and it would blend well with his own.

"Would you like to remove your jacket?", asked Shannon interrupting his thoughts.

"Sure.", Raymond said.

As he began to slide off his jacket, he couldn't pull his eyes away from her curves; the curves of her hips and her lips drew him in. He tossed his jacket aside aiming for a chair but missed. Shannon noticed and turned to retrieve it.

"Let me get that.", uttered Shannon.

Raymond quickly stopped her as his hand pulled her close by the waist. He had been wanting to do that the entire night and he wasn't going to miss his opportunity. Their noses touched and each could hear the deep breathing of the other until neither of them could refrain from the delight that lay within reach. Raymond possessively moved his hands to her buttocks and held her firmly in his hands as if he alone had a right to them and always would. He skillfully moved his tongue deep within her mouth as he imagined tasting other parts of her. She reciprocated his every movement and staked a claim to his body as well as her hands explored marking her territory on his muscled frame.

Shannon became drunk with desire with each kiss; as Raymond's kisses moved to her neck, she yearned and hoped that he would raise her blouse to reveal her breasts. He could rip her clothing from her flesh if he wanted to; she wouldn't hold it against him, she thought. The two stumbled in their passion as if with drunkenness as they approached her sofa while Shannon fumbled with the button of his pants. Shannon pushed Raymond to the sofa and straddled him, but somehow, he effortlessly flipped her to lay beneath him as he was determined to be in control.

He continued with kisses on her neck; he found her perfume intoxicating and he was desperate to lay kisses on the source. He swiftly slid his hands up her back and unsnapped her bra to free the soft treasures. To Shannon's delight, Raymond maneuvered her blouse up to reveal them and he buried his face within their comfort. Shannon released a moan of anticipation and it instantaneously brought him to a clear head. Just as quickly as their passionate exchange began, it ended.

"I'm sorry. I don't want us to move too fast.", Raymond whispered in her ear as he steadied his breathing.

He didn't want to rush her to have sex as he realized at that moment that he was truly falling for her and he didn't want it to be a fly-by-night hookup. He wanted to nourish their relationship so that they could have the coveted love story that they and so many others desire.

"It's okay, it's not too fast …", Shannon began then stopped herself.

She didn't want to sound as if she was begging him, but she was ready to explore his body. She didn't understand the reason for his restraint.

"For me, it is. I respect you too much. We'll have plenty of time for that.", Raymond reassured her as he kissed her forehead and then stood.

He began to tuck his sweater inside his unzipped pants, then he quickly walked to the chair to retrieve his jacket from the floor.

"Talk tomorrow, baby?", Raymond confidently asked.

"Yeah ... yes.", Shannon hesitated in her reply as she followed behind him to the door.

She was utterly confused by his actions and from his appearance, he seemed pleased by it all. Unknowingly, it was extremely difficult for Raymond when every atom of his body wanted to devour her, but he treasured what they were building too much to sacrifice it for quick pleasures. He knew it would be incredible when the time was right and he was man enough to take the lead on this.

"I'll have the driver to bring in the flowers. Good night, pixie.", Raymond said with a quick kiss on her lips.

"Good night.", whispered Shannon.

Raymond quickly jogged down the steps, hating that he had called her the nickname he had reserved for her in his head, but he adored her pixie haircut and thought the nickname was perfect for her. Pixie, thought Shannon as she smiled at the cute nickname; no man had ever given her one before at least not one that could be said in public. Raymond Brown, you are a tough one to figure out, thought Shannon.

Chapter 5

Shannon had been dating Raymond for weeks but it felt like months because they still hadn't been sexual yet. She didn't know how to handle it and she felt silly that she would even think there was a problem because of it. But her overactive imagination wouldn't let up and insisted there had to be one. Raymond had asked her out again for the coming weekend; they were seeing each other twice a week and talking multiple times on the phone. Despite that, the nagging voice persisted so she decided she wouldn't take him up on his offer and would plan something with her girls instead. She needed to hear their opinion on the matter.

She had offered to cook for the ladies, but both scoffed at the idea and insisted they dine out instead. So, the ladies agreed to meet up at Amore de Roma in the Eastern Market. She was excited about a visit to the market area; it was just in time for Flower Day. She and the ladies could do some flower shopping after dining at the restaurant.

Here she was, standing in her closet shuffling through her clothes once again; she had been doing that a lot as of late. Before Raymond, she would wear the same few styles over and over and let her new items sit in the closet with tags. But Raymond, unknowingly, and the girls had put a halt to all of that. She was putting extra care into her appearance more and more as she and Raymond dated. She had decided to wear something springy and feminine, but she didn't have much to choose from. Guess I'll have to go shopping with Vivian, she thought, as she shuffled past outfit after outfit until settling for a lightweight slate-blue crisscross V-neck off-the-shoulder Dolman-sleeved sweater with a slim waist and lace straps to keep the girls covered. She paired it with crisp flare-legged dark blue denim jeans and black leather platform wedged walking anklet boots with a side zipper. Finally, she'd carry the medium-sized YSL quilted clutch that Vivian bought her as a gift.

Shannon eyed the clutch before placing it on the passenger side seat of her car, if she and Raymond did work out, she'd be just like Vivian dropping a grand on a small purse barely large enough to hold a cell phone and car keys, she giggled at disbelief at the thought.

Shannon pulled into the parking lot of the restaurant; the building was built in the late 19th century. It was a two-story brick-style building constructed using red bricks and had red and white striped fabric awnings at the windows and entrance. She loved the coppered tiled ceiling of the interior and the cherry wooden bar area. It was classy and straight out of an interior design magazine; it represented the unique style and history of Detroit, a timeless classic.

She entered the restaurant and noticed her besties flagging her over to their table. She was thankful for their promptness because she was starving and from the looks of it, they were too. They had already ordered appetizers that were being served by the waitress.

"Hey, girls! Thanks for agreeing to meet with me. Your girl needs help.", sighed Shannon as she sat her designer bag on an empty chair.

"Hey. Oh, you're finally carrying the clutch!", exclaimed Vivian as if that were the most important thing.

"Hey, doll. We ordered your favorite appetizer. Sit and tell us what's going on.", instructed Gloria as she began nibbling on the appetizer.

"I'd better let you fill your bellies first before I spill the beans.", suggested Shannon as she reached for the bread.

"You better not have dumped Raymond.", Vivian fumed as her lowered fork clanked on her plate.

"Lord!", signed Gloria.

82

"Relax! I haven't dumped Ray, but I have thought about it.", admitted Shannon casually.

"Why? What has he done to piss you off?", questioned Vivian waiting to be annoyed by Shannon's response.

"Well, you know we've been talking for a while now ... It's getting pretty serious, at least for me and we haven't even had *sex yet*.", Shannon confided.

"You were right! We really did need to eat first before you told us this bull!", Gloria chastised and shook her head in disappointment.

"Shannon ... what is wrong with a guy wanting to wait and not sleep with you right away? Please tell me.", Vivian implored.

Gloria interjected before Shannon could speak; she was beyond frustrated with the younger woman.

"You've been mistreated by so many men, so frequently you think it's normal for a man to disrespect you and your body. They were probably trying to get your panties off on the first date.", whispered Gloria with discrete venom.

"Exactly and if they don't you speculate that they're gay.", Vivian added.

"Well, I have wondered that about Raymond too. Things will get heated and then just as quickly he's pulling away. Maybe I should give Joe another chance. He claims to be working now and his phone conversations are more mature.", explained Shannon.

"You're freaking kidding me.", huffed Vivian as she flung up her hands.

"Honey, I'm sure that Raymond is not gay, just a gentleman. If you want to pass up a rich good man for a broke one, go right ahead. I'm done trying to stop you.", Gloria proclaimed then flagged the waitress, "I am absolutely done.", Gloria added for emphasis.

"It's just that Joe, I think, has finally matured. Things could be different this time around.", explained Shannon.

"This time around? How many times has it been? You've given him chance after chance. And as his sister, I'm telling you he doesn't deserve another one!", insisted Vivian.

"Can we just enjoy a meal out? I don't want to discuss *my* love life anymore.", demanded Shannon.

Shannon was tired of defending her feelings and decisions; she was an inch away from ending things with Raymond so that she could focus solely on Joe regardless of what anyone had to say about him. However, she had decided before she made that rash decision, that she would go out with Joe first to make sure he wasn't faking being a changed man. The only thing that could get him off her thoughts was a hot waiter who passed by. The ladies had acquiesced and moved on to another topic but were drawn back by Shannon's comments.

"He is so fine and *that* body ...", Shannon's eyes and mouth conveyed her lust.

Gloria stared at the roughly kept man with straggly hair pulled up in a man-bun. She couldn't contain her anger.

"Really Shannon? God knows I don't like to judge, but he looks like he's straight from a halfway house and has a probation officer. So that's what you really want?", deliberated a confused Gloria.

"He doesn't look that bad. What can I say? I just really prefer white guys.", admitted Shannon out loud for the first time.

"There is absolutely nothing at all wrong with loving white men, but baby listen, you pick the bums every single time.", counseled Gloria with Vivian nodding in agreement.

"I just like them with an edge, a little roughness.", Shannon provided.

"Like my brother.", suggested Vivian.

"Yes, a guy who can handle his own that would punch a guy that offended him.", Shannon provided additional clarity.

"Yeah, but the problem is you might get punched too.", reminded Vivian.

"Thank you.", agreed Gloria.

The women didn't bring it up much, but there had been times when Joe's anger got the best of him and he threatened to hit Shannon. Fortunately, he had enough restraint in the past not to, but he destroyed everything in his path as a substitute. Shannon replaced countless items of furniture in the past while in a relationship with him.

"I'm not trying to tell Ray's business, but this is the very reason he's dated White women in the past because Black women have called him weak or gay because he's not thuggish.", Vivian disclosed.

"Maybe I should have let them have him. How can I compete with them? I don't have any of the features they have.", Shannon uttered.

"You need to uninvite yourself to this pity party! He prefers an educated *Black* woman and here you are about to do the same thing to him that other Black women have done in the past.", Vivian choked on the words.

"Doll, we just don't want you to be alone. You've been down that road with Joe and others like him enough times to know where it leads, baby. Every black man is not like your father; so, please do not throw a chance at real happiness away.", pleaded Gloria.

"If you don't want to listen to us, let your grandparents advise you. You should let them meet Raymond. You could invite the three of them to something.", suggested Vivian smiling.

Vivian knew that if Shannon's grandparents met Raymond, they would be his greatest cheerleaders. She knew that Shannon trusted her grandparents more than anyone. That was a reason Joe had never met them in nineteen years. Shannon's eyes were inquisitory as she didn't realize Vivian's plan; then her eyes softened.

"Perhaps. Maybe they will see something I don't and warn me about it. I could prepare dinner and invite them over. My folks haven't been over yet to see my new home.", Shannon planned aloud.

"Yes, that would be a great idea. But you'll have to cook soul food … since that's all your grandparents will eat.", replied Gloria as she smiled.

Vivian matched Gloria's smile as they both knew Raymond would fall in love with Shannon's cooking as soul food dishes were her specialty. Shannon didn't add up the reason for their giddiness; she just hoped that Raymond's bourgeoise appearance and his conversation would annoy the heck out of her grandfather. She too, mimicked their upbeat expressions at the thought.

The ladies managed to salvage some fun at the meal but decided to cut it short and not visit the flower vendors. Shannon's mindset had swallowed up the light-heartedness of their plans with gloom and no one was really in the mood for it, yet no one voiced it. It was a silent agreement; so, they called it a day.

Vivian had a one-track mind as they left the restaurant; she barely uttered her farewells before pulling out her cell phone to call her husband. She knew that drastic measures were necessary to prevent her good friend from making yet another mistake with her brother. She checked over her shoulder to make sure the two ladies had entered their vehicles.

"Hey, Vincent.", whispered Vivian.

"Hey, sweetheart. I thought you would still be with the girls. Is something wrong? Your voice sounds concerned.", Vincent queried.

"It's Shannon. That girl baffles me sometimes. As long as I've known her, I still don't know why my brother has a pull on her. She's talking about taking him back!", fussed Vivian as she slid inside her car.

"Damn! I thought things were good; at least that's how Ray feels.", voiced Vincent.

"Me too. Honestly, she's just afraid because everything that Raymond represents is new to her. I don't know what to do.", Vivian whimpered.

"I don't want you to worry. I'll handle this. Our best friends deserve happiness and I'll be damned if we let Joe fuck this up! Ok, sweetheart?", Vincent firmly reassured.

"Yes, thank you, baby.", sighed Vivian.

She knew that Vincent knew how to devise a plan and that she could count on him to do what needed to be done. She inhaled deeply to calm her nerves; she was relieved to know that none of the people who loved Shannon were willing to allow her to mess up a great love affair.

If only Shannon had known the fuss that her best friend was making over the newsflash she had dropped at dinner, she would have acted a complete fool. And Vivian would have reminded her that she's been acting a fool for Joe, for far too long and now it was time for a change.

As Shannon drove home, she contemplated when she would have Raymond and her folks over for dinner. She figured she would reserve the weekend for Joe and invite Raymond during the week for dinner. She had taken the week off to pick up Nicole from college since finals were over and Nicole would be coming home for summer break. Nicole was the absolute worst critic of anyone Shannon dated and she knew she would give her an honest opinion; Nicole wouldn't be impressed by Raymond's good looks or money. She would dig much deeper and examine his character.

Shannon was feeling good and subconsciously hoping that her family would give her any number of reasons to end things with Raymond so she could stay in her comfort zone. She didn't recognize that her comfort zone was more like a dysfunctional zone whenever Joe or men like him were involved. She spoke a command to the vehicle command center.

"Call Joe.", instructed Shannon.

"Calling Joe, baby daddy cell.", announced her voice activation system.

The phone rang longer than she expected and she was about to disconnect.

"Hey, how's my girl?", asked Joe.

Joe was shocked because Shannon had stopped calling him and they only talked if he called her.

"I'm good. I decided to take you up on your offer to go out.", informed Shannon.

"Now that's my Big Tit!", exclaimed Joe indiscreetly.

"You know I *hate* that nickname!", Shannon sternly whispered.

"Sorry, baby. I'm about to mess up before I even get the date.", laughed Joe.

"Exactly! Look, I'll pick you up Saturday at 8 pm and we can go to Charlie's for drinks.", suggested Shannon.

"No can do, babe. The owner told me if I show my face there again, he'll call the cops. I trashed that place real good the last time.", bragged Joe.

There was a quiet voice asking her if she really wanted this over what Raymond could offer. She sighed loudly, partly to quiet the voice in her head and also to show her frustration with his braggadocios story. The voice again reminded her of the respect Raymond garnered when they went out.

"Look, we can go to Buddy's and get a pizza. What about that?", asked Shannon.

"Sure, as long as I can order drinks, I'm good. Maybe we can go back to your new crib …", agreed Joe.

"Bye.", Shannon dismissed him.

For the first time in her life, she had two men interested in her at one time. As she prepared to call Raymond, the voice reminded her that only one was worth her time.

"Call Raymond.", instructed Shannon.

"Calling Raymond, fine ass cell.", informed the voice activation system.

The phone had barely rung before Raymond answered; it was night and day compared to Joe. Raymond instantly regretted answering so fast, but lately, they only talked when he called her; whereas before they both called each other as not wanting their time apart to end.

"Hey, Pixie. How are you?", Raymond responded.

He couldn't hide the excitement in his voice. He had missed her; missed hearing her and seeing her. It was definitely time for them to see each other again; it was well past due, he thought. Pixie, she thought, it made her smile every single time she remembered him calling her that for the first time.

"I'm good. How's my Ray doing today?", Shannon flirted.

She hated to admit it, but there was something different about talking to Raymond. His voice made tingles spiral through her body with one huge flutter between her thighs. She giggled as she waited for his response and the quiet voice reminded her of how good he made her feel.

"Pixie, I'm doing really good now that I hear your voice. I was just thinking about you. I wanted to take you out next Saturday.", Raymond flirted.

"I was thinking of you too. In fact, I was hoping to invite you over to my place for a casual dinner. I'll prepare dinner and you can meet my folks and my daughter. But I have weekend plans, so I was thinking … maybe Wednesday. Are you free?", Shannon invited.

Raymond was excited to hear that she wanted him to meet her family. He felt it was time to take things to the next level as well and maybe that was the reason things were stalling because they had been keeping their relationship at the same level when in fact it was time to grow.

"Yeah, Wednesday is good. I'll make sure my schedule is free. Just let me know what time and I'll be there.", informed Raymond.

"I think 6 o'clock is a good time for dinner. Is that okay?", asked Shannon.

"For sure!", proclaimed Raymond.

"Ok, we'll talk later.", Shannon said.

"Ok. Bye Pixie.", breathed Raymond.

His voice was so husky, that she could feel his breath on her neck as if he had whispered it in her ear. She was glad to be off the call with him; she was losing focus on the road and that could be deadly. She was glad that she didn't live far away. She wanted to replay that memory under her warm bedsheets as she remembered the touch of his lips on her cleavage.

"Focus girl! So, you can make it home alive!", shouted Shannon as she regained her concentration.

Chapter 6

Shannon hadn't seen Nicole this excited since she went away to college for her freshman year. It surprised Shannon how receptive Nicole was to the idea of her dating Raymond and Nicole seemed more excited than Shannon about the upcoming dinner guests.

"Everything needs to be perfect!", insisted Nicole as she took the once-forgotten China out of the cabinet.

"Let me help. You shouldn't be doing everything.", fussed Shannon.

"Nope. You just focus on making a delicious meal. I've got everything else covered.", reassured Nicole.

"Funny, when I ask you to clean up you don't. But for Raymond, you've cleaned this house from top to bottom and then some.", laughed Shannon as she swatted Nicole on the butt with the washcloth.

"Mommy! Stop! You're getting my pants wet.", laughed Nicole.

Mommy thought Shannon, it had been a while since Nicole used that term of endearment. Lately, it had just been mom or hey, since she was an adult now and truly understood the poor choices that Shannon had made over the years concerning men. Shannon felt that perhaps Nicole's knowledge of that took away some level of respect or endearment. The thought of Shannon possibly choosing a great catch gave Nicole hope and excitement about the future. Nicole had done some snooping of her own and asked her Auntie Vivian about him and she was excited about what she heard. She was going to do everything possible to help her mother make the dinner date a success.

Nicole's obvious excitement added to Shannon's own excitement and nervousness. Until that point, she had only focused on the possibility that Raymond would do something to piss off her grandfather, but what if he did the opposite. What if he won over her grandparents? That would make everything a game changer and validate what the quiet voice within her kept whispering, "Raymond will be your husband." At that thought, she nearly dropped the pan of macaroni and cheese she had just removed from the oven.

"Mommy, be careful!", Nicole shouted as she rushed over to assist, "What's wrong?"

"It's just getting real …", whispered a wide-eyed Shannon.

Nicole smiled at her nervous mother who was behaving uncharacteristically, but she had to remind herself that this was the first time her mother was dating someone worthy.

"Give that to me. Go check your appearance, your guests should be arriving any minute.", Nicole shooed Shannon away.

Shannon removed her apron to toss it on the hook near the pantry cabinet and headed to the powder room. Nicole thought her mother looked gorgeous and was perfect in every way, but Nicole wanted her to relax her nerves and thought if Shannon saw her reflection, that would put her at ease. Shannon had told Raymond it was a casual dinner, but she didn't want to look like she was just hanging with family. She had put the same effort into her attire that she had previously. She blew the dust off yet another outfit that had been sitting in her closet waiting to dry rot. It was a white one-piece jumpsuit with a cross collar that bared her shoulders then draped down to the elbow. The waist was snatched and form-fitting and it hugged her round derriere. She added a touch of gold when she paired large hoop earrings and a pair of open-toe slingbacks to her ensemble. Shannon pressed her lips together to renew her lipstick and smiled; just then the house camera detected movement outside the house at the curb.

"I'm surprised Shannon wants us to meet this Raymond guy. She's never introduced us to anyone.", Larry pondered.

"I say this one must be pretty special.", speculated Evelyn, "Slow down, you're about to pass up her house".

"That's the house! Our baby girl has done well for herself.", Larry's voice quivered.

"Yes, Lord! Who would have thought she'd turn out so good after being dropped off to us in dirty clothes and a loaded diaper.", whimpered Evelyn.

"We've got to pull ourselves together. We don't want Raymond to see us like this. He'll think we're all crazy.", laughed Larry.

"I think that's him in that fancy car that pulled up behind us. What type of car is that, dear?", asked Evelyn.

"Money … it's called money.", Larry said as he looked in his rearview mirror.

Raymond pulled his Bentley behind the Washingtons and assumed that the couple must be Shannon's grandparents as they looked and pointed at the rearview mirror as if they were summing up who he might be. Larry noticed that the young man was smiling at them.

"Stop making a clown of yourself. He's watching us.", fussed Larry.

Larry scurried out of his car as quickly as his stiff legs would allow. Raymond thought he should do the same so that he could introduce himself and assist with anything the couple might need. Larry rushed to Evelyn's side to open the door so they would be prepared to greet Shannon's suitor. Raymond could see that she was not steady on her feet. He could hear them playfully fussing.

"Dear, do you need the chair?", asked Larry.

"And how do you think we're going to get that up the stairs?", inquired Evelyn with her hand on her hip.

"We didn't really think this through, did we?", surmised Larry.

"Not at all. I'll just use my walker or cane to get around inside; I won't be moving around much. You can get that.", insisted Evelyn with a heavy sigh.

Raymond greeted them with a wave as he approached the couple.

"Hello, there young man! You must be Raymond.", informed Larry.

"Yes, sir.", confirmed Raymond as he stopped in front of the couple.

"I'm Larry and this is my wife, Evelyn. We're Shannon's grandparents.", Larry informed as he extended his hand.

"Nice to meet you both.", beamed Raymond with his captivating smile and a firm handshake.

Larry admired a man with a firm handshake and direct eye contact. So far so good, thought Larry.

"Do you need some help?", Raymond offered.

"Yes, I need to get the cake from the trunk that Evelyn baked for our babies and her walker. Can you get that so I can assist my wife?", instructed Larry.

"The cane will be better for getting up the steps and moving around in the house.", insisted Evelyn.

"Why don't you get the items and I'll assist her instead." provided Raymond as he took Evelyn's arm.

It wasn't a question, but instructions.   As the two approached the stairs of the porch, Raymond lifted Evelyn effortlessly and walked up the stairs carrying her like a life-size doll. Larry chuckled as he watched the young man not just show off, but show his heart. My baby has struck gold after years of digging and finding rocks, Larry smiled at the thought. He wasn't the only one impressed; Evelyn beamed with delight that Shannon just might have found a man as kind as her grandfather or at least as strong as he had been in his youth.

Shannon heard the signal on her phone again going haywire announcing the arrival of a guest and she was so nervous. She could see her hand shaking in the mirror as she ran her fingers through her hair to make sure it was perfect. She took several deep breaths, but she was immobilized.

"Mommy! What are you doing? Never mind, I'll get it.", shouted Nicole from the kitchen as she ran to the front door.

Nicole leaned against the thick mahogany craftsman door to peer out the square glass panel. She was ecstatic to see that Raymond was an absolute gentleman by carrying her great-grandmother up the stairs. She knew without a doubt the evening was going to be successful and it was very important that she get to know this dark knight; the first of his kind to ever be introduced to the family. She flung open the door with anticipation.

"Hello, Granny!", then Nicole moved her attention to the handsome stranger, "Raymond, right? Hello, I'm Nicole. Come on in!", squealed Nicole then she cleared her throat.

Darn girl, she thought, don't make your mother look like she doesn't ever date.

"Hello, Granny's babydoll.", giggled Evelyn as she pulled her in to plant kisses on Nicole's face.

"Come this way, Raymond. Granny, let me help you to the living room. We can sit here until we are ready to eat.", informed Nicole as she guided everyone.

Shannon was headed to the entrance when she saw Nicole take Raymond and her grandmother to the living room. She was distracted however by her grandfather who was struggling to enter the house. Larry managed to juggle the items as he struggled to open the hefty door to bring the cake and walker inside.

"Where do you want this cake?", asked Larry.

"Big Daddy!", exclaimed Shannon as she skipped through the narrow hall past the stairs to greet her grandfather, "I'll take the cake. Hey Raymond … Granny! Make yourselves comfortable. I'll be right back.", Shannon shouted as she walked to the formal dining room near the entrance.

"Why do you have that walker? You never listen.", fussed Evelyn as she waved for Larry to come near.

Evelyn and Larry sat on the high-back chairs that provided more height, making it easier for them to get up and down. Raymond and Nicole sat on opposite ends of the sofa allowing space for Shannon to sit between the two when she returned. Shannon had not paid much attention to how Raymond looked when he entered the living room, but now that she had joined them, his very essence commanded her attention and he stood to approach her.

Raymond dressed casually, but nothing that touched his skin could ever downplay his magnetism. He wore a slim-fit pair of Rock Revival denim jeans with a long frontal signature patchwork that traveled down his thighs and stopped just below the knee. The white detailed stitching and embroidery of the rear pockets gave him an extra swagger that couldn't go unnoticed whenever he walked into a room. She watched fixated as he glided toward her in his white-soled cognac Rockport shoes. His white textured slim-fit hoody clung to each rippling muscle of his arms and laid snugly against his tight abs. She had never seen a man as attractive and the more she got to know him the more attracted to him she seemed to become. It was indeed frightening and she became even more so when he stood in front of her. He took her possessively in his arms and whispered in her ear as she had fantasized about him doing so many times. She inhaled him deeply becoming drunk from his cologne.

"I've missed you, Pixie.", he whispered as his lips brushed against her ear.

Then he surprised her and everyone in the room when he kissed her lips then stared at her as if he had never seen anyone as beautiful as she. Then it was her turn to surprise everyone including herself when she pulled him close and kissed him again as if no one but the two of them were in the room.

"Dessert comes after the meal. You two can do that later!", joked Larry as Evelyn and Nicole joined his laughter.

Okay, mommy, thought Nicole, you actually do know what to do to get a man. Raymond and Shannon realized that they had forgotten where they were and blushed as they heard the laughter. Evelyn decided to change the topic, attempting to allow the pair to compose themselves as they sat down.

"Honey, we are so proud of you. Your home is absolutely stunning, Cupcake.", complimented Evelyn.

"Thank you, granny!", blushed Shannon.

"Yes, baby girl. You have done well for yourself and babydoll. And I can't *wait* to eat!", agreed Larry.

"It does smell delicious. It hit me as soon as I walked in!", Raymond confirmed.

"Mommy is a really good soul food cook.", Nicole added.

"Cupcake, what did you cook?", smiled Evelyn.

"I prepared mac-n-cheese, collard greens, cornbread of course, beef short ribs with potatoes and gravy, white rice and candied yams.", explained Shannon.

"Yes, Lord!", shouted Larry, "Nicole, make sure I get a healthy plate!", Larry laughed.

"Yes, Big Daddy.", Nicole giggled.

"I've never had soul food before.", Raymond was embarrassed to admit.

That would be strike number one thought Shannon as her family gasped; she thought she would have been happy for her grandparents to dislike him, but now hoped they would let that slide.

"Oh, boy! You are in for a treat! Especially the way Shannon cooks it. She took everything she learned from her grandmother, here, and her great-grandmother and added some of her own touches. Yes, Lord!", bragged Larry as he nodded his head.

"I can't wait! If it tastes as good as she looks, I'm hooked.", laughed Raymond.

"My man! Those two things caused me to propose to this one right here!", Larry pointed at his wife as he joined Raymond's laughter.

Shannon couldn't help but blush at the compliments and the implied acceptance of Raymond. Subconsciously, a part of her was excited that such a put-together man wanted her and could possibly even want to commit his life to her. Not only that, he was the first man that she had ever introduced to her family and the first they seemed to think worthy of her. She cleared her throat to redirect everyone.

"Well, we better not sit too long. I don't want the food to get cold.", informed Shannon as she stood.

"Yes, indeed!", agreed Larry as he smacked his lips, "I can almost taste those greens now".

Raymond smiled at Shannon; she looked so delicate and innocent as she blushed at their compliments. He hoped that their courtship would be energized by their evening together. He caught a glimpse of Evelyn smiling at him. She had been observing the way his eyes were devoted to Shannon.

"Let me help you up from the chair, Mrs. Washington.", offered Raymond as he quickly jogged to Evelyn.

Everyone was all smiles as they entered the kitchen to fix their plates. Raymond was a little unsure of what to do as he was accustomed to dinner being served on serving dishes and platters on the dining room table whenever there was an intimate family dinner or even the wait staff serving the food. Larry noticed his confusion.

"Young man, this is how we do things in the Washington household. We serve ourselves.", laughed Larry.

"Everyone but him. If it's not me fixing his plate, it's one of these two.", snickered Evelyn as she grabbed two plates.

"Granny, let me fix Big Daddy's plate. You'll make it too skimpy.", teased Nicole as she took the extra plate.

"That's my girl! Look out for your Big Daddy.", chuckled Larry.

Nicole set the plate down and washed her hands in the kitchen sink.

"See your granny wasn't even going to clean her hands.", Larry playfully chastised his wife.

"Shut up! It wouldn't be the first time you've eaten a little dirt.", fussed Evelyn as she reluctantly set her plate down to follow suit.

Raymond spotted the powder room off the kitchen and headed there to wash his hands.

"Not comfortable washing your hands in the kitchen sink?", inquired Evelyn.

"No, ma'am.", Raymond admitted as he looked back to comment.

"Well, we are just simple folks. You can relax and just go with the flow.", revealed Larry.

Everyone nodded in agreement and Shannon smiled to reassure Raymond that no one was judging his decision. Shannon had just finished washing her own hands in the kitchen sink when Raymond returned, so she handed him a plate. Raymond looked at the pots and pans on the stove and didn't know where to begin. Shannon decided that she would take the lead and guide him through the process.

"In this stock pot, we have greens. Get you a spoonful.", she instructed as she held the lid and pointed toward the serving spoon.

Raymond was obedient and did as he was told then looked to her for further instructions.

"Okay, slice a piece of cornbread.", Shannon instructed then touched his hand to stop him, "That is way too small of a piece. You need more than that to soak up the broth.", she giggled.

"Okay ...", Raymond said hesitantly hoping he liked the unfamiliar food.

Nicole could see the doubt on his face as she stood nearby scooping a large portion of macaroni and cheese for her great-grandfather.

"Trust and believe, you will love it!", Nicole reassured him.

"Okay, Nicole. I'm going to trust that you are being *real* with me.", joked Raymond.

"Oh, most def.", giggled Nicole as she took a bite off her grandfather's plate.

"Stop that and fix your own! There's plenty.", fussed Shannon as she shooed her daughter away, "Ray, let me give you a little more."

"This is good. I just don't want to get too much. I don't like wasting food.", admitted Raymond.

Shannon had begun fixing her plate when she decided to set it down so she could take a fork from a drawer; she only knew one way to squash his fear. She took the fork and cut off a piece of candied yams from the cast-iron skillet and fed Raymond without asking permission. He opened his mouth like a love-sick puppy willing to do whatever she asked of him. He chewed the morsel and with each bite, it seemed to unlock more and more delicious flavor; his eyes grew wide with each discovery of his taste buds. They had been brought to life by the indescribable flavor.

"That was incredible!", he blurted not realizing how loud he had become.

"Boy, I told you!", shouted Larry from the dining room then he whispered to Evelyn, "We need to start planning a wedding."

Larry leaned to his left to kiss his wife on the cheek and they hugged at the thought of finally seeing their baby girl happy. Nicole carried a plate to her great-grandfather and set her plate down. She knew exactly what sparked their display of affection.

She decided she would join in the excitement and began hugging her grandparents.

"We don't need to get carried away. We all know how she can mess things up.", warned Evelyn just loud enough for the three of them to hear.

Larry and Nicole nodded as they sighed, but a light of hope remained within all three despite Evelyn's warning. Soon after that, Nicole passed Shannon and Raymond as they entered the dining room and she went back to the kitchen to get a beverage. Raymond balanced a hefty plate of food and Shannon was beaming with joy. She waited to see where Raymond wanted to sit and then sat beside him.

Larry reached for a phantom glass only to find an empty spot where one should have been.

"Babydoll, can you bring me some red Kool-Aid!", shouted Larry to the kitchen.

"Pop will do for me.", informed Evelyn.

"Mommy … Raymond, what do you want?", asked Nicole.

"I'll take a pop. I'll let you and Big Daddy drink up the pitcher of Kool-Aid.", provided Shannon.

"Well … what about a bottle of water?", asked Raymond.

He didn't have a clue what red Kool-Aid was and he wasn't about to ask. However, it was quite apparent to everyone from his expression that he didn't know, but they would play along with him if he liked.

Nicole returned with glasses of Kool-Aid for her and her great-grandfather then skipped out to bring the bottles requested by the rest.

"You don't have a clue what Kool-Aid is do you?", laughed Shannon.

"Not even a tiny one.", Raymond laughed.

His boisterous laughter completely put him and everyone at ease. Nicole returned quickly with the second order of drinks. It was an evening of firsts and she didn't want to miss anything else.

"Well hell, since we're making confessions. I've never sat down to dinner with a rich guy before.", blurted Larry.

"Nor have we ever had a meal with one of Shannon's boyfriends.", Evelyn added with a giggle.

"Granny!", Shannon muttered slightly embarrassed.

Nicole was about to join in with the "nor have I ever" when her phone rang. It completely disrupted the mood as it loudly announced, "Jackass calling, Jackass calling".

"Oh, my goodness. Is that how you identify your boyfriend? That's horrible babydoll.", contended Evelyn.

"Of course not! That's just my sperm donor, Joe. He probably wants to borrow money.", explained Nicole.

Raymond cringed and decided to take another bite of the delectable beef short ribs and allow the family to speak on that.

"Don't you think that's a bit much baby girl?", questioned Larry.

"That's all he's ever been to me and mommy. That's practically his name, Joe Jackass Johnston Jr. I bet his dad was one too; it probably runs in the family.", insisted Nicole.

"You think?", Evelyn said sarcastically as she peered at the young woman over the rims of her glasses.

"No matter what he's done, he's still your father and you should respect him.", Larry proclaimed.

"Nowadays, Big Daddy, a person has to earn that!", Nicole defended her actions.

"Let's forget about Joe, please. I don't even want to hear his name!", Shannon scolded.

Praise Jesus, thought Evelyn, Raymond you are really having an impact on my cupcake. Unknowingly to her family, Shannon was feeling physically ill at the thought of Joe and even more so that she had agreed to go out with him that weekend. What on earth had she been thinking?

"Pixie, are you all right?", Raymond asked while placing his arm around her shoulders.

"I'll be okay. Some good food will do me some good.", Shannon reassured.

Raymond leaned over to kiss her cheek and she was then able to refocus on him. The mood was as thick and heavy as a brick and he wanted to do something to lighten it.

"The weather is finally breaking. It would be nice to take you all out boating on a Saturday.", suggested Raymond.

"That would be lovely...", Shannon glowed.

"Like a yacht? The only boat I've been on is Bid Daddy's fishing boat.", interjected Nicole.

Nicole was visibly excited as she thought of all the videos and pictures, she could take to post on her social media platforms. Shannon could see the lights, camera and action in her daughter's eyes.

"When?", questioned Nicole.

"In a couple of weeks, if everyone is available.", Raymond supplied.

"If everyone is available? They are retired.", Nicole pointed at her great-grandparents, "I'm on summer break and Mommy will *get* available. This gives me and Mommy time to shop. Let me text Auntie Vivian about going shopping."

Nicole's slender fingers began moving at superspeed like the Flash. Perfect, thought Shannon, now they all could freely move on from that extremely awkward conversation about Joe Johnston. Shannon was thankful that everyone was able to move forward and the evening was restored to a playful and hopeful evening together.

The family and Raymond sat in the family room following dinner and the coziness of the room matched the feeling between all parties. They had laughed and talked for hours. Shannon was flabbergasted by how effortless the conversation was between Nicole and Raymond once they started conversing. Nicole had always been intrigued by law and would often discuss it with Vincent and now she had found another cohort in crime so to speak. Shannon marveled at how things could be with Raymond and could always have been, had she chosen better love interests in the past.

Raymond glanced at his Shinola watch and was surprised by the time; he couldn't believe how it had flown by and even more surprisingly he nor anyone else was much interested in leaving.

"Where did the time go? I could go on for hours about the law and legal precedents. I hope I didn't bore anyone.", Raymond apologized as he dazzled them with his smile.

"No, not at all! I was glued to every word.", provided Shannon.

She might not have grasped every single topic, but she sure was fixated on the man, his lips, the way he articulated every word and his confidence. And she knew she wasn't alone.

"I appreciated the insight from a successful attorney. I don't know if Mommy told you, but I've wanted to be an attorney my entire life.", Nicole informed.

"No, she didn't, but she's very guarded and protective of you though. I'd love to be a mentor for you and guide your career. I can even put in a good word for you when you apply to Law school and assist you with the LSAT. I'm sure between me and your Uncle Vincent helping you, you'll be all set!", promised Raymond.

"Thank you! That's awesome.", Nicole beamed.

It was the first time that Nicole ever felt supported and heard by any of her mother's love interests. She felt that she was always viewed as an obstacle to whatever plans those boyfriends had and being a step-father was not one of them. Raymond stood to leave and politely said his goodbyes to the family before Shannon escorted him to the front door.

"Pixie, this was so much fun. Your grandparents are hilarious.", chuckled Raymond as he wrapped his arm around her waist.

"You put it kindly. My grandparents are a trip! Just wait until they get comfortable with you!", giggled Shannon, "But seriously, I'm so glad I planned the dinner ... It was perfect.", confessed Shannon as she leaned on his shoulder.

"I hope I can see you before we go boating.", Raymond whispered.

"Definitely.", Shannon purred before she kissed him.

Despite a satisfying meal, neither was full. They could have easily devoured each other. It took every ounce of strength they had to remember that they were not alone. Raymond had put off being intimate because he wanted her to know that he valued her, but now he felt that they both were ready. However, he had to remind himself it was neither the right time nor place. Perhaps, he was old fashioned, but he wanted to take her away, take her somewhere special for their first time.

"Talk soon, Pixie.", Raymond whispered and hit her bottom beneath its curvature before leaving.

Shannon often considered why it was always *him* pulling away from her leaving her feeling like a horny lovesick puppy. She desperately reminded herself, he was just different and a cut above any man she had ever dated. Unknowingly, Nicole was in the hall and witnessed the passionate kiss; she was close to tears and decided to do a silent prayer. Nicole wasn't big on religion, but if there was ever a time God was needed it was now to prevent her mother from messing things up.

Chapter 7

Instead of going to the office that Saturday as he often did when he wasn't taking Shannon out, he decided to stay in and reflect. The stark contemporary décor and design of his Birmingham condo were no longer inviting and it had begun to feel foreign to him. Everything in the interior was black, white and grey; there was no life in the sprawling rooms. Perhaps empty was a better word, he thought as he surveyed his living room. He had been contemplating a lot of things that day and Shannon was number one on that list. Shannon, Nicole and perhaps a little one could bring something that was missing to his world. He had been lounging on his living room sofa journaling when his phone rang. Raymond reached for his cell phone on the ottoman in front of his sofa and noticed that it was Vincent checking in.

"Hey Vincent, how's it going?", hummed Raymond as he resumed his outstretched position on the sofa.

Vincent could hear the elation in his best friend's voice. He couldn't wait to find out the status of things as he walked the second-floor hallway toward the stairs.

"Great! But that's the question I should be asking *you*. So how was the dinner with Shannon's family?", urged Vincent.

Vincent stopped mid-stride on the stairs and leaned against the wall to listen to all the details.

"The whole thing surprised the hell out of me. Her grandparents were friendly and very down-to-earth. They joked and laughed with me. You know I'm not used to family members being so open and warm.", laughed Raymond.

"Tell me about it.", chuckled Vincent, "So what's the next step? I mean …", paused Vincent.

"Just to get to know everyone better. I invited them to go boating in a couple of weeks and they agreed ... Bro, I think I'm ready to take things to the next level with Shannon ... and I think she's ready too.", Raymond elaborated.

"Bro ... I'm happy for you. Speaking of coupling up. I spoke to Giovanni last night and he thinks we should plan a couples' trip to the cabin. It'll be a fun way to celebrate the remodel completion.", offered Vincent.

"When were you thinking?", asked Raymond.

"What about next month? That will give Giovanni enough time to secure his hoe of the week.", joked Vincent.

"Bro!", laughed Raymond, "You know he moves fast and his ladies even faster. He could have one lined up for tonight if he wanted."

"That's for damn sure!", agreed Vincent.

"Look, I'll catch up with you later. Let me know if you need any help setting things up for the cabin.", offered Raymond.

"Sure will. Talk later.", Vincent responded.

Vincent couldn't wait to share the good news with Vivian. He dashed down the stairs and decided to search her favorite spot to see if she was relaxing there. As Vincent entered the study, he was glad to see she was there as expected; she was catching up on some of her interests.

"Have you heard the news?", Vincent was elated to inquire.

Vivian set her fashion magazine down to listen to what her husband was saying.

"About what? I hope the news is about Shannon's family introduction.", Vivian concluded.

"Yes love.", Vincent said as he leaned to kiss her on the forehead and then sat beside her on the sofa.

"No, because Shannon hasn't called me and I've been too nervous to reach out to her. Interestingly, I did get a text message from Nicole about shopping and I couldn't make out the rest. It was in that text lingo the kids use.", declared Vivian.

"Well, there's no reason to be nervous. I don't know why Shannon hasn't called when it was a smash hit! Her grandparents and Nicole loved Raymond. He feels that they have a real connection. They are even planning to go boating in a couple of weeks.", informed Vincent.

"Really? If that's the case, I hope she canceled her date with Joe for tonight, but I doubt it because he's been bragging all week that he finally won her back!", fussed Vivian.

"Shit! Raymond thinks he's in.", fumed Vincent.

"I know, right!", agreed Vivian, "What are *we* going to do to help our best friends?"

"What am *I* going to do … It's time for some drastic measures; otherwise, we can forget about things working out for Ray and Shannon.", concluded Vincent.

"Yes, *please* do something … *anything*!", insisted Vivian.

Her eyes begged her husband and reassured him that she wouldn't stand in the way no matter what he decided to do.

"I'll get the ball rolling today, I promise.", Vincent reassured, "Excuse me. I need to make a call."

Vincent left Vivian to head to his office for privacy as he did not want anyone to know the details of what he had planned.

Saturday evening came too fast for Shannon. Although, there had been a time when that would not have been fast enough for her to see Joe. At one time, Joe held such a hold on her heart, body and mind that family and friends feared that she was obsessed with him. She never wanted to feel that way about him ever again. She had always insisted it was because he was her first love and nothing more. But now as she thought back to those days, she could secretly agree that she had been sick and crazy for him and in need of some serious therapy. Hell, she *might* still need therapy, she thought, to help her figure out why she was going out with him now.

Damn, thought Shannon, as she drove to pick up Joe for *their* date. Falling back into old familiar patterns did not feel good. It felt awkward and unnatural since dating Raymond. She imagined her dates with Raymond, the limos, the flowers and the staff stumbling over themselves to serve them at dinner. Those memories brought a smile to her face, but they were quickly hijacked as she approached Joe's home. She sighed heavily as she pulled into his driveway then again when he walked out of his dilapidated house. It was much like him, in need of an overhaul. His home was in a rough neighborhood on the east side of Detroit off McNichols Road, not far from a prison that had been built in the 1990s smack dab in the middle of a community. His home was a bungalow-style frame house in much need of a new paint job, but since he was renting there wasn't much he could do about its appearance even if he wanted to and he didn't.

Joe walked toward the car as if he owned it and motioned to her to get out and let him drive. Anyone with common sense would know that it wasn't his car; it didn't match his tatted-up arms and scruffy short beard and tousled brunette hair. They truly were an odd couple; she was the uptown black girl and he was a white boy definitely from the poor side of the tracks, the epitome of a bad boy. She instantly waived her hand to shoo him to the passenger side; she did not have time for his antics as she was an inch away from telling him she had changed her mind. As she should have, she thought.

When she agreed to go out with him, she suggested a neighborhood restaurant, Buddy's Pizzeria. It was one of the remaining staples of the once-picturesque neighborhood of hard-working Polish immigrants and middle-class workers. It was basically around the block from his home and within walking distance. Earlier, she had had half the mind to tell him to just meet her there even if he had to walk. Reluctantly, she had not and now she decided that she would make the best of the evening since she had agreed to the date. Could she truly call this a date now that she had experienced so much more in the short time of dating Raymond? No, not even, she thought.

"What's up? You've been making a lot of huffing sounds.", Joe asked as he lit a cigarette.

"Not in my car!", ordered Shannon.

He reluctantly lowered the window and tossed it out.

"Damn! I'm sorry. Baby, I see that I'm going to have to work overtime in bed tonight to relax you.", Joe laughed as he reached for her thigh.

"Please …", groaned Shannon as she rolled her eyes and pushed his hand away.

It was not a request, but a dismissal of the offer. She hadn't realized that she was making audible sounds of her frustration; she thought it was just in her head. They hadn't even made it to the restaurant and she was so annoyed by everything he was doing and not doing. Even the smell of him was a turn-off; there was no way he was touching her tonight. That's not happening Joe, she thought. He reeked of cigarettes and booze; she hated that smell combination. In the past, she often would make him bathe before they were intimate otherwise, she couldn't stomach him.

Finally, she thought, as she whipped the car quickly into the parking lot and into the nearest spot she could find. Joe reached for the handrest above the door as his body moved with the jerking motion of the car.

"Shit! If you don't want to be here …", blurted Joe.

He was about to say more but was stopped by Shannon's steal glance that silenced him. Joe quickly exited the car and entered the restaurant leaving Shannon in the car getting her purse. She shook her head in disappointment, but she quickly reminded herself that this is what dating Joe Johnston looks like. She exited the car after gathering her purse and entered the restaurant to find him sitting at a table waving and whistling to get her attention. The hostess approached Shannon, but she pointed at the dog whistler so the hostess would know that she was the *bitch* that he was calling. She had told him for years not to whistle at her like she was a dog, but Joe did what Joe wanted to do no matter how it made her feel.

Shannon sprinted to the table; the quicker she arrived the faster the date would end, she hoped. The server must have thought the same because she arrived right behind Shannon to take their order.

"Give us a large Detroiter, a beer and a Pepsi for her.", Joe ordered.

Any other time this would have been one more thing that would have pissed her off, but she wanted to get it over with and go back home. Joe was expecting her to fuss and complain about ordering for her, but to his shock and disappointment, she did not. He was starting to feel that there was something different about her. Even when she went through periods of dating other guys, Joe could still count on her jumping at his every beck and call. He wasn't *feeling* this new Shannon.

"So, what's up with you? Are you acting *different* because of this big house I hear you bought? I want to see it.", insisted Joe.

"No, I'm not acting *differently* because of my new home. I've been in a reflective mood this week. I've been rethinking a lot of things lately ...", Shannon informed.

"Oh, you've been *rethinking* things. I guess I'm one of those things, huh? Are you too good for me now? So, the father of your only child is not good enough for you. Oh, okay.", fumed Joe.

"You are going to argue by yourself if that's what you want to do. With you every single date has an argument.", explained Shannon.

"Don't forget about the wild makeup sex afterward.", smiled Joe.

"Do you realize that's sick?', questioned Shannon, "Is it too much to ask that we have a normal date, a normal conversation or do you not do 'normal'?"

The hostess slash waitress hesitantly walked toward the fussing couple with their drinks. Shannon tried to stop fussing when the waitress approached, but not Joe. He loved an audience and was gearing up for round two.

"Here are your drinks. Your food will be out shortly.", informed the server.

"Thank you. Can you bring a to-go box out with the food?", whispered Shannon.

"Sure.", the waitress said as she nodded.

Shannon felt that the waitress completely understood the rationale for the box. The quicker the date, the better for Shannon and her.

"You and Vivian are one and the same. She married that rich prick Vincent and she hasn't given her family a dime.", complained Joe.

"Not this shit again. Are you all supposed to sit on your asses and collect money from her like she's the government paying a welfare check? She's given to you all enough over the years, long before she ever met Vincent. If I were her, I wouldn't even be bothered with any of you.", confessed Shannon.

"You two are like sisters. You can convince her to spot me a few dollars or buy me a Corvette or something. I bet she gave you a down payment on that big house of yours.", asserted Joe.

His comment was a huge insult and a slap in the face; Shannon was about to tell him the hell Vivian didn't, but the waitress returned with the pizza and the carry-out box. Joe started taking a slice before the waitress could place it fully on the table.

"I'm so hungry!", informed Joe as if that excused his behavior.

"I'll be back. I need to use the ladies' room.", Shannon announced.

Joe barely acknowledged her words as he grabbed his second slice to scoff it down. God help me, thought Shannon as she walked away. It took everything within her not to cuss him out; she needed to cool off. As an adult, she never took a dime from anyone. She took too much pride in making it and being successful to give that credit to anyone other than herself and she never would have her hand out wanting to collect on Vivian's fortune of marrying a wealthy man.

Joe was about to signal to the waitress that he wanted another glass of beer when he received a call from Vincent.

"Speaking of the fucking devil.", whispered Joe before answering, "Brother-in-law! Shannon and I were just talking about you."

"Really? I would ask what about, but I have something more important to discuss. Can you step away?", inquired Vincent.

"Sure, what's up?", asked Joe.

Joe grabbed another slice and then headed outside.

"I'll cut out the bullshit and get to the point. You need to leave Shannon alone. I'll give you 100 grand to leave town and not look back.", Vincent proposed.

"Are you fucking with me?", whispered Joe.

"No, I'm fucking serious.", sounded Vincent.

Joe began nervously looking around as if someone could hear Vincent's offer despite the phone being pressed intensely to his ear so that he could verify what he actually was hearing. Joe was so caught up in the offer he started walking home as if in a trance.

"Fuck yeah, I'll accept it!", Joe confirmed.

"So, help me God, you better keep up your end of the fucking bargain.", blared Vincent.

"Yeah, yeah. When do I get it?", Joe snickered.

Joe found the threat of the preppy boy hilariously funny and doubted that Vincent had anything to back those words. Joe was from the streets and could smell a real threat a mile off and that was not one from what he could decipher.

"Come to my office tomorrow at 2 pm. Since It's a Sunday, there won't be a lot of folks there.", informed Vincent.

"Yeah, don't want anyone seeing you with your poor *brother-in-law*.", Joe sneered.

"Just fucking be there, shit!", Vincent yelled before disconnecting.

Joe came out of his trance to realize that he was halfway home, so he continued his trance-driven track there. He figured he would deal with Shannon later after he had a chance to make up a good excuse. Shannon exited the ladies' room to find that Joe was gone and the waitress assumed that they were running a scam. The waitress nearly accosted her to demand payment.

"You haven't paid your tab and your friend left!", the waitress accused as she shoved the receipt in Shannon's hand.

Shannon was completely confused. Whenever Joe left the restaurant, he would be outside smoking a cigarette but he would always call her and tell her to hurry up. Not once had she not known what was going on.

"No one's trying to skip out on paying.", insisted Shannon as she retrieved her wallet from her purse, "Here!"

Shannon shoved her credit card in the woman's hand and then headed to the table to box up the leftover pizza. She was so embarrassed; this time was the worst because she had experienced better.

"I'm going to wring your neck, Joe Johnston, just wait and see.", she murmured.

Shannon rammed the pizza into the box and rushed past all the glaring eyes of guests as she headed back to the waitress for her receipt and credit card.

"Sorry for the confusion. My friend had an emergency that he needed to address and he panicked.", Shannon lied to cover her intense embarrassment.

Shannon assumed that she would spot Joe smoking in the parking lot, but he was nowhere to be found. She decided to swing by his house to see if he had walked home. She could imagine him now, explaining that one of his buddies called him about a job or some get-rich-quick-scheme. She was curious to see what lie he would provide. Sure enough, she thought, there he was walking home with a gigantic smile on his face.

"You motherfucker!", hollered Shannon.

Shannon cut him off by driving up someone's driveway to block his passage. Without hesitation, she jumped from her car and started throwing slices of pizza at him. She did not think about how her actions could be perceived by the homeowner nor the danger she could have put her and Joe in by pulling into a stranger's driveway at night.

"What the hell is wrong with you? You're smiling like an idiot while I'm embarrassed at the restaurant because it looks like we are trying to stiff the waitress!", shouted Shannon.

One of the neighborhood dogs began barking as if it were trying to remind her that it was night and her actions were highly inappropriate.

"I got an important call. So, I had to bounce.", insisted Joe.

Joe hadn't had enough time to come up with a good excuse, so he was sure that Shannon wouldn't be satisfied by that.

"That was more important than saying goodbye or telling me that you needed to get home?", Shannon surveyed.

"Yeah, it was pretty fucking important!", yelled Joe.

"I am so sick of your ass! I've dealt with your shit and disrespect for too damn long.", cried Shannon.

She began punching him on his chest, arms, head and wherever she could reach until she was out of breath. Joe had allowed her to hit him until she started punching his head then he started blocking her blows.

"Joe Johnston, you can go fuck off and die for all I care! I am done! Do you hear me? Done!", Shannon shouted then ran to her car.

Shannon was so disappointed in her response; she had removed herself from her throne and she was in the muck and mire

119

with him. She had reverted to that angry frightened teenage girl whom he had gotten pregnant nineteen years ago. She was not behaving like the educated, classy and six-figure income earner who had raised a smart and dignified young woman. This was the evidence and proof that she could never advance with Joe as he was determined to keep her stagnant and dysfunctional.

Shannon glared at the road through her tears as she cried out to God and made promises to herself and to Him.

"I swear my entire focus will be on Raymond. He's everything that I need in my life. God, please forgive me for playing with his emotions. He deserves a good woman and I want to be that woman … his woman.", cried Shannon.

She decided that she needed to do something that she had never done to ensure that she kept her promise. While at a traffic light, she took out her phone and blocked Joe. She didn't trust herself to be as strong as she needed to be. It was finally time to set her childish ways and her childhood love aside to give Nicole and herself the family they both wanted.

Shannon was not the only one fed up with her choices. Vivian felt she was failing her friend if she continued to sit silent and not voice her opinion about Shannon reconnecting with Joe. She decided she needed some muscle behind her so she called Gloria to back her up.

"Hey, Gloria. I know it's kind of late, but do you mind if we call Shannon on the three-way?", suggested Vivian.

"No, I don't mind. Is everything okay with our girl?", Gloria inquired nervously.

"Just the same ole thing … Joe.", provided Vivian.

"Oh, Lord. Yeah, I have time. Call her!", insisted Gloria.

Shannon was about to ask God to give her the strength needed to resist Joe when her cell phone began ringing. She looked at the display to see that it was Vivian calling. She hoped everything was fine as Vivian usually didn't call that late since getting married.

"Hey, Vivi. Is everything okay?", inquired Shannon.

"That's what we want to know. I have Gloria on the phone with us.", insisted Vivian.

"Everything is okay. Why?", Shannon asked wondering what had prompted the question.

"Joe has been bragging that the two of you are back together. Is that true?", demanded Vivian.

Shannon paused hating that Joe was overplaying his hand over just a single date.

"Look we just went out …", Shannon began but Vivian didn't want to hear it.

"So, you went back to the bullshit!", shouted Vivian.

"Un-freaking-believable! I know you think Joe is sexy as hell, but hell is all he brings to the table.", sighed Gloria.

"Wait! Hold on a minute. I admit that I was foolish enough to go out with him tonight, but you'll be glad to know that I quickly realized it was a horrible mistake. Trust and believe, it will be the last time!", Shannon informed.

"Oh, I pray so!", whispered Gloria.

"We've heard this all before.", doubted Vivian.

"This time was a real doozy! Things played out the way they have so many times in the past, but this time … it felt worse that at my age I would be acting like a lovesick hood rat. I finally realized that I should want better… I deserve better.", confessed Shannon.

"Thank you, Jesus!", shouted Gloria, "Just focus on our Raymond and you'll be good!"

"Ok, I hope things really sink in because Raymond is the absolute best man that has ever come your way.", cautioned Vivian, "Please don't throw him away."

"Amen! He's top shelf, baby. If I were younger, I'd take him off your hands if you don't want him. But I'm sure there are a ton of other women waiting in the wing to do just that, so don't toy with him.", warned Gloria.

"You both are right. I've said these things before and gone back to Joe. But this time it's different because I have an awesome man wanting to be in my life.", Shannon admitted, "You both can rest easy tonight. Your girl has finally learned. Though it's taken me over twenty years ...", laughed Shannon, "Good night, ladies. Love you."

"Love you too!", Gloria and Vivian replied.

Chapter 8

Joe was flying high with his newfound wealth; he thought he had finally tapped into a goldmine that wouldn't run dry. At least if he played his cards right. Nothing was too good for Joe now; he bought the best weed, alcohol and a new set of wheels. Moving out of town was never in his plans, especially after contemplating the price Vincent was willing to pay. He would tap into that well one more time then, he might leave, he wasn't sure but for now, he planned to live it up and that he did. The streets were talking and everyone was trying to figure out what job Joe had committed to have the type of money he was throwing around. The fellas in his circle were very curious; some of their theories were that perhaps loan sharks had given him the money or he had finally scored big in a heist.

It had been years since he bought his mother anything; there usually wasn't anything left after booze, women, marijuana and the occasional supply of pills. Joe felt like the big man as he parked his brand-new ride in front of his mother's house. The neighborhood dogs alerted Peggy that someone was outside. She realized that the streets hadn't lied when she saw her son exit the new sports car. He had barely entered before she gave him an ear full.

"So, you're trying to get some more jail time, huh? How did you get all this money folks say you're spending?", Peggy interrogated her son, "Did you get it from loan sharks again? You barely survived the last time you didn't pay up on time."

"No, no. It's all legit and there's more to come.", swore Joe.

"Legit? Really?", questioned Peggy.

Peggy found that very doubtful as she had never known her son to hold down a minimum wage job let alone any that would pay a high school dropout that type of money.

"I found a way to make your rich son-of-a-bitch son-in-law pay up and I'm going to milk it for as long as I can.", bragged Joe.

"Just don't let your uppity sister find out that he gave it to you.", warned Peggy, "If Vivian can get a man like Vincent to change, she must have learned how to wrap him around her finger and she'll put a stop to it!"

"I'm sure he won't admit to it to her if he's pecked like that. Besides, the ball is in my court this time, Ma and I'm playing to win!", confirmed Joe as he reached inside his pocket to pull out a jewelry box, "This is for you."

Peggy was flabbergasted; her eyes couldn't believe what they were seeing. She opened the ring box to find a small diamond ring inside. She had never owned a real diamond of any kind. To think it was her son of all people to buy it; the child that had given her so much grief and frustration over the years.

"There's more to come!", promised Joe.

The word on the Detroit streets made its way to the Barrington Estate and Vivian was surprised that Vincent hadn't handled things and Joe was more active in the streets than ever before. She decided she would speak with Vincent before he headed to the Detroit Club to hang with the guys and her father-in-law.

"Darling, I thought you dealt with my brother a couple of weeks ago.", Vivian stated as she entered the study.

"I did. Everything went as planned.", Vincent reassured.

"Want to bet on it?", sounded Vivian as she plopped down on the sofa.

"Don't tell me that son-of-a-bitch is still in town.", growled Vincent.

"Yes, and spending money all over town. My mother couldn't wait to brag about the diamond ring he got her and his new sports car.", Vivian clarified, "I wonder where he got the money? I don't guess he got another loan from a loan shark.".

Vincent couldn't contain his anger at being played by Joe. He should have known better than to believe that Joe would leave town of his own will; he should have taken a more hands-on approach, he thought.

"That fucking bastard! He agreed to leave town if I gave him a hundred grand.", Vincent cursed, "I'm going to have to think of a new strategy. Let me call Giovanni …"

Vincent picked up his cell from his desk and then paused; he decided to leave the room as he didn't want Vivian to know any of his plans, especially since he had to bring Giovanni into the mix. But Vivian knew that if Giovanni was brought in, like his father before him, that meant he needed to do some heavy lifting. The kind that Barrington men don't do directly and the least she knew the better; so, she could be shocked by the incident like everyone else.

"What's up bro?", asked Giovanni, "Are you canceling poker night?"

"No, but I need you to arrange something … something we can't speak on in front of Raymond or my father.", explained Vincent.

"Speak.", relished Giovanni.

"I thought paying Joe Johnston 100k to leave town would solve Raymond's problems with Shannon, but the con artist is spending cash around town with no intentions of leaving. I wouldn't put it past him to try to get more.", explained Vincent.

"Fuck yeah, bro, for sure he's going to try. You should have leaned harder on him than that. Let me handle it. I'll get it done and no one will have to deal with him afterward.", Giovanni promised.

"Thanks, bro. We need him out of the picture.", Vincent concluded.

"Consider it done! Let me make some calls.", Giovanni assured.

Vincent was relieved that he could count on Giovanni as a friend, a brother and a confidant. Raymond's happiness meant just as much to Giovanni as it did to him. Vincent valued the two men too much to sit on the sidelines while anyone plotted against either of them. And right now, Joe was plotting to ruin things for Shannon and scheme him in the process. Vincent realized that Raymond was too caught up to even realize that a snake was lurking in the shadows trying to destroy what Raymond was building with Shannon.

And caught up he was. Raymond had been speechless when Shannon called him that weekend following their dinner date. It was a very late Saturday night call and he almost thought it was a booty call; he would have been excited had it been. However, he was even more exhilarated by the actual reason for her call; she echoed what he had been feeling. She expressed that she was ready to take things to the next level and was tired of wasting time. Raymond felt it was almost apologetic in nature.

As if arranged by God, himself, it had seemed like a perfect time to invite her to the cabin. So, he shared Giovanni's plan for the guys to bring their girlfriends and she readily accepted. There was so much anticipation and even relief in her voice. That weekend felt like a reset or recharge for their relationship to bloom.

Raymond didn't know what had gotten into her, but he was thankful. Thereafter, they went out multiple times leading up to the boating outing. He wanted that excursion to be perfect for Shannon and her family. He had arranged for his favorite caterer to prepare a variety of hors d'oeuvres and sandwiches served with sparkling wine and fruit juices as a light and fun way to cruise the Detroit River. He thought that was simple enough to be cozy, but with just enough class to be sophisticated.

He had instructed everyone to meet at the Detroit Yacht Club on Belle Isle, an island park that was a part of Detroit; he advised Shannon that he would meet them inside and suggested that Shannon tell the booth attendant that they were his guests. Despite having already met her folks, he felt slightly nervous. This time her family was meeting him on his turf so to speak and this would be a better test of their comfort level.

Shannon was fighting back nerves as well. Yes, their first gathering had been exceptional, but she didn't want to press her luck. To reduce any chance of time delays, she had suggested that her grandparents spend Friday night with her and Nicole so that she wouldn't have to rush across town to pick them up. She didn't want to feel on edge before going boating and she didn't want anything to interfere with their plans, but her grandmother had refused because she felt that the stairs would have been too much of a strain on her knees. So, Shannon was stuck rushing across town to pick them up hours before they were scheduled to meet Raymond at the yacht club and then taking them by her home until it was time to leave.

"What are you doing Granny?", asked Shannon.

She walked into the kitchen to find her grandmother placing sandwiches into a small picnic basket.

"Raymond didn't say we needed to bring anything.", Shannon reminded.

127

"Well, he didn't say we didn't. All he said was that we were going boating. And you know we need to eat something. Your Big Daddy and I have to take medicine at lunchtime. And we can't take it with just snacks; we need real food.", insisted Evelyn.

"Well, okay.", whispered Shannon.

They were going to look like country bumpkins carrying a bunch of bags, thought Shannon. Nicole entered the kitchen shortly after and shared the same thoughts, but she wasn't going to remain silent.

"Granny, we don't need to lug a bunch of bags with us. You already have a bag in the car filled with jackets and a bag in the living room with blankets and water. Dang, we are going to look like street bums.", teased Nicole, hoping Evelyn would leave some items behind.

"That's enough talk. We need to leave out so we are not late.", fussed Larry in true coach fashion.

Everyone fell in line as if Larry were calling the shots and it was his affair. He pointed Nicole to the bags so she could carry them to Shannon's car. He was going to do whatever he could to ensure the outing went well and that his future grandson-in-law would not be kept waiting. As if Shannon needed his direct assistance, he decided to sit in the front passenger seat and directed Nicole and Evelyn to the rear. As Shannon and her folks drove to Belle Isle, she guessed that she was the only one nervous. Everyone else was laughing and conversing; the more they talked the more nervous she became.

"Oh, Lord!", panicked Evelyn.

"What's wrong Granny?", inquired Shannon.

Shannon was fearful that she would have to turn around and head back home; if she did that, they would definitely be late and look like ghetto folks, late and lugging a bunch of bags.

"I forgot our motion sickness pills.", informed Evelyn.

"I'm sure we can buy that at the clubhouse if needed.", Shannon reassured her and breathed easy that it wasn't anything serious.

"Okay, if you say so. You know how sick I can get in your Big Daddy's fishing boat.", insisted Evelyn.

"I'm sure Raymond's boat is way better and bigger than that little old thing.", laughed Nicole.

Shannon drove the bridge from the mainland, Detroit, to the island which was a state park. The family had been to Belle Isle hundreds of times over the years, but never had they once been to the Detroit Yacht Club. There were two worlds that partied on the island; the poor common folks, like themselves, that had picnics and family reunions on the park grounds and then there was the rich elite that partied and socialized at the yacht club.

All their laughter stopped as they neared the yacht club; they looked at the facility in awe. The structure was picturesque and stately; it was a restored cream 1920s Mediterranean-style villa with an orangish roof and boasted of being the largest yacht clubhouse in the United States. The gate attendant noticed their expressions as the car approached the entrance.

"Hello, Ma'am. How may I help you?", asked the guard.

"Excuse me.", Shannon swallowed her words and cleared her throat, "Hi, sir. We are guests of Raymond Brown II."

"Yes, ma'am. The young sir told me his girlfriend would be arriving. I've known that young man since he was a youngster running around the club with his grandparents. He spent a lot of time with them.", chuckled the guard, "I'm running off at the mouth, but I had some great laughs with his grandfather. I truly miss that man. Well, I've talked your ears off enough. Just, park your car in the guest spot near the entrance and ask for him at the desk if you don't see him in the lobby. Enjoy yourselves.", informed the guard.

"Wow, they know him like that?", Larry inquired.

"I felt the same way when I witnessed it for the first time. His family is well-known and respected. When he takes me to his frequented hang-outs, the waitstaff practically falls over themselves to wait on us.", explained Shannon.

The pride in her voice and on her face did not go unnoticed by her family; they all were so excited for her and were in anticipation of what the future would bring. Shannon pulled into an empty guest spot and took several deep breaths to steady her nerves. Just as before, her family noticed her response and her grandfather wanted to reassure her that all would be well.

"Cupcake, you've got this. It's your time to finally shine.", declared Larry.

Shannon opted to nod at her grandfather as she didn't trust herself to attempt to speak at that moment. She felt any attempts would lead to tears and now was not the time for the ugly cry, she thought. Afterward, Larry went into coach mode again and directed Nicole to assist him and Evelyn with the bags.

"Who's getting Granny's walker?", speculated Nicole.

"I don't think I'll need it for this short distance. I have my cane if needed and your Big Daddy for support.", Evelyn informed, "And maybe even Raymond."

"Watch it, woman. You already have a good man!", laughed Shannon.

"Yes, I do.", Evelyn giggled then kissed Larry on the cheek.

"That's all I get for carrying all these bags.", laughed Larry.

"Yuck! Not you too! I'm already preparing myself for Mommy and Ray.", teased Nicole.

"Grab the rest, Nicole so we don't keep the man waiting.",
instructed Larry.

However, despite Larry's instructions, somehow, he
entered the building carrying the bulk of the bags. Evelyn became
self-conscious of the bag she was holding and her wardrobe when
she noticed the elegant ladies carefree and sashaying in the lobby
in their fashionable attire. She and Larry looked more like they
were going fishing. They should have taken a note from the
playbook of Nicole and Shannon. Both had gone shopping with
Vivian where they bought new outfits.

Nicole wore white baggy joggers, a long-sleeved navy-blue
cropped hoodie with a mock tank top and thick-soled white Chucks.
Shannon was just as modernly fresh and carefree in the matching
color; she wore a cotton navy-blue tie-belted jumpsuit with ruffles
on the high round collar and wide sleeveless bodice. She was a
delectable sight from head to toe; her pixie curls were perfectly in
place, her lashes and cat-eye makeup outstanding, and her pouty
glossed lips were ready to kiss Raymond. She finished her look with
a pair of gold embellished thong flats, a small gold-beaded handbag
with an interloping top handle, vintage gold metallic leather fish-
hook earrings, a matching wide bracelet and a vintage mirrored
ring in the shape of a sunflower.

Nonetheless, Evelyn reminded herself that this new world
belonged to her granddaughter and great-granddaughter and it
didn't matter what she looked like. Subsequently, Evelyn would
brush off those feelings, sit, watch and enjoy the ride that they
would embark upon. Raymond stood in the lobby talking to an
acquaintance when the family entered and he instantly lost interest
in that conversation and abruptly began walking off until he
realized the rudeness of his actions then he turned back to his
fellow club member. Love had got a hold of him and didn't want to
let go.

"Forgive me, Henry, my guests have arrived.", Raymond apologized for his behavior.

"It's completely understandable.", Henry concurred.

Henry noticed the beautiful vixen and he completely understood Raymond's urgency to be close and acknowledge the beauty before another man even attempted to head her way. Indeed, several had noticed that she entered alone and were openly eyeing her. Raymond nodded and said good morning to those men as he approached her making it known to all that she was spoken for and off limits. While the men and Raymond might have been captivated by her, Shannon was definitely engrossed in Raymond. He was dashing, handsome any number of words that meant fine as hell, thought Shannon.

Raymond was all about the blues as well; he sported a contemporary stretch wool-linen blend navy blue suit with gold buttons, black loafers, a plush buttonless white polo shirt and a gold-tone Shinola watch. Shannon felt like a different woman in his presence; she felt elegant, confident, sexy and seen. Her movement said as much as she glided toward him with her hips swaying and demanding attention.

"Pixie! You look incredible as always.", Raymond announced as he reached for her hand.

"Thank you.", Shannon whispered in his ear before greeting him with a kiss.

"They look so good together, Granny.", giggled Nicole.

"Yes, they do Babydoll. Yes, they do.", smiled Evelyn.

Larry nodded in agreement. The three observers thought the pair was picture-perfect; perfect enough to exchange vows despite not being in traditional colors. Everything was near perfection; it was a bright and sunny day and Shannon had everyone close that meant everything to her, most of all.

"Hey guys.", Raymond greeted the family, "Ready?"

"Good morning, Ray. I just need some motion sickness medicine just in case. I forgot to bring mine. Can I buy that here?", asked Evelyn.

"No need to worry. I have some on the ship for when my grandmother joins me. She has the same issue.", informed Raymond.

"Great so we're all set if you are.", Larry added.

The family followed behind the love birds giving them a little privacy for flirting and their hands to explore discreetly. As they walked along the expansive dock, Raymond indicated that the larger ships were farther away from the building.

"How much farther?", asked Evelyn.

She paused to hear Raymond's response.

"It's just a little farther. Do you need me to help you?", offered Raymond.

"No, I guess not. I'll use my cane and I should be fine.", informed Evelyn.

She then removed her folded cane from her large purse to provide the needed support. They soon neared Raymond's yacht and two other ones that were docked nearby. Nicole became excited as she saw the family connection.

"Is that Aunt Vivian and Uncle Vincent's boat?", beamed Nicole as she pointed at one of the yachts.

"Yes, it is! Vincent named it, Vivian, next to it is Giovanni's ship, the Bianchi, and lastly my ship, Pixie.", Raymond expressed with the broadest smile.

Shannon blushed; she had no idea that the name Pixie meant anything to him. She just thought it was something cute he had decided to call her. Now she was extremely curious to know exactly what the significance was. She was about to ask when Raymond noticed the questions on her face.

"I loved fantasy stories as a kid and I was fascinated by Pixies. I thought they were cute and some downright sexy.", Raymond whispered with his dazzling smile.

Never had Shannon been given a nickname of such importance or so adorable. It was just another sign and proof that she and Raymond belonged together, but was she listening? Her family and friends definitely were listening and believed.

Raymond gathered Shannon closer as he engulfed her waist and guided her to the Pixie. It was a moderately sized yacht; the largest size allowed at that marina. It was a modern and sleek black and white ship with a main and lower deck. The word Pixie was scripted in white on the black hull of the ship. The two-man crew and two-person catering staff were waiting outside the ship to greet the party. It was a far cry from the small boat Shannon's grandparents took out fishing some weekends. The Washington clan was speechless at the majestic view of it all; the waitstaff, the boat staff and the refinement of the ship. Shannon was much different from her best friend, she never aspired to have anything like this. The most she ever wanted was just a good honest man, a nice home, a happy child and a good career. But this was almost unreal to think that people lived like this and that this could be her life permanently, thought Shannon.

"Hello, Mr. Brown. Welcome, Miss Washington and guests.", the captain greeted the party.

"Hello.", greeted Shannon and her family in unison.

"Hello, Simon. Simon has been captaining our vessels for more than twenty years now.", informed Raymond.

"Yes, I captained the Princess before his grandfather retired it. The elder Mrs. Washington-Brown was very particular about her namesake.", chuckled Simon.

"Washington-Brown?", Evelyn whispered the question.

"Particular is a very nice way of putting it.", Raymond laughed.

It was indeed fate that had paired her cupcake with Raymond, Evelyn thought. Her eyes mirrored those feelings; Larry and Nicole noticed and nodded in agreement. Shannon blushed at the mention of the elder Mrs. Washington-Brown and to think, her husband christened his ship after her nickname as well. Would history repeat itself so to speak, Shannon thought; Vincent spoke incessantly about how much the elder Raymond Brown adored his wife and thought she was everything. It was awe-inspiring to think that one day little Bernie and Nicole's little ones might speak of her own love affair with so much admiration and fondness.

Raymond guided Shannon onto the ship and her thoughts back to the reality before her. The ship was even more impressive once aboard and none of the Washingtons tried to hide their opinions; Nicole was even more expressive as she released an audible squeal of delight. She followed Raymond and Shannon past the cockpit as they entered the cabin on the main level. The ship's crew assisted Evelyn onto the ship and up the steps to the main level.

"Your ship is breathtaking Raymond!", announced Shannon as she entered the cabin.

The cabin was decorated elegantly in muted tones of cream with brown wood trim around the ceiling of the cabin and wooden floors. There were thickly cushioned sofas that lined both sides of the room with a table beside one and a kitchenette nearby. In the center of that table was a huge flower arrangement that showcased Raymond's excellent taste in bouquets. The caterer had their hors d'oeuvres, desserts and beverages laid out in wait for them. There was an array of choices from Mediterranean cucumber square sandwiches, to individual charcuterie appetizers in small bamboo cups with fruits, cheeses, turkey breast, salami and prosciutto deli meats. For their sweet tooths, there were clear square glass cups of lemon parfait.

After noticing the elegant presentation of hors d'oeuvres, Evelyn self-consciously tossed her bag on the floor, out of sight before sitting down, embarrassed that she didn't realize the level of comfort at which Raymond would be treating them. Shannon sat on the south side of the room and her grandparents and Nicole sat across from her while Raymond looked over the display. He was pleased that the caterer met all his requirements.

The ship began its voyage along the Detroit River and the family settled in the sitting area. Evelyn seemed quite at ease despite stating that she usually had issues with motion sickness.

"Mrs. Washington, do you seem to be fine or do you want to take the motion sickness meds?", asked Raymond.

"No, I think I'll be fine. This boat is a lot bigger than I'm used to, so the ride seems much smoother.", informed Evelyn.

"Wonderful. Is anyone ready to eat?", expressed Raymond.

"Hey Raymond, speaking of that, Evelyn brought some snacks that can be added to the table.", Larry innocently offered.

If Evelyn's eyes could slit his throat, they would have. Nicole giggled at her great-grandmother's reaction. Raymond was a little surprised that they had brought anything.

"Oh, sure. Feel free to add it.", offered Raymond, "What did you bring?"

Raymond hoped it was a homemade dessert of some sort; he was sure it would be divine if it matched the meal they shared at Shannon's home.

"Just some sandwiches, nothing fancy.", Evelyn whispered as she fanned her hand wanting to end the conversation.

"Okay. Let's take a look. Place them here.", instructed Raymond.

Evelyn, Shannon and Nicole dreaded the sandwiches being placed next to the dishes the caterers had prepared; even the catering staff looked trepidatious as Evelyn pulled the sandwich bags from her sack and placed the five pre-packaged deli meat sandwiches on the table. She cleared her throat of embarrassment as she walked away.

"Thank you, Mrs. Washington. I'm sure they're delicious.", smiled Raymond.

"Wanna bet?", mumbled Nicole.

"What was that, Nicole?", asked Raymond.

"Nothing.", interjected Shannon as she eyed Nicole to watch herself.

"In fact, let me get one now. Help yourselves as well. If you want to freshen up, there's a powder room toward the back.", suggested Raymond.

Raymond rubbed his hands together in anticipation of the homemade sandwiches. He took a healthy bite and each chewing motion became slower and slower as if his taste buds were trying to figure out what on earth he was chewing. His eyes were confused and begged for an explanation.

"It's bologna. Ray, have you ever had that before?", giggled Nicole almost choking on her petite gourmet Mediterranean sandwich.

"That's what this is?", questioned Raymond, "No, I've only seen it in commercials. What condiment is this? It's not mayonnaise."

More giggles filled the room, this time it was not only Nicole, but Shannon as well.

"It's a salad dressing.", laughed Shannon, "From the look on your face, you've never had that either."

"Look! Don't talk about my sandwiches. That's your Big Daddy's favorite snack.", Evelyn fussed playfully.

"Sorry, but he can have them!", Raymond said straight-faced.

He said it so resolutely that no one could contain their laughter, even the staff couldn't hold back. It seemed the perfect thing for the perfect time, to slice through Evelyn's embarrassment and lighten the mood once more. As the ship left the marina, the staff left the cabin to provide privacy to the family as they talked and laughed; it seemed so effortless and natural for all of them. It was utterly refreshing; Shannon sat wrapped in Raymond's arms as he planted playful kisses on her hair and claimed her with each kiss.

This was a first for Shannon's grandparents; they had hoped for years that she would meet someone worthy and they could get to know him. Before Evelyn had time to consider her words carefully, she spoke what the rest had been thinking.

"You are a very smart man, Raymond; dating our cupcake through us is perfect. We all have a chance to get to know you.", expressed Evelyn.

"Thank you. I know how much you all mean to her, so I want to get to know you and get your approval. Your cupcake … my pixie … means everything to me.", Raymond enlightened.

"You've got our vote.", reassured Evelyn as she squeezed Larry's hand.

"Mine too!", seconded Nicole.

"What about you, Pixie?", asked Raymond.

Shannon smiled at him as her eyes lit up with joy.

"How could you not?", teased Shannon before planting a sweet fleeting kiss on his lips.

"Yeah, this is a first! We all agree that you are the one for our Shannon. Hell … we've never even met any of the others.", confessed Larry.

Raymond's expression and his eyes displayed his confusion; he must have somehow misunderstood Mr. Washington, he thought.

"Not even Nicole's dad?", wondered Raymond.

Shannon began to fidget and look embarrassed. Raymond regretted asking the question, but by God, he had to know. It was no way possible that could be true, thought Raymond.

"Nope.", Larry flatly replied.

"Raymond, it's like that old song Big Daddy listens to, 'he's not the kind you bring home to momma'.", laughed Nicole.

"He was not even there when our baby doll was born, even though Vivian called him to let him know we were taking Shannon to the hospital.", noted Larry.

Raymond was horrified; that brief conversation shined a bright light on the reason Nicole felt the way she did concerning her father. What type of man ignores the greatest joys a man could have, the love of a good woman and the fruit of his essence, a child? He had to be a real bastard, thought Raymond, no wonder Vivian wanted to escape her family's curse. Raymond tightened his embrace around Shannon and looked deeply into her eyes as he made a vow.

"I will always stand at your side to support you … to love you, Nicole and our little ones.", Raymond declared.

Raymond thought his declaration was only in his head but as he glanced across the room, he realized he had uttered the words aloud. Shannon couldn't restrain the tears that welled in her eyes; a feeling of relief and release came upon her as if a burden had been lifted. The burden she carried in her past relationships where she was expected by the guys and herself to be the mature one … the put-together one that handled the business or made important decisions. It finally hit home just how heavy that burden had been. She quietly rested her head on his shoulder. She thought about her past actions and how she had started to give time to Joe again and she was baffled by her actions. It made absolutely no sense to give Raymond the cold shoulder; he was way too hot and sincere to be put on ice, she thought.

Raymond and the Washington clan hadn't had that much fun in ages and the time seemed to fly by as the captain returned the ship to the marina. Evelyn wanted to know everything about the upcoming trip to the cabin and Raymond tried his best to oblige. It was quite apparent that she and Nicole were just as excited as Shannon. He told stories of when the old heads took him and the other grandchildren of those power men there for weekends. It was then that Shannon truly saw that the love he had for his grandparents equaled her love for hers.

After docking at the port, Shannon and her family gathered their things to debark. Neither she nor Raymond wanted to see the evening end. Nicole and her great-grandparents said their goodbyes as they exited ahead of Shannon.

"Bye Nicole … Mr. and Mrs. Washington.", echoed Raymond.

"Talk later.", Shannon whispered before kissing him.

"Most definitely.", confirmed Raymond.

As Shannon and her family debarked the ship and headed back to the clubhouse, Raymond reboarded the ship and stood on the deck as if staring off into the future. The majestic view from the island helped him to reflect on the bond he was developing with Shannon and her family. It inspired him and confirmed that there was no doubt in his mind that he needed to propose to Shannon. He wanted her to know his intentions were sincere and dependable; that he was different than the rest. That he was willing to commit himself and everything he owned to her. He decided to call his jeweler to make an appointment. The romantic in him had decided to propose to her during their cabin trip. He planned to ask Vivian to find out her ring size as he did not want Shannon to have any idea of his plans.

Chapter 9

Spring had indeed been a rebirth for Shannon and Raymond and now summer was in full bloom. It was the most mature and satisfying relationship that either of them had experienced. They had borne their souls to one another in words spoken and unspoken. The pair had even included Nicole on some of their outings and they looked like a happy family.

They were just days away from the cabin trip and Raymond was getting concerned about the ring. The jeweler had called him the previous week indicating that there would be a delay in the ring being ready. Raymond was starting to fear that his plans to propose would be delayed until he received a call from the jeweler.

"Hello.", greeted Raymond.

"Hello, Mr. Brown. I have good news. The ring is ready. It is gorgeous and definitely worth the wait.", reassured the jeweler.

"Excellent, Benito! I'll come right away.", Raymond provided.

"And sir, for the delay … I found a unique and exquisite ring box for it.", bragged the jeweler.

"That's great. See you soon.", Raymond said before disconnecting the call and then summoned, "Roberta!", Raymond blustered as he dashed from his office.

"Yes sir.", Roberta uttered as she stopped in mid-motion at the filing cabinet.

"I just heard from the jeweler that Shannon's engagement ring is ready. Don't expect me back until next Monday. The next time you see me, I'll be her betrothed.", declared Raymond.

"Oh sir, that's wonderful", she complimented.

If only his grandfather were still alive and his grandmother well to witness this day, Roberta thought. Despite that loss, he would have her along with his other loved ones and close friends to be there to support and cheer him on, Roberta thought.

Raymond drove the short distance to the jeweler on Jefferson Avenue not far from the Bianchi mansion. His childhood was full of memories of Ricky, Bernard and his grandfather showing him how to be a man and the things men did for the women they loved. And that jeweler was one of their favorite jewelry makers. Raymond knew that he wanted something unique for Shannon as she was like no other woman he had ever met; so, there was no one better equipped than Benito. Raymond pulled his Bentley in front of the building and took several deep breaths before exiting the car.

Benito anticipated his arrival and buzzed Raymond in; he had a glass of champagne to celebrate the upcoming proposal and the arrival of the magnificent ring waiting for Ray. He handed the glass to Raymond upon his entry.

"Have a seat while I get the ring. I made this ring with the finest materials I could get from Italy.", boasted Benito.

Benito brought out the ring in a unique ring box that looked antique and vintage and made of glass. It was square-shaped with brass filigree around the top edge of the box and along the sides. Benito opened the fragile box to reveal red felt in the shape of a rose with the engagement ring atop. The engagement ring was made of platinum, a flawless clarity ten-carat cushion cut solitaire on a halo setting with a pave diamond-surround band. It was a brilliant piece of craftsmanship that Raymond couldn't wait to place on her hand. He was ecstatic that he was going to propose at the cabin with those he held dear as witnesses of his profession of love.

"Benito …", began Raymond.

"I know, sir. It's gorgeous. ... perfect for your pixie.", concurred Benito, "If you want you can replace the felt with a real rose as would have been the custom at the time the box was designed."

"Thank you ...", Raymond breathed.

Raymond passed the ring back to Benito for packaging. He was beyond emotional; the words he wanted to say were fighting with the tears that threatened to come forth. He never imagined that he would have found love with the woman of his desire, the woman of his dreams. He could almost feel the hand of his grandfather on his shoulder saying, 'You chose well my son'. Benito presented the package to Raymond.

"Good luck, Mr. Brown.", Benito offered.

He too remembered the elder Mr. Brown bringing the young Raymond to his store as a child. Raymond nodded as he took the prized possession and put it inside his inner blazer pocket for safekeeping. He decided he would share his awesome news with Vincent who would be more excited than Giovanni. He hopped into his Bentley and called his pal.

"Bro!", exclaimed Raymond, "I picked up the ring. Shit's getting real, Bro!"

"Congratulations! I can't wait to witness the proposal.", cheered Vincent.

"Bro, did you feel this way when you picked up Vivian's ring?", pondered Raymond.

"Not for the first set of rings, I was a different person back then with a different mindset. But for her replacement set after our one-year anniversary ... hell yeah.", affirmed Vincent.

The two shared a boisterous conversation while Raymond began his drive home when he remembered that his parents had returned home from their vacation. He was in such a celebratory mood that he surprisingly even wanted to share it with his family in Franklin, a suburb not far from his penthouse. Instead of going home, he made a detour to his route and headed to his grandmother's home. He parked in the expansive driveway in front of the massive structure he had once called home. He then headed to the front door; as usual, the butler opened it to greet him. It always seemed that Lawrence, the majordomo, knew his every move and seemed to always sense his arrival.

"Master Raymond, you're just in time to catch your parents.", informed Lawrence.

"Thanks, Lawrence; that's what I was hoping. I have some exciting news to share with the family.", chuckled Raymond.

Lawrence was shocked and pleased to hear that; the Washington-Brown family needed something to be excited about, he thought.

"Where are they?", asked Raymond.

"They're in the drawing room.", informed Lawrence.

"The drawing room?", chuckled Raymond.

It always amused Raymond that Lawrence got a kick out of being old-fashioned and using terms most people didn't even understand nowadays.

"Yes, sir.", replied Lawrence as he patted Raymond's shoulder.

Raymond raced down the hall like he did so many times in his youth whenever he wanted to show something off to his grandfather and grandmother, be it his report card, recognition from his school or even his state bar exam. This moment was no different; he was about to embark on the most thrilling time of his life. He entered the room to find his parents sitting on the sofa and his grandmother on a chair.

"Mother, Father how was Paris?", Raymond chattered more eager to get to his news.

Eleanor sat in her favorite chair smiling as she waited eagerly for him to acknowledge her. He quickly rushed over to kiss her on the forehead as his mother began to speak, and then he made himself comfortable on the sofa next to her.

"It was wonderful as usual. Your grandmother told us you're dating. Is that true or are her memories jumbled?", asked Angela, his mother.

"It's true. Her name is Shannon. She's the most beautiful and complicated woman I know.", bragged Raymond.

"I thought your grandmother wore that crown.", smirked Richard, Raymond's father., "Tell us about this gem."

"For starters, I'm going to propose this weekend. I just picked up the ring from Benito.", informed Raymond as he patted his blazer pocket, "Shannon is highly educated and accomplished. She has a highly driven daughter as well.", Raymond boasted.

"She's divorced?", asked Angela.

"No ...", Raymond paused.

"No?", questioned a confused Angela.

"She's never been married.", Raymond uttered.

"So, I know she doesn't come from money then. Where did you meet this woman?", Angela cross-examined.

"Vincent and Vivian introduced us; she's a good friend of Vivian.", Raymond detailed.

"Do you have any pictures of this bombshell?', inquired Richard.

"Yes, I took some pictures when we went boating with her daughter and her grandparents. Before that, she invited me and her grandparents over for dinner.", elaborated Raymond.

Raymond passed his cell phone to his mother who held it so that Richard could see the photo as well.

"She cooked?", asked an astonished Richard.

"Yes, and very well.", admitted Raymond.

"Oh, she's cute for a dark-skinned girl.", sneered Angela, "I thought you and Veronica were good together.

"That's old news, Mother.", Raymond dismissed.

"Well, Veronica does come from old money like us and ...", paused Richard.

"And what Father? She's white and she will keep our bloodline fair-skinned. Is that what you want to say? I can't believe this family is still color-struck and elitist in the twenty-first century.", objected Raymond.

"That's enough! Leave my precious baby boy alone. He's finally found someone who makes him happy. Don't mess this up for him. Do you want him to be miserable like the two of you? You're afraid to be still for a moment and be in the presence of each other without all the fanfare of entertainment. I adored my husband and he alone was enough!", shouted Eleanor.

It was the first lucid thing she had said all day. Richard and Angela were embarrassed that someone suffering from dementia could see the truth behind their actions; that their love was built and centered around shallow things and not as mature as Raymond's love appeared to be.

"My precious boy, please show me the ring.", Eleanor asked.

Raymond was thrilled to ignore the negative comments of his parents to focus on his grandmother's request. He could always depend on her for her support and love. Besides, the last thing he needed was the words of his parents burrowing a hole in his brain that weekend.

"Oh, it is exquisite! You have such great tastes like your grandfather! You become more and more like him every day. I guess that's why people always thought you were our son born in our middle-aged years.", Eleanor beamed.

Richard and Angela sat quietly as they could not even take credit for Raymond's success. As Eleanor hugged Raymond, she looked over his shoulder disappointedly at her son and daughter-in-law.

The anticipation for the weekend was contagious and everyone was feeling the excitement. Shannon decided to leave work early as well; she, too, decided to take the rest of the week off in preparation for the weekend getaway. As she exited the building, she decided to call Vivian.

"Hey, Vivian. What are you up to? I'm going home to start packing.", jabbered Shannon.

"That's what I'm doing now. So, are you looking forward to the weekend?", asked Vivian.

"Yes! All week, I've been feeling like Raymond has a big surprise for me or something.", chatted Shannon.

"Maybe? I know one thing for sure and that's, the two of you are *so* good together. Almost as good as Vincent and me.", giggled Vivian.

"I totally agree. He makes me feel like there's no other woman in the world but me.", Shannon tweeted.

"Love it!", exclaimed Vivian

Vivian joined Shannon's laughter.

"Oh, let's get Gloria on the line. I need her to hear this.",
laughed Vivian.

"Yeah, call her. Maybe the two of you want to come over
for drinks while I look over my wardrobe.", suggested Shannon.

"Ok, hold on; let me add her.", instructed Vivian.

Shannon continued walking to her car while Vivian got
Gloria on the line.

"Hey, girlie!", chuckled Gloria, "I hear you're excited about
the cabin trip. I'm still a little peeved that you haven't introduced
me to one of his uncles. I'm still waiting."

The ladies laughed at Gloria's teasing; they knew she
wasn't really pressed for a boyfriend and if they did introduce one
to her, he had to measure up to a very high standard.

"You know ...", paused Shannon, "I haven't met any of his
family yet. The only one he's close to is his grandmother and she is
struggling with dementia. So, I understand the delay in meeting
her."

Gloria could hear that old devil of doubt trying to rear its
ugly head and she wanted to squash it immediately.

"Yes, that *is* the case. Just like you aren't rushing to
introduce him to your mother. It's the same thing ... different
scenarios.", reassured Gloria.

"Exactly! Trust me, you'll meet everyone you need to
before that big day.", concluded Vivian.

"That big day ...", whispered Shannon.

"Yes indeed! That big day is on the horizon, baby. Just sit
tight and hold on!", avowed Gloria, "In the name of Jesus!"

"Amen!", shouted Vivian.

"Don't play with the Lord now.", cautioned Gloria.

"Oh, I meant it! Amen, from your lips to God's ears. There will be so many people shouting hallelujah at *that* wedding.", declared Vivian.

"Oh yes! Evelyn and I will be doing the holy ghost dance around the sanctuary.", laughed Gloria.

"Okay!", Vivian laughed, "Hell, I'll be right there with you. I've been with her on the front lines from hell and back! So, trust and believe, I will dance with you!"

"You two are a mess!", snickered Shannon.

"Gloria; Shannon and I were thinking that we should meet up at her house and help her pack. I want to be sure she's going to be really sexy this weekend. What time should we come over?", inquired Vivian.

"Well, I am headed home now; so, you can meet me in an hour if you want.", suggested Shannon.

"That's good for me. In fact, I can leave now and swing by a pizzeria. How does that sound?", offered Vivian.

"Good. I can leave home now as well. I can do one cheat day and have pizza.", announced Gloria.

"Yeah, pizza and wine.", giggled Shannon.

"You know it! See you soon then. Bye.", Vivian added.

"Okay, girls.", added Gloria.

"Bye", Shannon finalized the plan.

It was times like this that she was grateful that her granny stressed the importance of keeping a clean home. She could comfortably have anyone over at any given time without worry. As she pulled into her driveway, Vivian's words played on repeat, that she would help her pack something *sexy*. Oh Lord, she's going to rag me about my pieces again, Shannon thought, oh well that's what I get for agreeing to it. Shannon announced her arrival to what she hoped would be an empty house, but Nicole was home from her summer job.

"I'm upstairs Mommy!", shouted Nicole.

"Your Auntie Vivian and Auntie Gloria are coming over to help me pack. We're going to have pizza and wine.", informed Shannon.

"Great! I'll have some too … the pizza I mean.", giggled Nicole, "And I can help you pick out outfits too?"

"Oh boy! Not you too?", sighed Shannon as she walked upstairs

Nicole peeked out her bedroom door to tease her mother as she walked down the hall.

"Yeah, I can't have you embarrassing me. Raymond is fly and you need to match his vibration.", teased Nicole.

"Oh, I match his vibration all right.", teased Shannon, "Hold on, let me text Vivian that you are here, so she can bring enough pizza."

"Hold on? No, I need you to know that I don't want to hear about your sex life, yuck!", fussed Nicole.

"We actually haven't had sex yet. Can you believe it? *I* barely believe it.", laughed Shannon.

"Really?", questioned Nicole.

Nicole was flabbergasted that her mother hadn't had sex with him yet. She felt that her mother rushed into sex with every guy she'd dated since Nicole had learned anything about dating and sex. Nicole felt that much more convinced that Raymond was the one; he was that crazy about her without having sex! She knew a man like that was a keeper; she just hoped that her mother realized it too.

"Don't look so shocked.", insisted Shannon as she tickled Nicole, "Go check the door, that's probably your aunties."

Shannon had heard the notification from the app on her phone indicating someone triggered the motion sensor. Vivian and Gloria had pulled up at the same time and were waiting at the door. They were even more excited than the last time they were there to assist her in selecting an outfit. Nicole jogged to the front entrance and peered out the window atop the door to verify their guests before she flung open the door with excitement.

"Auntie Vivi … Auntie Gloria! Hi, come on in. Let me take those pizzas to the kitchen.", Nicole greeted.

"Where's your mother?", asked Vivian.

"She's upstairs.", informed Nicole.

Nicole grabbed the pizza boxes and headed to the kitchen as Shannon began walking down the stairs.

"Hey, ladies!", Shannon greeted them and then hugged each one.

"You are glowing! Isn't she Vivian?", complemented Gloria.

"Yes, Raymond looks good on *her*!", Vivian agreed.

"Girl, I look the same. Come on; let's go to the kitchen.", refuted Shannon.

"No baby girl, happiness has a different look altogether.", Gloria enlightened.

"For sure!", Vivian chimed.

As the ladies entered the kitchen, Nicole made it quite plain that she had been listening to every word.

"Yes, Mommy; you look happy and act happy. Anyone that knows you can see how you're different now.", described Nicole.

Shannon blushed at her daughter's words; she knew that she indeed did feel different lately. She was more relaxed, calm and hopeful; and if she were honest with herself, she knew that Raymond was to blame and in the most wonderful way.

"Did you have your interview?", asked Vivian.

"I did; I had it last Friday. I thought HR had decided not to fill the position since it took so long to get the request for an interview.", informed Shannon.

"How did it go?", inquired Gloria.

"I think I nailed it. *Like* you said, things have been different for me. Because I'm relaxed, I am even more confident.", admitted Shannon.

"A new big-time promotion, an engagement to a big shot ... you've got it going on!", affirmed Vivian.

"Slow down ... neither has been confirmed ... unless you know something I don't know.", Shannon pointed out.

Vivian's cheeks turned crimson with excitement; she wanted to keep quiet about the news. God knows she knew how to keep a secret, she thought, but she had wanted this for her bestie for *so* long.

"Oh, my Lord, Jesus!", sang Gloria.

"Yes!", shouted Vivian.

Vivian turned in a circle at the kitchen counter and she flared her arms with excitement. Nicole started jumping in place and squealing, almost knocking the pizzas off the counter; while Shannon stared in disbelief.

"Yes, he told Vincent that he had an engagement ring designed by the family jeweler from materials from Italy. The jeweler even threw in an antique jewelry box of some kind. The same one that made my new set of rings!", cried Vivian.

"Oh my God … *oh my* God.", breathed Shannon deeply trying not to faint, "This is really happening."

Shannon instantly stood and started squealing and running around the kitchen like a little girl. It was contagious, even Gloria couldn't contain her excitement. Gloria decided she could do the holy ghost dance because this news was cause for a celebration. It felt surreal to Shannon; she had finally found what so many girls desire. Vivian would no longer be the only one with wealth and felt obligated to cover the costs of things. Vivian swore that she did it because she loved Shannon and not out of obligation, but soon would come a day for real when either could freely buy or pay for one another without a thought. They could even take shopping trips around the world as they dreamed of as teenage girls.

Shannon was overwhelmed by excitement, fulfillment and love. She grabbed Vivian and stared her in the eyes; their tear-filled eyes said what their hearts felt as they nodded at one another before hugging. The ladies continued to laugh, cry and laugh some more while they scrutinized outfits and lingerie for the trip. Nicole beamed as she observed her mother's joy and newfound happiness; soon, Nicole would finally have a man she could proudly call father.

The night was drawing near when Raymond realized he and Shannon had not discussed what time he would pick her up and the trip was in the morning. They had talked all week about everything, but that; subsequently, he decided to give her a call. Shannon had just insisted Vivian and Gloria leave so that she could get some rest. As she threw herself on the bed, she laughed at the thought of how tiring laughing and dancing could be.   Yet she perked up instantly when she noticed Raymond calling; she wouldn't have to imagine his voice that night.

"Hey, how's my pixie.", flirted Raymond.

"Great, just wishing you were here. I was just thinking about you.", admitted Shannon.

"Really? Good.", flirted Raymond, "because you have me wanting you and thinking about you all the time."

Shannon's blush caused her to giggle.

"This weekend will be really good for us … special.", Shannon concluded.

"Yes, it will, Pixie. What time should I pick you up?", asked Raymond.

"Well, I was thinking. You should let me pick you up so you can see how the other side lives.", teased Shannon.

"Okay. Did you forget that you have a luxury vehicle?", laughed Raymond.

"That's a beginner's luxury. The average Joe can manage to save up a few coins and buy a Cadillac. Most people have never even seen a Bentley up close.", laughed Shannon.

"Okay, if you say so. I'll let you pick me up this one time. I'm not used to my girlfriends driving me around. I don't mean to sound old-fashioned, but that doesn't sit well with me.", conceded Raymond.

"Got it! Just this one and only time.", insisted Shannon.

"Okay, so you can pick me up at 6 a.m. My place is not as spotless and cozy as yours, so don't tease me about it, okay? I just texted my address.", joked Raymond.

"I promise I'll tease you in other ways.", laughed Shannon.

"Pixie … you're trying to start something you can't finish tonight.", chuckled Raymond, "See you in the morning."

"Good night, baby.", purred Shannon.

Raymond decided to call Vincent before he went to bed to make sure there were no glitches; he wanted everything to be perfect for his special weekend getaway with Shannon.

"Hey, Vincent. I just wanted to make sure you have everything covered for tomorrow.", Raymond informed.

"Yes, for sure. Everything will be perfect for you to pop the question.", insisted Vincent.

"Great! This weekend will be the next step for me and Shannon on all accounts.", supplied Raymond.

"All accounts?", questioned Vincent.

Raymond could not mean, what Vincent thought the words implied.

"Yeah, all accounts. This will be our first time being intimate together.", Raymond admitted.

"Bro … really? I've never known you to take this long.", Vincent confessed.

"Yeah, it's been a shock to me too. But what I have with her is so unique, so special that I've been nervous about moving too fast. So much, that I might have moved too slowly.", chuckled Raymond.

"Well good luck, bro, but I don't think you really need it.", laughed Vincent, "Please don't tell Giovanni that you two haven't had sex. He'll rag you nonstop about it."

"I feel you on that!", laughed Raymond.

The sunrise was glorious; Shannon hadn't seen a morning as beautiful. It was as if the heavens felt her excitement about their weekend getaway. Raymond teased that she should not expect it to look like hers; in fact, she knew better than to think that. She doubted it could be anything less than fabulous and as she approached the attached parking structure, she was reassured that her expectations were in fact correct. It was a gated building and she had to provide his name and her identification so that the guard could call him to verify that she could enter the structure. The guard smiled, nodded and opened the gate.

She had assumed it was a high-rise building, but it was not very tall. He had told her that he stayed on the tenth floor; but when she entered the elevator, she noticed the number stopped at ten and the button read 10P with a keyhole below it. It was quite apparent that meant he owned the penthouse unit. Unexpectedly, she heard Raymond speaking through an intercom after she had pressed the button.

"Hello.", greeted Raymond.

"Oh, my goodness Ray. You startled me.", gasped Shannon.

"Sorry, I didn't mean to scare you. I'll send the elevator up.", informed Raymond.

Despite dating him for months, him spending time with her grandparents and her daughter, she stood there staring at the penthouse button and became nervous all over again. The reality of his wealth was again making her stomach flutter and doubt fill her heart. She reminded herself that she was his pixie and there was nothing to fear.

The elevator must have used a warp-speed drive to get her there so quickly; the doors opened, it seemed just a moment after speaking to Raymond, to reveal a wide gallery to his entrance. She stepped off the elevator as if stepping into a museum. She glanced forward from the ceiling to the floor and then turned back to stare at the wall adjacent to the elevator. The elevator doors were brass with intricately detailed artwork. She had never seen anything as elegant; she turned again to observe the details more closely.

The walls were painted a pearl white with a tray ceiling and recessed lighting and hanging on the walls were multiple undulating circular mirrors with a hand crafted antique silver-toned finish. The floor was a grey marble with a white marble pedestal table in the center with a silver-tone Sputnik sphere chandelier above it. There were even two marble busts atop two white marble pedestal tables, one in each corner near the entrance and a large painting on the opposite wall next to the elevator. She was so drawn in by the beauty of the gallery, that she did not notice when Raymond opened the massive white ornate wooden doors and stood in the double doorway. He rested his right arm above his head on the door frame and his left hand was inside his pocket.

"Good morning, Pixie, my love.", Raymond's voice echoed, "Welcome to my home. Come inside."

She skipped to him like the excited girl fluttering inside and kissed him as she laid her hand upon his chest and the other cupped the back of his shoulder. He returned her kisses passionately, then he kissed her on her forehead.

"Oh, Raymond, your place is so elegant and beautiful! You have such great tastes.", Shannon complimented.

Shannon entered the unit and paused at the doorway as if afraid to walk upon the marble floors that flowed from the gallery inside. She was in utter awe as she glanced around the spacious interior.

"I selected a great interior decorator and designer.", chuckled Raymond, "I have no problem paying others for their expertise. If it were up to me, I would just have a bed, books and a television."

Raymond closed the doors behind them and took Shannon's hand to guide her inside. As she stepped farther inside his penthouse, she marveled again with her eyes at the elegance that lay before her. His place was stylish, some might even say trendy; it was definitely the home of a person without children. It was sophisticated and contemporary with black leather furniture with grey and white accent pieces to soften the feel. It screamed power, money and the home of a bachelor; a woman's touch could bring even more life and invitingness to the space. Yet, she sensed that he would not want to live there after marrying; she could easily picture him in a mansion, running on the grounds with his children. Children, she gasped at the thought, would she want to start all over with a little one? As she stared at him, he was explaining something, but what … she didn't know. Shannon contemplated motherhood; she thought she could do that for him since he was a man who would give her the world.

"You and I will buy another home together.", Raymond blurted.

He knew she was not listening to anything he was saying; so, he thought he would have a little fun with it and say what he was fantasizing about.

"What was that?", asked Shannon.

She realized he had said quite a bit and she had no clue what he was saying. She couldn't stop her mind from imagining a life with him. It was something she had not done in ages, but it felt exciting.

"Nothing really.", laughed Raymond.

"Tell me.", teased Shannon.

She pulled his collar as if she were going to force it out of him.

"You're a tough cookie, huh?", teased Raymond as he kissed her hands.

"That's right! Southwest Detroit by way of the west side. Don't you forget it.", laughed Shannon.

"The west side, huh? That's where the bougie and stuck-up Detroiters live.", chuckled Raymond.

"Okay, you can believe that if you want to.", laughed Shannon, "And what do you know about Detroit anyway?"

"You'd be surprised.", smirked Raymond.

There was that irresistible smile again; she could not imagine her life without it now. It was everything, warm, flirtatious, sexy, bashful and happy. He picked up his luggage that sat just inside the entrance.

"I promise I will give you a tour later. I've been planning some things.", supplied Raymond.

"Really? Oh, my goodness I can't wait. You really know how to spoil a girl.", Shannon complimented.

"Oh, that little stuff? You haven't seen anything yet.", Raymond boasted.

Shannon put her arm around his waist and exited his penthouse beside him.

Chapter 10

The ride to the cabin was fun and seemed to fly by. Raymond and Shannon laughed constantly and he got all her jokes. He really got them; he did not feign laughter like Joe, she thought. He even imaginatively added to them, so she knew he really got them.

"Your feet look so small, but you really have a lead foot. Who knew such delicate feet could be so heavy.", laughed Raymond.

"I do not drive fast. I'm only doing the speed limit.", vowed Shannon.

"You think?   Have you checked the speedometer?", questioned Raymond.

"Uh, no ...", Shannon whispered.

She then took a quick glance at her speedometer and noticed that she was driving eighty miles per hour in a seventy-mile-per-hour zone.

"Ok, I guess I am driving a little fast.", conceded Shannon.

"Yeah, a wee bit.", laughed Raymond.

"Okay, old man. I'll slow down.", teased Shannon.

"Hey. I just want us to make it there alive.", Raymond defended his opinion.

Giovanni and his girlfriend of the week, Markita, were on the highway headed to the cabin as well. He was determined that he would end the Joe Johnston problem once and for all, to be the hero of the story for his good friend. Even if it meant he would have to be distracted by it and not give his full attention to his date.

"That's like the fifth time you've answered your phone.", complained Markita.

"Bae, you know I have multimillion-dollar businesses that I run.", explained Giovanni.

"I know Bae, but I like all your attention.", flirted Markita.

She had begun to massage his manhood when he received yet another call.

"Damn, Bae!", fussed Markita.

"Talk to me!", Giovanni ordered the caller.

"Your plan is in motion boss. It'll be handled before morning.", reassured the lackey.

"Make sure of it!", ordered Giovanni.

"Are we almost there? Shit, I'm tired of riding.", Markita complained.

"There's the cabin.", Giovanni pointed to the luxury cabin atop the hill.

Giovanni pulled his Bugatti up the driveway and parked next to Vincent's Corvette Stingray. Markita opened the console to place her snacks inside.

"Leave that closed. You know my gun is there.", ordered Giovanni.

"Oh, I forgot.", Markita apologized.

"Don't play with me, Bae.", warned Giovanni.

"I'm not, Daddy.", Markita purred.

Vivian had told Shannon how beautiful the cabin was, but her description paled in comparison to reality. The asymmetrical mid-century modern exterior design was stunning and a marvel of its era; there were windows everywhere and some looked like they went from the floor to the ceiling. It was built partially on a hill and had a walk-out basement on one side and a traditional basement on the other. Shannon couldn't wait to go inside. Shannon and Raymond pulled up the driveway behind Giovanni and Markita. Markita resumed her dick massage he had stopped earlier, but that wasn't enough to satisfy him at that moment. As a result, Giovanni lifted her dress and began tasting her as she raised her leg and pressed it against the window.   So, it's going to be like that Gio, thought Raymond. Shannon cleared her throat; she had no idea that she would witness something like that.

"Shannon, meet Giovanni and his trick of the week.", laughed Raymond as he pointed to the car in front of them.

Shannon assumed that Raymond was not being serious about his friend's love life.

"I thought he had a serious girlfriend.", Shannon whispered.

"He doesn't, but he can always get a flavor of the week.", teased Raymond.

"Oh, so he wanted some chocolate this weekend.", teased Shannon.

"That's his favorite flavor.", laughed Raymond.

Shannon laughed also, but she secretly feared that they might be the only couple not getting it in that weekend. If there was a perfect time for them to have sex for the first time, that was it. Raymond saw her thoughts on her face.

"We are not going to sit on the bench this weekend. We're all going to see some play time.", Raymond affirmed.

Shannon giggled at his sports analogy as he leaned over to kiss her. The practice was starting and neither of them could wait for playtime. Giovanni and Markita were unloading the trunk when they noticed Raymond and Shannon kissing. Not bad, bro, a little tame but that's good for you, thought Giovanni.

"Wait till you go to your room, Bro!", shouted Giovanni hoping to embarrass the couple.

Shannon blushed and Raymond looked annoyed, much to Giovanni's pleasure. They reluctantly opened their door to exit and join the pair.

"I thought you said all of your boys were rich. What's up with this basic Cadillac?", questioned Markita in her mock whisper.

"It's my car.", Shannon explained, "I told him he could leave his Bentley at home."

"Girl, you better let your nigga upgrade you!", laughed Markita, "My nigga is a real plug; he bought me a Porsche."

Markita giggled as she snuggled Giovanni and rubbed his buttocks.

"Soon, she'll have it all; not just a car.", Raymond foretold.

Shannon blushed again, hoping that meant he would propose that weekend. Markita noticed the way the couple looked at each other and knew what they shared was more significant than anything she could possibly hope for with Giovanni. Giovanni noticed a twinge of jealousy sweep across Markita's face and he knew he needed to lighten things up again.

"Let's get this thang jumping!" shouted Giovanni.

"Yeah Bae, let's get it bussing!", Markita joined in the excitement.

Markita and Giovanni ran up the stairs to the porch to find Vincent there to greet them. Raymond and Shannon were less animated and walked up the stairs to enter the cabin. The guys were surprised at how revamped the cabin was compared to the days of their youth.

"Fuck bro, this is hot!", complimented Giovanni as Markita followed him speechless.

"Damn, Vincent! Yeah, this is nice. You really made this place your own.", Raymond offered.

"Oh wow!", added Shannon as her eyes searched the interior.

"Thanks, guys. Come on in and get comfortable.", offered Vincent.

Shannon rushed over to Vivian who was already sitting in the sunken family area; it was the only feature of the cabin that remained the same.

"Everyone, this is Markita.", Giovanni introduced.

"Hey!", Markita greeted then clung close to Giovanni.

Vincent had given the cabin a much-needed overhaul and lightened the dark wooden blocks on the wall leading to the kitchen. He had wanted to put his signature touch on it since he had decided to keep the once-unappreciated gift from his father. The interior decorator white-washed the wooden blocked wall and bamboo ceiling. The designer swapped out the dark wooden floors for white oak floors throughout. Vincent had the old windows replaced with black framed new ones and installed two tri-fold patio doors that lead to the deck off the family room; it was adjacent to the fireplace that had been upgraded with a floor-to-ceiling dark grey quartz with white veining.

The party motioned their way to the family room to join Shannon and Vivian who sat joking, laughing and hugging. The two sat upon a pale grey Italian leather sectional with two large oval dark grey river stone Roman coffee tables in the middle of the sectional atop a pale grey hand-woven shag rug. It was a modern touch that added additional elegance to the décor. Vincent and Raymond approached the ladies to stake their claim to their respective loves as the ladies made room for their lovers to sit next to them. Giovanni guided a nervous Markita to the large sectional to sit with the party. She was starting to feel like a fish out of water. Giovanni noticed and decided to plant a kiss on her forehead to calm her.

The guys discussed how different the cabin was from the days of their youth when they came as children and the conversation quickly went down memory lane with Raymond and Giovanni telling stories of their childhood with an embarrassed Vincent nodding in agreement. Shannon loved hearing the stories for the first time and seeing Raymond's face light up with admiration as he discussed his grandfather. She and Vivian laughed nonstop at the stories, while Markita was thinking of ways to participate in the conversation.

"Something smells delicious.", complimented Markita.

"Thanks, Markita. The chef and his staff are preparing an incredible spread for us. I wanted this weekend to be something special.", Vincent winked at Raymond.

Raymond was anxiously awaiting the right moment to remove the ring box from his Louis Vuitton cross-body bag. Shannon noticed that Raymond was gripping it for dear life after Vincent hinted at the weekend being special. Shannon blushed as she leaned against Raymond's strong frame; everything about Raymond was surreal. She almost didn't believe everything she had experienced with him was tangible; it was things that dreams were made of.

"I know the ride was long; so why don't you freshen up and get changed? Our meal should be ready by then.", suggested Vincent, "Gio, your room is next to ours off the family room. Raymond, you and Shannon are on the lower level with the walk-out to the patio and pool."

Since Vincent knew that Raymond had been putting off being intimate until his proposal, he wanted them to have privacy for that special moment. Vincent winked at the couple causing both Shannon and Raymond to blush. Raymond had wanted that moment the first time he saw Shannon; it was something about her that drew him yet frightened him all at once. He guessed that's how a man knows when he had met the one and she was definitely the one for him.

"Sounds good. Pixie, let me get our bags from the entrance.", Raymond offered Shannon.

"Yo, Vincent. Next time hire a butler for us. Nobody's got time for lugging bags around.", joked Giovanni.

"Okay, I'll let you handle that when *you* host an event.", laughed Vincent.

"Right!", Giovanni said sarcastically as he walked to get their bags, "Markita, your bag is heavy as fuck compared to mine. What's in here?"

"Daddy, don't play. You know I brought our sex toys.", Markita laughed boldly.

"Oh, yeah. I forgot.", laughed Giovanni.

Everyone chuckled as they knew the purpose of his antics. Yeah right, thought Raymond; it was just a way to let everyone know just how freaky they were going to be that weekend. Shannon shook her head at Giovanni in disbelief at his boldness; she was now grateful that Vincent offered them a more private suite. The last thing she wanted to hear during the night of their first would be obscenities from Markita and Giovanni. Raymond motioned to her and nodded toward the kitchen which led to the walkout basement where they would sleep.

The master suite was warm and inviting just as the rest of the cabin had been; it was decorated in shades of grey, blue and white. Shannon found a muted grey wooden canopy bed in the room with two long sheer white silk draperies elegantly sprawling down its four posts. Shannon felt like a princess entering her bed chambers. Raymond was pleased by her expression and he hoped to bring even more moments of pleasure to her.

"Would you like to shower first?", Raymond offered.

"No, you go ahead.", Shannon said mischievously.

Raymond saw the glint of mischief in her eyes but was unsure what she had planned. However, he had plans of his own. He removed his shirt so that she had a glimpse of his muscular physique and then he removed his pants to reveal his thick muscled thighs. He tossed them on the floor and looked over his shoulder at Shannon. Shannon stared at him with desire and lust in her eyes; yes, she had a plan indeed. He entered the bathroom very hopeful that they would share a romantic night together. Once she heard that he had turned on the water, she began to remove her clothes. She boldly approached the bathroom door, the closer she was the more confident the sway of her hips and the bounce of her huge breasts.

Shannon thought it was time out for being old-fashioned and letting Raymond dictate when they would make love; because she was ready to express her love and desire for him. She quickly turned the doorknob and entered the bathroom. Raymond had his back to the door as the water slid down his caramel-sculptured back and onto his muscled buttocks. She wanted to taste him from head to toe; so, she would do just that. She stealthily entered the room like a spy on a mission as she quietly opened the glass shower door and got on her knees. She gently encompassed his thick thigh with one arm as her tongue moved gently over his buttocks and her hand tenderly touched his testicles. Raymond had been leaning his head down against the shower wall in deep thought about his upcoming proposal; he wanted it to be heartfelt and romantic.

"Pixie?", questioned Raymond as his manhood got in formation.

"Yes, Ray.", whispered Shannon.

As she stood, she continued working her tongue up a trail on his back until he turned around. Raymond couldn't speak; his breathing had become heavy, deep as if a growl. He had restrained his desire for too long and he was out of his mind with desire. Gone was the man whose every move was to ensure that he didn't go too far too soon with her; she had given a clear sign that she wasn't going to take no for an answer and the word no was not in his vocabulary at that moment. With one hand, Raymond slipped his hand around her buttocks to her vagina to claim it and lifted her to press against his chest as his lips devoured hers.

Shannon gasped at his sheer strength that he could lift her with one arm; at that gasp, Raymond slipped his tongue deep within her mouth as he imagined his tongue entering her other two delicate openings. The two moaned in desperation for the other like two wild beasts devouring a much-needed meal. Shannon fumbled with the nozzle to turn off the water as if reading his mind; then he carried her drenched body to the bed and laid her atop the comforter. His imagination did not do her body justice; it was a masterpiece of ebony softness. He buried his face in her voluptuous breasts and pressed them against his face then he inhaled as if coming up for air, then flicked his tongue rapidly over her large black nipples. He used every nerve ending to stop his eruption from happening too quickly; because any man would erupt at the sight of them and would even be willing to lose his soul for a taste of them.

Shannon urgently pulled him forward so that his penis would lay atop her breast then she placed it between them so he could simulate his sexual thrust. She rested her mouth atop her breasts to welcome his entry. Raymond's body began to shake and he growled to command his dick to hold its load for a little longer;

he had no idea what type of lover Shannon would be, but now he knew this was just the tip of the iceberg.   Raymond's hazel eyes were transfixed on Shannon and displayed every emotion that he felt; at that moment he was at her will. Shannon could have used him and done with him any and everything she wanted. She gently nudged him down and he knew what he had permission to do. Raymond reached frantically for his bag on the nightstand to get a condom. Shannon realized what he was in search of and reached for his hand.

"There's no one else, Ray.", Shannon reassured.

Raymond nodded; he knew that he wouldn't be able to hold back much more, so his hand guided his member inside her and his thrusts were deep, hard and firm. Raymond claimed his Pixie that day and she would only belong to him and he to her; even if she didn't fully realize it.

Shannon was utterly surprised that his passion matched her own. She thought she would have to be the dominant one, but he proved to her that it was in him to display power. She guessed Vivian and Gloria had been right all along that he had held off on sex because he truly loved her, she thought as she locked eyes with his beautiful eyes.

"I love you … I love everything about you.", Raymond whispered as he thrust deep and steady.

Just as Shannon was going to utter that she loved him, she orgasmed and squealed the words as she wanted nothing to stop her from expressing her feelings. Shannon's voice traveled the staircase to the kitchen for anyone nearby to hear. Giovanni had gone to the kitchen to get a cold beer when he overheard the pair.

"Shit! Damn Ray.", laughed Giovanni, "That's why I'm going to make sure you've got *that* on lock!" Then he yelled downstairs, "Damn, we're waiting on you. You were supposed to dress not fuck."

"Did I hear what I think I heard?", laughed Shannon.

"Yup, that's Giovanni …", laughed Raymond, "We better get dressed and not keep them waiting."

Giovanni decided to make a quick call before he joined the rest in the dining room.

Just as Shannon had been discovering a new world so had Joe; he was basking in his newfound wealth and was the man around town. He had another windfall at Motor City Casino and was headed home north on the Lodge Expressway. He couldn't believe how well things were going for him.

"I could really get used to the high life.", laughed Joe as he tapped his chest pocket full of cash.

"We've got eyes on the fuck.", informed the hired hand.

"Cool. Get it done!", ordered Giovanni.

"You got it Reap!", he reassured.

"Damn, what the fuck! Slow down bitch!", shouted Joe at the erratic driver, "Don't fuck my shit up!"

Joe was annoyed that a car was tailgating him and he was losing his buzz. He swirled his car from the middle lane to the left one so he could slow down and ride alongside the tailgater. He let the passenger window down so that he could shout directly at the driver, but instead, the driver shot several bullets at him and his vehicle. Joe attempted to speed up to avoid more gunfire but to no avail. He and his car were hit multiple times by the bullets which caused him to lose control of it. His speeding car hit the median barricade and flipped multiple times landing on the other side of the expressway barely missing other vehicles as it sat on its side.

Giovanni heard his phone beep; he checked it out to see that he had received a text message with one word, 'Done'. That was all he needed to know; it was time to get his party on, he thought. Markita noticed how excited Giovanni was when he joined them at the table. He nodded at Vincent as if they had a surprise or some secret agreement. She did not understand why he insisted on dressing up for dinner when they weren't dining out. Subsequently, she decided to wear the Chanel items that he had bought for her.

Markita had draped an oversized black and white silk Chanel scarf around her neck, down over her bare breast and wrapped a large buckled black Chanel belt around her tiny waist. Her long hair was the only thing covering her back; she knew that Giovanni loved to see her lean back out. She paired it with skinny-coated black jeans. Gio had also given her a pearl necklace with a silver diamond-encrusted Chanel signature emblem that she paired with her Chanel stud signature earrings and an oversized faux pearl fashion ring. Lastly, she wore a pair of four-inch Cinderella slingbacks with a silver sequin-covered bow. She thought she had done a decent job of piecing something together; those stuffy hoes wouldn't outdo her, she thought.

Vivian felt like Markita; she wanted to look nice but not overdressed since they were not going out on the town. But unlike Markita, she knew the real reason for the evening's attire. She wore a grey off-the-shoulder puffy top made of chiffon. It had long blouson sleeves with elastic cuffs and a sash that she tied in the back to snatch her waist; she paired it with skin-tight shiny silver leggings. She finished the look with peek-a-boo grey leather booties with crisscross straps and a zipper in the back. She wore her hair in an updo so that her anniversary gift was clearly displayed. She loved the platinum choker of pear-shaped diamonds and matching stud earrings; she felt it made her simple outfit pop. As much as she wanted to look nice, she hoped that Shannon would dress up for her upcoming surprise and outshine them both.

Sure, enough she did, thought Vivian, as Shannon entered the dining room. Shannon had found yet another treasure that she

172

had been saving for a special occasion that seemed to never come. She wore a bright yellow chiffon maxi dress that was off the shoulder with long puff sleeves attached with a band waist and a waist-high split that seemed endless. The dress was a perfect contrast to her dark ebony skin that flowed from the dress; her gorgeous legs and her voluptuous bosom. She kept everything else simple; she just wore a pair of large gold-tone hoops, light makeup and beige strapped heels.

"Glad you two could join us.", Vincent laughed beating Giovanni to the punch.

"Yes, we know you had *thangs* to do.", Giovanni teased.

"Well, you know …", laughed Raymond.

Raymond couldn't joke more than that; if he said another word about it everyone would know just how excited he was and he didn't want to lose any cool points with Giovanni. So, he played it off as the group engaged in conversation while the two-person cooking staff served their meal. After the staff filled their champagne glasses, Vincent decided that he would make a quick toast.

"To friendship!", announced Vincent.

"Friendship!", chimed the group.

Raymond decided that there was no better time for him to make a speech of his own than to follow the words of his best friend. He stood, then cleared his throat and said the words he had envisioned over and over.

"There are moments in our lives that are momentous and you hold on to them forever. In those moments you want those you love and hold dear to share them with you if possible. I have two of the most resilient and steadfast men, I know, supporting me. It feels good to know that I have two of the baddest motherfuckers on my side, Vincent and Giovanni.", laughed Raymond, "But most importantly, I have Vincent to thank for introducing me to the most incredible woman I've ever known ... my Pixie.", Raymond confessed.

Raymond assisted Shannon from her seat and then bent on one knee. He removed the ring box with a shaky and nervous hand.

"Shannon, my beautiful Pixie, will you marry me?", Raymond asked as he opened the box.

Shannon was overwhelmed by the beauty and presentation of the ring sitting atop a velvet rose. Markita and Vivian were astonished by it as well; Markita so much that she released an audible gasp at the remarkable piece.

"Oh, my God! Yes, I'll marry you!", Shannon cried.

Raymond bounced from his kneeled position to place the ring on her finger then squeezed and lifted her. He buried his face in her bosom to prevent anyone from seeing the tears that threatened to spill from his eyes. He had never been so happy and couldn't imagine being happier than he was at that moment.

The evening was filled with congratulations, stories and laughter as the couples ate, drank and danced the evening away. Raymond was determined to cut the night short so that he could spend some much-wanted alone time with his Pixie. He wanted to take his time and explore her body instead of being the lust-hungry lover he was during their first lovemaking experience.

"Excuse us, folks. We're going to call it a night.", informed Raymond.

Shannon blushed and shrugged her shoulders at Vivian then set her drink down to follow her fiancé.

"Handle your business.", chuckled Gio, "Markita, want to try out the new beads?"

"Beads?", asked Vivian.

Giovanni was about to explain when Vincent interrupted, "No thanks. Come on Vivian.", laughed Vincent.

Raymond and Shannon left the other two couples and briskly walked to their suite, but before she could enter, he swooped her up and carried her inside.

"Okay … you're going to get enough of lifting me. Don't blame me if you hurt yourself.", teased Shannon.

"Don't worry baby, I got you Pixie! I can handle all this delicious chocolate.", chuckled Raymond.

"Okay …", giggled Shannon.

He carried her to the bed and laid her upon it; he straddled her and gazed upon her face.

"I can't believe just how lucky I am to have you in my life.", Raymond declared.

"No, Raymond, I am the one who is truly blessed to have *you*.", Shannon whispered.

Raymond kissed every inch of her face then slowly moved down to her neck and shoulders before he delighted in her cleavage. He reached beneath her to unzip her dress to reveal her fullness. The sight of her seemingly restricted his airflow causing him to breathe heavily as he devoured her breasts and nipples. He could have stayed there forever; he felt the depth of her love there as she ran her fingers through his wavy hair. Then he laid on his side propped up on his elbow to discuss something, he felt that he needed to address.

"Pixie, I know you've probably been wondering when you'll meet my family.", Raymond began as she nodded, "You already know where I stand with my parents … it's more important that you meet my grandmother. I spent so much of my youth with my grandparents that people often thought they were my parents.", Ray chuckled.

"I understand … I won't rush you, but it would be nice to meet them all before our wedding day.", joked Shannon.

"True.", agreed Raymond," I will set something up in a couple of weeks so you can meet everyone, promise. But the most important person is my grandmother. I just hope she'll be thinking clearly.", informed Raymond, "What about your parents?"

"That would be a hell no!", laughed Shannon, "I don't want you taking this ring back. But seriously, I haven't seen her in who knows when and never met my father. That just means there are fewer people for you to impress."

The couple laughed, talked, cuddled and made love seemingly endlessly; they made the tenderest of love until they fell asleep in each other's arms. Shannon often woke up before daybreak, so she lay there lost in thought; she could finally see a different life, a better life, was within reach after years of searching high and low. Mainly low, she thought. She had a peace that had been unobtainable until now; one she hoped would never escape her grasp ever again.

Vivian heard her cell phone ring and she wondered who in the world could be calling her that late. She glanced at the phone and noticed that it was her mother; she and Vincent were in the throes of passion and nothing her mother could be calling about was more important than what she was doing at that moment.

Shannon heard her phone vibrate on the nightstand and she decided to check it. She read the text message from Peggy, Joe's mom, 'Joe was shot causing a horrible crash and he might not make it. He's at St. John's near his home in the ICU ward.' All of Shannon's peace and joy were ripped from her heart and fear replaced it. She knew that Peggy was a drama queen and she might not be able to trust the severity of Joe's condition as told by Peggy, but she couldn't chance it. Subsequently, without a thought, she threw on her clothes, grabbed her purse and car keys then rushed out of the cabin to race to the hospital to be at Joe's bedside leaving everything behind, her luggage and most importantly Raymond.

Raymond was a solid sleeper and didn't budge while Shannon was racing out of the room; eventually, he realized that his soft Pixie was not in bed beside him as he felt the bedsheets. He turned on the lamp atop the nightstand as his opened eyes burned and adjusted to the light. He looked around and noticed that her purse and discarded clothes from their arrival were gone along with her keys. He quickly grabbed his boxers and put them on so that he could go look for her. He desperately wanted to make sure all was well, but she was nowhere in sight. A nagging voice urged him to look outside for her car, but surely, she wouldn't leave. He hesitantly inched closer to the window and under the moonlight saw that her car was in fact gone.

Shannon did top speed as she made the long drive back to Detroit; at her high rate of speed, she shaved a lot of time off her trip. She rushed inside the hospital like a frantic woman, afraid that her daughter would be without a father. She hadn't even thought about calling Nicole, but she would have wanted to have more details before she did. She hated to admit that she would be more affected than Nicole if something happened to Joe.

She nervously asked for the room number of Joe Johnston, but the nurse advised that visiting hours would start shortly but only for family members due to his condition. Shannon quickly informed the nurse that he was the father of her daughter and as she did the nurse got a glimpse of her engagement ring. The nurse assumed Shannon was his wife and quickly provided the room number along with directions to get there.

Shannon feverishly walked to Joe's hospital room fearing the worst and imagining his mangled body in the bed. She prepared her mind for what she might see when she inhaled deeply and entered the room.

"What the hell are you doing here?", shouted Rita forgetting where she was.

Joe had been sleeping but was awakened by Rita's angry outburst. He was still slightly groggy when he turned to the entrance to see Shannon enter the room. A part of him was thrilled that she cared enough to come; her best friend, his sister, hadn't even shown up with the rest of the family.

"Shannon?", Joe questioned.

"Like I said, why are you here?", demanded Rita.

Shannon ignored his off-again and on-again lover so that she could tend to Joe; she guessed that Rita didn't realize that he was only bothered with her when she wouldn't be bothered with him.

"Oh, my God! What happened?", questioned Shannon.

"He was shot!", exclaimed Rita.

Shannon pulled his covers over his chest to cover his wounds.

The two ladies ignored Joe's attempts at speaking; instead, Rita snatched the covers and moved them back to his waist causing an argument.

"He gets hot under a thick blanket. You ought to remember that!", fussed Rita, "But now he is my man so I guess that's why I remember."

Joe despite being in pain was getting off on the fact that his teenage love and his current lover were arguing over him and when it became physical, he wished he could record it. He looked on the nightstand for his phone but was too sore to reach it and too out of it on pain pills to try. The two women started to tug at the cover with such force that it ripped; then Rita slapped Shannon. Rita had wanted to do that for years and there was no better time than the present, she thought.

Shannon collapsed to her knees. The sting of the slap caused Shannon to pause when all she wanted to do was punch Rita; she placed her left hand on her face and felt the diamond on her cheek. The ring had turned inward and was rubbing her face and it was a stark reminder of what she had jeopardized by coming there. Suddenly all the memories she had suppressed surfaced; the years of Joe's lies, disappointment, violence, mistrust, control and infidelity rushed over her causing screams to gurgle forth. She had never cried from the depth of her soul or honestly acknowledged the brokenness left in his quake until then; the years of being a fool for Joe by accepting him back time and time again knowing nothing would ever truly change.

Rita and Joe thought her cries were a result of her desire for him and her defeat at the hands of Rita, but it was a culmination of years of pain at the hands of the pitiful man who lay before her smiling. The huge diamond was barely visible through her tears as she stared at the massive stone. She flipped it around as she continued to stare at it and then thought of the incredible man she had left behind at the cabin. Shannon looked at Rita and Joe in disbelief at her own actions; how could she be so foolish? She stumbled to her feet and felt sick to her stomach; her stomach wanted to vomit up her stupidity if it were possible. The nurses entered the room after racing down the hallway to determine the cause of the horrifying screams only to see Shannon dizzy from crying. She gripped the bed rail to steady herself.

"Are you okay, ma'am?", inquired one of the nurses.

"I will be, once I leave here and make things right with the most incredible man I've ever met.", confessed Shannon as she composed herself and then left the room.

Raymond sat on the bed in the dark until daybreak; he barely had the energy to bathe, dress or even breathe. He had called Shannon countless times to no avail. He was heartbroken beyond words and he felt as if she had ripped his heart out and dragged it by the bumper of her car to wherever it was that she had gone. He felt like a damn fool; like she had bewitched him into believing that she cared, but it had been nothing more than a game. Perhaps it was just that, a ruse to see if she could break the rich Black nigga, he thought; maybe that's all he was to her since she only dated white guys. Maybe, he should have stuck to his pool of rich White debutantes.

It seemed to be taking Raymond and Shannon forever to come out for breakfast; of course, the guys thought they were probably having sex. But something in Vivian's gut thought differently as she remembered the voicemail her mother left. Shannon wouldn't, she couldn't, thought Vivian as she walked to the window to look out only to find that Shannon's car was gone. Vivian panicked as she ran down the stairs to Shannon's suite and knocked on the door; she hoped that they both were gone into town for something. The door creaked open to reveal a heartbroken Raymond slumped on the side of the bed with his face resting in his hands. When he looked up at Vivian, she instantly began to cry as she witnessed the depth of his hurt and confusion.

"Oh my God, Shannon, what have you done?", whispered Vivian.

Shannon was numb as she made the drive home and everything was a blur. When she threw herself across the bed, she didn't even remember turning onto her street let alone walking up the stairs. She did not know how she could ever face Raymond again, but the diamond on her finger shouted that she owed him that and more. She didn't even know if he would accept an apology from her; she knew she wouldn't blame him if he never wanted to see her again.

Chapter 11

Shannon had been in autopilot mode for the days and weeks after her betrayal. She had no real memories of anything she had done since that fateful night she left Raymond at the cabin. She even started her new position not fully self-aware. She missed him terribly and cried every night when she thought of him and then cried again when she ignored his calls. She wanted desperately to answer, but she was embarrassed and scared to confront him. The reality of what she had done was too great to face.

Raymond couldn't sleep, think or even eat since Shannon disappeared. He felt that he was going to lose his mind if he didn't figure out a way to get her to talk to him. He had been avoiding going to her home in fear that he would find a cocky Joe there; Raymond knew if he saw Joe, he would beat the living shit that was left, out of him. He had begun to call morning and night without Shannon answering not even once, but he would try again. Once again, he had notified his secretary that he wasn't feeling well and would not be in. He had reassigned a couple of cases because his mind was a wreck; he knew he couldn't abandon his practice, but at that moment he cared about nothing more than reaching Shannon. He decided that he would try calling again, but Shannon refused to answer.

"Fuck!", shouted Raymond as he threw his phone.

He stood and began to pace his living room when he heard his phone ring. He dashed across the room praying to God Almighty that it was Shannon, but it was Vincent.

"Fuck! What is it?", demanded Raymond.

"Bro, calm down.", Vincent suggested, "Look, my father thinks it would be a good idea for you to come and spend some time with him, Giovanni and me. He reserved a private room at

Motor City so we could gamble and hang out. I called Giovanni and he agreed to leave his office early.", informed Vincent.

"Damn, John knows?", fussed Raymond.

"Yeah, what can I say? I pretty much tell him everything. He doesn't like how this is affecting you. Will you come?", asked Vincent.

"Yeah, okay. Let me hop in the shower and I'll be right there.", conceded Raymond.

"I'll call you when I arrive so you know where to meet us.", informed Vincent.

"Sounds good.", agreed Raymond.

Raymond had never been this distraught over losing a girl, breaking up with a girl or even not getting a girl. He didn't trust himself to drive that distance to the casino; he called the family chauffeur to pick him up and take him there. As he rode to the casino, every mile, he imagined John giving him some old-timey chauvinistic pep talk that would make him feel less of a man. He really needed his grandfather at a time like this; hell, even old Ricky Bianchi would be better than John, he thought.

The luxury sedan pulled into the valet section in good timing; Raymond was glad that he wasn't late when he noticed that Vincent had just arrived and was handing the car over to the valet. Giovanni in pure Bianchi fashion pulled up with his music thumping and commanding everyone's attention.

"Bro! It's good to see you. I've been concerned.", voiced a sincere Giovanni.

"Yeah, for sure, Bro.", Vincent agreed.

"Well, I've barely been keeping it together. Gio, thanks for not ragging me.", admitted Raymond.

"No worries, I'll rag you later.", laughed Giovanni.

Raymond and Vincent joined Giovanni in laughter and started into the building when a man attempted to accost Vincent. Roger had been eyeing the men from a distance but the more he looked he was sure that he knew one of them; but how could he know those heavy hitters, thought Roger.

"Bro!", shouted Roger as he reached for Vincent.

"My man, back the fuck up!", warned Giovanni as he discreetly showed the handle of a small pistol, "You don't know us, the fuck!"

"Sorry dude. I don't want no trouble.", Roger apologized fearful of the brazen man.

Roger was embarrassed, but certain he knew the guy. Although, there was no way his brother would be in that circle. The wealthy double-ganger was furious and snarled at the thought that Roger would even think that they knew each other.

"Come on before some other broke motherfuckers approach us.", fumed Giovanni.

One of the security guards snatched Roger and pulled him to the side.

"Those are the owners of Greektown Casino. You're lucky they aren't pressing charges. Get out of here!", scowled the guard.

Just then, Vincent received a text message from his father informing them of the reserved room. The three men headed there and Raymond felt a little lighter; maybe that was what he needed after all, thought Raymond. The guys entered the game room; there was a poker table and roulette wheel set up for them. A waiter asked the men for their drink orders and then scurried off to get them.

John joined the young men and greeted them all with hugs. It helped to ease Raymond even more; he finally felt comfortable enough to discuss the incident with his pals.

"I don't get the pull this Joe has on Shannon. Maybe she thinks he'll change like you did, Vincent.", confessed Raymond., "Who knew how you would change when you used to party all the time and be into the drug scene? It's possible she might be holding on to that."

"I hate to hear how I used to be because I'm literally not the same person. It's rare that people change; but it's obviously not impossible, but rare never-the-less.", Vincent admitted.

The waiter returned with the drinks and then departed quickly to provide privacy.

"I don't know what to do.", sighed Raymond.

"Joe needs to be dealt with. I tried by giving him $100k to leave town, but we see that plan failed.", Vincent revealed then sipped his drink.

"Well, you're not the only one with an epic failure; mine just landed him in the hospital. And we see how that turned out.", whispered Gio.

"What the fuck? Really?", Raymond questioned as he stared at his friends.

"You need to think of a good plan.", plotted Giovanni.

"Listen to your friends, Raymond.", urged John, "Men of our stature and power take what we want. Don't we, my son?"

John looked at Vincent admiringly as he gripped the back of his neck.

"Yes, we do Father.", laughed Vincent as he hugged his father vigorously.

"Vincent knows that well. He's more of a Barrington than I am and his grandfather put together.", chuckled John proudly.

"I don't know about that because y'all were some real motherfuckers in your day.", laughed Giovanni.

"Trust me, Raymond, and think about what I've said. How do you think your grandfather, a black man in the 50s, had the power he had? It was because the three of them, he, my father and Ricky, stood as one unmovable force and they helped each other. Allow your friends, your *brothers*, to help you.", insisted John.

John walked away from the men so that his words could sink in and headed to the roulette table.

"He's right! We *are* men of power and I will have Shannon. Let me take over from here.", announced Raymond.

"Hell yeah!", cheered Giovanni, "What do you have in mind?"

"I have a few thoughts …", Raymond divulged.

Vincent smiled in support of his friend.

"If you need anything, whatsoever, we have your back!", Vincent reassured.

Giovanni patted Raymond on the back in support of the promise Vincent made on their behalf.

The evening with his friends and John was the shot in the arm he needed to get his life back in order. The next day Raymond awoke with a new resolve. He was determined that his vow would be more than bravado; he would start to set everything in motion. He called a private detective that he had used in the past and asked him to keep an eye on Joe who had made a remarkable recovery for someone who was reportedly on his deathbed.

"Spivey, I need you to watch and dig up some dirt on a guy. His name is Joseph Johnston Jr.; he goes by Joe.", requested Raymond.

"You got it. Tell me about this Joe character.", Spivey responded.

"He's from Southwest Detroit, white, poor and a street guy. He's been rumored to be involved in some shady dealings over the years.", added Raymond.

"I've got the perfect dude to keep an eye on him. He has some great connections in that part of town. Let's meet up so you can give me a photo and anything else you come up with.", informed Spivey.

Raymond agreed and set up a meeting time with him. It was time out for doing things strictly by the book and letting fate have its way; not this time, he was taking charge. Nothing was going to stop him from having his Pixie and making her a permanent part of his life.

The next part of his plan was to return to the land of the living by diving back into his work. If he were going to stake a permanent claim to Shannon, he had to ensure that he maintained his empire to provide nothing short of the best for her and Nicole and the little one they were sure to have. Additionally, he ordered a flower arrangement that he would pick up and take to her home after work. He would surprise her and not give her an opportunity to scurry out of seeing him.

His day had been a busy one; he was shocked by just how much he had abandoned his work. Nothing passes like a busy day, he thought, as he drove to Shannon's house that evening. It seemed like ages ago that he had visited there for the first time; he remembered how nervous he had been. Oddly, those feelings renewed in him as if it were his first visit; he prayed to God that the bastard Joe was not there. He didn't know if he would have the self-control to be polite when all he wanted to do was bash Joe's head. He sighed a sigh of relief when he noticed her car in the driveway. He took several deep breaths and grabbed the enormous bouquet arrangement and exited the car. Nicole heard the ring doorbell and she assumed that her mother was approaching the door. She was glad that her mother had returned early; so, she quickly dashed to the door and began speaking as she flung it open.

"How was dinner with Auntie Gloria?", asked Nicole to a confused Raymond.

"Hey, Nicole. I was hoping your mom was home since her car is in the driveway.", informed Raymond.

"No, sorry. Auntie Gloria picked her up. She's trying to talk some sense into her.", admitted Nicole, "Come on in."

"I'm here to do the same.", Raymond uttered.

"Mommy is crazy about you and feels ashamed of herself for leaving the cabin.", Nicole disclosed.

"Really? I can't tell; she won't answer my calls. I was starting to think that maybe Joe had won her back.", grumbled Raymond.

He walked into the living room and set the flower arrangement on the coffee table next to a pitiful arrangement of carnations. Nicole spied Raymond's curious expression as he looked at the skimpy twigs.

"Mommy and Joe? No, not at all. Let me move this out of the way. Mommy threw them in the trash when Joe gave them to her today. Auntie Gloria took them out.", Nicole elaborated.

"He was here?", Raymond inquired.

Raymond was very confused as to why Gloria wouldn't allow Shannon to throw the flowers away; especially, if she truly was in his corner.

"Joe showed up unexpectedly and we don't know how he even got the address. Mommy wouldn't let him inside, but she reluctantly accepted the flowers. Auntie Gloria told Mommy that she needed to keep the flowers … to help Mommy make a choice. Auntie said Mommy had two choices, the pitiful past, the carnations represented, or you, her future.", Nicole revealed.

Surely, Shannon would have a clear picture of how her past compares to her future when she returned to see the flowers standing side-by-side. It was a visual for Raymond as well that made him even more determined to win her back.

"I don't want to be out of line, but you need to know that mommy loves you. She still wears your ring every day and I believe as long as that ring is on her finger, she's still your Pixie.", Nicole philosophized.

"You are a pretty wise kid. You know that?", laughed Raymond.

"Yeah, I do.", laughed Nicole.

The two talked for a bit about the law profession and law school as they had many times before. Nicole enjoyed her conversations with Raymond every single time; he was the type of man that would make the best father and she looked forward to the day when she could call him, Daddy.

"You know what?", conspired Nicole to a curious Raymond, "I am going to help you.",

"How so? What do you have in mind?", Raymond marveled.

"I can prepare dinner in celebration of Mommy's new job…", began Nicole.

"Wait … you can cook … and Shannon got the promotion?", pondered Raymond.

"Yes, Mommy and Granny taught me well. Oh, yeah, Mommy got the promotion, but she hasn't been excited about it, at all. So, like I said, I'll cook and set the table really nicely. Then you can surprise her by coming over!", Nicole revealed, "Let's plan for this Saturday. I need time to grocery shop."

Raymond smiled at his future stepdaughter who beamed with excitement; he knew then more than ever there was no way their efforts would fail. That simple talk with Nicole was just another fire that was lit in his bones; that week had been more like normal than any since the cabin fiasco. He was determined that once he secured his position with Shannon, he would tackle the task of introducing her to his parents. There was no time like the present, he thought, he would be bold, man up and proudly introduce the love of his life to them even if they wouldn't accept her. He absolutely had zero fucks to give when it came to anyone or anything standing in his way of settling down with Shannon.

Friday had rolled around quicker than expected and he was over the moon with excitement for Saturday. Even receiving a call from someone other than Shannon was no longer an annoyance, he thought, as it began to ring as it sat on his office desk face down. He flipped it to see that it was Vincent checking in. He had already talked to Giovanni earlier that week. He could always depend on his boys acting like mother hens to see if he was okay.

"Hey dude, what's up? I'm putting in a late night; I'm still in catch-up mode.", informed Raymond.

"Just thought I would see how things are going with you and Shannon.", admitted Vincent.

"Well, I dropped by her house, but she wasn't home; however, I did have a great conversation with my future stepdaughter. She's on board to help me. I have a surprise in store for Shannon tomorrow.", Raymond advised.

"That's great ... you know I'm no expert on women, especially black women... but there has to be a reason Shannon keeps going back to that scum. If you can figure that out, I think you'll solve your problem.", confessed Vincent.

"I think that it boils down to the fact that Shannon doesn't trust black men except one, her grandfather. Any other is thrown in the category with her no-good father who abandoned her. Hell, she barely gives black women a pass; if Gloria didn't remind her of her grandmother, I think she'd be out. The pain of that abandonment runs so deep; it's almost hatred. I pray it's not to the level of self-hatred.", Raymond concluded.

"Shit, that's deep.", blurted Vincent.

"Yeah, so you see it's much deeper than Joe. He's only a part of it.", Raymond proclaimed.

"Well, damn. I don't know what to say …", admitted Vincent.

"Abandonment issues are a motherfucker.", proclaimed Raymond, "Hell, I have those same issues with my own parents. They were present, yet absent all the same."

Vincent sympathized with Raymond and related more than Raymond could have ever imagined. Vincent was determined to keep things positive so he switched gears to gossip about Giovanni's latest girlfriend; if that's what she even was.

"So, what do you think of him and Markita? Do you think they are serious?", snooped Vincent.

"Bro, when has he ever been serious… but honestly… I don't think so. He needs a woman that makes him work for her affection.", concluded Raymond.

"Yeah, I agree … a chick that's hard to get and he goes nuts trying to win her over.", Vincent agreed.

"Oh, like Shannon, you mean?", laughed Raymond.

"My bad!", chuckled Vincent, "Yeah, just like her or even worse."

The two men continued to share jokes and laughter about their best pal. Raymond decided it was time to call it a night and get off the phone when he realized he had been doing more laughing than working since Vincent's call. Besides, he could only think of how things would play out with him and Shannon; and if things went as he planned, he and Shannon would be sharing her bed Saturday night. That occupied his thoughts as he slept that night.

Raymond felt exhilarated; that week he had been living by a schedule closely and that Saturday morning was no different. He had scheduled a meeting with Spivey for that afternoon, so he'd swing by there before surprising Shannon. He had two large flower arrangements on the back seat waiting to be presented to his Pixie and a thin file folder of information about Joe on the front passenger seat. He had gathered as much information from Vincent as he knew and was able to gather from Vivian. Raymond included that along with a picture of Joe; he snarled every time he looked at the photograph. Raymond couldn't believe that there were so many men who didn't appreciate a gem, but it reminded him of what his grandmother often said. She repeated a saying her mother often told her as she was starting to date young men, 'You don't throw pearls before swine'. There were just some people who didn't deserve nor even recognize something good and that was Joe, a pure pig, thought Raymond.

Raymond pulled into the small parking lot on the side of Spivey's office. He hoped that Spivey would find all the dirt on Joe, a pig like that definitely had been rolling around in the muck and mire with the sleaziest of characters, thought Raymond. Raymond entered the small simple office; there was only a desk, a couple of chairs, a few file cabinets and a mounted television on the wall.

"Hello, Mr. Brown. Good to see you again.", greeted Spivey.

"Hey. Same here. I'm excited to get this project done.", announced Raymond as he passed off the folder.

"So, this is the infamous Joe Johnston Jr.?", Spivey stated.

"Yeah, and I want to know all the dirt. Dig deep. I don't care how ugly it gets; the uglier the better! No matter the cost or the resources you have to throw at it. I want the evidence to be zip-lock tight!", instructed Raymond.

"Anything for you, boss.", informed Spivey to his top-paying client.

"Keep me updated as you find out the smallest details.", instructed Raymond as he prepared to leave.

"Sure thing. Talk soon.", agreed Spivey.

Raymond's hope was to present all the evidence as quickly as possible so that Giovanni's contact could fast-track the case for a winter lock-up.

"You're going down motherfucker.", whispered Raymond.

Raymond strolled to his Bentley with confidence; he caught a glimpse of himself in the sideview mirror and winked as he entered his car. He wore an Italian tailored trim fit burgundy cotton shirt; it had a burgundy paisley print trimmed in gold on the reverse side of the cuff which was visible when he folded it up. He wore the crisp shirt with a pair of black trim-fit slacks, black alligator loafers and his favorite Shinola watch.

"Let me go claim my Pixie!", grinned Raymond as he turned up his music.

Raymond and his car thumped with the music as it played; his excitement and confidence grew with each mile. Nothing on earth was going to stand in the way of him getting his Pixie and making her his bride. His grandfather would be proud of his resolution and the way that his best friends supported him. The next mountain to tackle would be introducing Shannon to his parents. Originally, he had planned to wait until he had sure-up things with Shannon; instead, he would be confidently proactive and do it now. He instructed the hands-free feature to call his grandmother's butler.

"Hey, Lawrence.", Raymond enthused.

"Hello, young sir. What may I do for you?", inquired Lawrence.

"I want the folks to meet my Pixie. Can you instruct the chef to prepare a formal dinner for a couple of Saturdays from now? Also, I'll need you to notify my parents and Crystal as well. I don't want them planning to leave the country before then.", instructed Raymond.

"Yes, of course, sir. Your baby sister will be thrilled to meet her future sister-in-law. Come to think of it, their next trip is actually a few days afterward. I'll make sure everything is in order, sir.", informed Lawrence.

"Excellent!", exclaimed Raymond, "Talk later."

"Yes, good day, sir.", Lawrence beamed.

Raymond knew that everything was in good hands with Lawrence on the case. Lawrence was like another second father figure and runner-up to his grandfather when it came to support. Raymond knew the evening would have flair and be top-notch; he just hoped that his parents' behavior would match. He imagined the proud moment of presenting Shannon to his family then suddenly, a sensation fluttered through his body; he checked his manhood. He didn't want an erection like he was a teenage boy on his first date. Cool, he thought, when he noticed that his pants controlled his bulge well.

Shannon was shocked when Nicole told her that she was preparing a celebratory dinner for her promotion. She hadn't been in tune with anything since her fiasco, so she never would have planned to do anything in celebration. In celebration of what, she thought, another promotion with the rest of her life being in shambles? Nevertheless, she was appreciative of her daughter's gesture and would accept the one time that her daughter wanted to pamper her. Nicole had prepared breakfast for her, ran a bubble bath and even washed her hair while she soaked in the tub. It was all so ultra-surreal; especially, when she noticed that Nicole had laid out an outfit on her bed. Shannon fought suspicious thoughts and forced herself to enjoy the special treatment.; yet those thoughts persisted.

"I'm not in for some bad news, am I? You haven't dropped out of college, have you?", questioned Shannon nervously.

"Mommy!", laughed Nicole, "Don't be silly. I would never do that. Let's get you dressed."

Nicole had picked out a sunny yellow maxi dress; it had a solid bodice with a cage-style neckline and white and yellow geometric print from the waist down to her ankles. Nicole had searched through her mother's jewelry until she found white square hoops and a wide square white plastic bracelet. Nicole paired it with a pair of beige 4-inch platform stilettoes. There was no doubt in Nicole's mind that Raymond would be blown away by her mother's beauty. After Shannon dressed, Nicole pulled her mother to the full-length mirror in her bedroom. She wanted Shannon to see the beautiful woman that she saw before her.

"You look stunning!", giggled Nicole, "Come on, let's go down to dinner."

"Okay …", laughed Shannon as she followed behind her daughter.

As Shannon neared the bottom of the stairs, she could smell the delicious aroma of the food more clearly and as she walked closer to the dining room, she could see that Nicole had beautifully decorated the table.

"Baby girl!", Shannon beamed, "You did all of this for me?"

"Yes of course Mommy! You deserve the best.", affirmed Nicole.

Shannon was close to tears as she realized that despite her many mistakes, raising her daughter was one of her greatest accomplishments. Nicole was so precious, thought Shannon. She hugged Nicole and planted several kisses on her forehead.

"Mommy, stop! I don't want your makeup on my forehead.", giggled Nicole.

"I still don't understand why I needed to wear makeup…", began Shannon.

"Just so you look and feel special.", insisted Nicole, "Go back to the living room. I need to add one more touch.", instructed Nicole.

Nicole had hidden Shannon's phone so that she wouldn't hear the ring notification when someone approached and so her mother would be taken by surprise when Raymond rang the bell. She quickly went to the kitchen to remove the serving dishes from the oven and placed them on the dining room table. She had prepared lasagna, sauteed spinach and garlic bread. Then she quickly lit the candles on the table then eyed the silent notification on her cell revealing that Raymond had pulled into the driveway.

Raymond had taken several deep breaths as he parked in Shannon's driveway behind her car. He subconsciously was not going to give her a chance to hop in her car and dash off. He quickly exited and grabbed the two huge flower arrangements from the back seat. He placed the arrangements in front of his face, perhaps another subconscious move, as he approached the door. He regained his confidence and rang the doorbell.

"Mommy, can you get that? I had a delivery scheduled for you.", informed Nicole.

"Wow! I feel so special!", giggled Shannon.

Shannon wiggled toward the door as she excitedly opened it to see her surprise.

"Oh, my gosh Nicole they are beautiful.", exclaimed Shannon as she reached to take them from the assumed delivery person.

Raymond handed one of them to Shannon to reveal his face.

"But not nearly as beautiful as the incredible woman in front of me.", whispered Raymond.

"Ray … Nicole …", whispered Shannon as she looked back at her approaching daughter.

"Ray, come on in.", welcomed Nicole from the hall.

Raymond entered and walked past Shannon as she stepped aside in shock. It all made sense to her, the candles on the table, the makeup and the pretty outfit. But how could she be angry with either of them for giving her what her heart truly wanted, time with Raymond? Raymond boldly entered the living room and set the arrangement on the coffee table. He eyed the pitiful arrangement that Joe had sent days ago. He picked it up and handed it to Nicole.

"Please put these where they belong.", instructed Raymond.

Nicole winked and headed to the kitchen to toss the carnations into the trash. Shannon smiled at her daughter as Nicole walked past her.

"So, you and Nicole have been busy?", teased Shannon as she walked toward the sofa.

She motioned for Raymond to join her as she sat down on the sofa.

"Yes, that day I left the other flower arrangement, we decided to work as a team.", explained Raymond, "I hope you aren't upset with us."

"Me upset? I don't have a right to be.", confessed Shannon, "If anyone should be upset, it's you."

Raymond opened his mouth to interject, but Shannon interrupted him.

"Raymond, please let me finish... You are the best man I know and you don't deserve what I did. To tell you the truth I don't even know why I did it. It's like I was in autopilot mode, just doing what I've always done... run to Joe's rescue. When I got there, I felt like a fool; perhaps for the first time. I realized then that I had to leave him and our past, right there, in the past. Please forgive me.", Shannon explained apologetically.

"Shannon, of course, I forgive you. You mean everything to me. That ring you're wearing proves that.", Raymond reminded.

Raymond was so relieved to hear her heartfelt words that he leaned to kiss her, but she stopped him.

"You deserve a better woman than me Ray.", admitted Shannon as she removed the ring.

She set the ring on the coffee table and they both stared at it for a while, then Raymond began to speak as he reached for her hand.

"That's just the lie you're telling yourself to make it easier to push me away. I'm going to prove to you that I am not like Joe or even your father. I am willing to fight for you!", professed Raymond.

Tears began to well up in Shannon's eyes as she bowed her head, but Raymond wanted to stare deeply into her eyes, into her soul, so he placed his hand under her chin to raise her head and turn it to face him.

"Don't cry Pixie. I will always be by your side to protect you, to provide for you and even to defend you. You and Nicole are my family now and my world.", vowed Raymond.

He kissed her tears away then his lips moved to her nose, then her neck until he finally reached her lips. She thought he was being ultra-romantic by kissing other areas before finally moving to her lips, but the truth of the matter was that Raymond thought he would devour her if he started there. He tried to remember that Nicole was present somewhere in the house, but once he kissed her lips, all thoughts left his mind. All he wanted to do was taste her and feel her in his arms. Nicole peeked in the living room from the hall and was so pleased that they were on track to make up. She had already texted her best friend to pick her up and her phone notification indicated that her friend was outside. Nicole quietly exited the house with the two love birds kissing and groping each other not aware of anything but each other's lips.

Raymond and Shannon's breathing was heavy and labored so they stopped to breathe. Raymond quickly snatched the ring from the table and placed it back on her finger.

"I want nothing but my death to be the cause for you to remove this ring. I vow to be the best lover, friend, confidant, husband and warrior for you.", confessed Raymond, "Will you accept my ring again?"

"Yes!", squealed Shannon as she nodded a tearful agreement.

Raymond stood and effortlessly lifted Shannon so that she straddled him as he jogged up the stairs.

"Which way to your bedroom?", Raymond huffed.

"To the left. Oh God! Don't die on me now.", cautioned Shannon.

"Oh, I got you Pixie!", laughed Raymond.

He jogged into her bedroom and the two of them flopped on the bed laughing.

"Okay, maybe the next time we'll just run up the stairs on our own. You've got that good-good in the trunk.", joked Raymond.

"Oh yeah.", laughed Shannon as she tickled him.

"Yeah, you do. You know I love every ounce of it!", laughed Raymond as he began to kiss her.

Shannon flipped the script on him and his body then climbed on top to take control. They began to kiss passionately and slowly. They wanted to savor each touch and each sensation. Their minds were solely focused on each other, not on Nicole or the meal waiting for them downstairs. Raymond explored Shannon's entire body from head to toe and back up again as he introduced it to his lips and his touch.

Shannon loved his attentiveness and the fact that he wasn't rushing things to get to his own orgasm, but explored her body and tested her skin to see how she would react to each touch. And when they locked eyes, she could see the overwhelming and overflow of love he had for her; growing up she saw that same look in her grandfather's eyes whenever he looked at her granny. It was the type of love that stories were written about and here she was seeing it reflected from the eyes of an incredible and gorgeous man. She didn't feel that she deserved him, but unknowingly, he was in tune with her and could read her like a book.

"You deserve the best and I'm going to make sure I give you that and more.", whispered Raymond.

He skillfully unhooked her dress and slid it down to her waist so that he could bury his face in her bosom as he unsnapped her bra. He teased her nipples with his tongue before pulling with his lips to make their arousal grow. He loved the size of her breasts and her large nipples that he hoped would one day soon nurse their little one. Shannon loved him so much; he was masterful at bringing her body to life. She gripped his head to bury him deeper in her soft mound. This time they savored each touch, each lick and each taste of one another as they made love throughout the night leaving Nicole's labor of love sitting on the dining room table. When Nicole finally returned home after midnight, she noticed Ray's car remained in the driveway and that the meal remained untouched. She smiled knowing that Ray and her mother were a couple once again and nothing made her happier.

Chapter 12

Evelyn heard a knock at their door. They didn't often have guests, especially not unannounced ones. She used her cane to walk to the door, but not without fussing.

"Larry, did you invite someone over without telling me?", demanded Evelyn.

"Of course not! I know you don't like surprises.", reassured Larry.

Larry had no interest in being put in the doghouse. He hadn't been there for a very long time and wasn't about to go back after all those years. Evelyn stared at him as a warning that he'd better be telling the truth. She peeked out the peephole and her heart almost stopped; she barely had the strength to open the door.

"Bernadette?", questioned Evelyn.

Larry looked up from his sports magazine in shock. He just hoped that their daughter had not come to start trouble or beg for money. It had been almost two decades if not more since they last saw her. Larry placed his magazine on the coffee table and braced himself as she entered.

"Hi, Mommy. Hi, Daddy.", greeted a nervous Bernadette.

Evelyn wasn't one to tolerate foolishness no matter how much she loved a person and her daughter wouldn't be an exception.

"What brings you here? The last time, you were here you still looked like a young woman. Now I barely recognize you.", Evelyn blurted.

"I don't blame you for being suspicious. I just wanted to stop by and see you now that I'm clean and doing pretty good.", Bernadette explained.

Larry and Evelyn had heard that same tale during her last visit and then they noticed she had stolen some of Evelyn's gold jewelry. So, neither was very trusting of the visit. Bernadette began looking around the living room and noted that the place looked different.

"Yeah, our cupcake makes sure we are taken care of. Have a seat.", Larry ordered as he pointed to the living room chair.

He didn't want her to even think she had a chance to roam around and snoop out something to steal. Bernadette noticed the accusatory looks of her parents and reluctantly sat where she was instructed.

"Wow. So, Shannon is doing good for herself?", inquired Bernadette.

She had eyed some boxes sent by Shannon that were stacked near the chair.

"Yes, thank the Lord! Our cupcake landed a good job after college. She's gone on and earned a graduate degree.", bragged Evelyn.

"Oh wow!", Bernadette gasped.

"Yeah, you would have known about her successes if you ever called or stopped by for anything other than money.", Evelyn accused.

"Well, like I said, I'm not here for that this time.", claimed Bernadette.

"I hope not. Shannon nor we need any drama in our lives; especially not Shannon. She has a daughter to think of; she's our baby doll, Nicole. Nicole is in college and she wants to become an attorney.", Evelyn continued.

"Shannon's done more than I ever thought she would especially since she got pregnant right out of high school.", Bernadette declared.

"Well, she listened to us. We told her not to give up and that things could turn around. Speaking of … Shannon just got a huge promotion and is engaged to a hell of a man, a rich one!", bragged Evelyn.

Larry cleared his throat to notify Evelyn that she was telling too much. Evelyn caught the hint and changed the subject quickly.

"Are you still living in the city?", asked Evelyn.

"Yeah, I am. I was just set up in a tiny house by a non-profit company a year ago. Like I said, I'm doing all right.", informed Bernadette.

Evelyn's heart softened a little as she realized that her daughter was looking for affirmation and acknowledgment of her progress.

"That's good doll, I just hope and pray you stick to it this time. God only gives us just so much time and then it's over.", preached Evelyn.

"You're right. I'm hoping that this is truly my time, that I am on the right path and might even hit a windfall.", expressed Bernadette.

Bernadette stayed a little while as they all tried to talk and reconnect in some way, but it was awkward. Time had changed them all and they realized they were strangers to each other. Larry offered to pack up some food to give to Bernadette and she accepted. She seemed to be appreciative of the gesture as she left, but neither of her parents truly trusted Bernadette's reaction or reason for visiting.

"If she comes back, don't let her in if I'm not home.", warned Larry.

Evelyn nodded in agreement as she fought back tears of heartache; it pained them both to see how the years of drug use and hard living had ravaged the looks of the once beautiful woman. Bernadette's once vibrant dark chocolate skin looked ashen, dry and lifeless.

"Should we tell Cupcake that her mother stopped by?", asked Evelyn.

"No, that will just upset her. I don't know if she'll ever get over the pain of being abandoned. Yet I thank God, every day, our daughter had the sense to leave Shannon with us. Come on baby, let's get ready for bed.", concluded Larry.

Everything had been divine since Shannon and Raymond rekindled their love story. Shannon had been so joyous and excited ever since she and Raymond made up; they took turns entertaining at his penthouse and her home. It was hard for Nicole to keep up with Shannon's comings and goings. As happy as Shannon was, her cynical side was on edge as it waited for the bottom to drop off and had she known about her mother visiting her grandparents, she would have been sure it was bound to happen. Additionally, her nerves were draining her as the days approached the dinner. Sleep had been a stranger to Shannon the night before and she spent that Saturday morning preparing her mind for her evening meal at the mansion.

"Mommy, do you think you will stay the weekend at Ray's?', Nicole quizzed.

"Yes, I will; I'll probably come back Monday after work. Don't go throwing a wild party.", teased Shannon.

"Oh snap, I'll have to cancel.", giggled Nicole.

"Yeah right! You can help me pack a weekend bag.", laughed Shannon.

"How about we pack up all of your stuff and you leave the house to me?", joked Nicole.

"No way! You're coming straight with me when I do and this house is going up for sale.", ordered Shannon and then she tossed her bra at Nicole playfully.

"Watch it! You can suffocate me if I get tangled up in that thing.", laughed Nicole, then she moved to a more serious conversation, "Are you nervous about meeting his folks?"

"Heck yes! Who wouldn't be?", Shannon petitioned.

"Me! And you shouldn't be either. Raymond wants you and doesn't care how anyone else feels about it!", Nicole declared, "Besides, he's chosen well. You'll always keep him on his game."

"That's a nice way of putting it.", laughed Shannon.

She was about to tease Nicole more when her cell phone notification indicated movement in front of the house.

"Are you expecting someone?", asked Shannon.

"No, not this early. My bestie is coming over later.", informed Nicole.

"Finish putting these things in my bag while I go see what this woman wants.", instructed Shannon.

It was very uncommon for strays to walk around her neighborhood, she thought, as she walked down to the entrance. That was what her granny called them, people who walked aimlessly like they had no home, no purpose and no life. She definitely was not going to open the door; instead, she talked to the woman through the app on her phone.

"Hello, how may I help you?", Shannon requested.

"Hi, are you Shannon? I'm your mother. I stopped by my parents' house yesterday for the first time in years hoping to see you there.", informed Bernadette.

"That's a lie! I've never seen you before.", Shannon's inner child accused.

"You were just a little baby the last time I stopped by while you were there. Any other time, I waited until you were in school or asleep at night.", Bernadette explained.

"What do you want? How did you know where I live?", demanded Shannon.

"Can I come in? The neighbors don't need to hear our business.", Bernadette pleaded.

"Hell no! Answer my question.", demanded Shannon.

"I saw your name and address on a package you sent to your granny.", Bernadette explained.

Bernadette regretted telling the truth as it did give deceitful vibes and Shannon instantly regretted her past laziness. She had found the perfect outfit for her granny, but she had been too busy to drop the items off and decided to mail them instead.

"So, you figured you'd come here and beg or con me out of something!", Shannon accused.

"No baby girl, I just wanted to see you ... I've been clean for over a decade now ... you know. I don't want any money.", explained Bernadette.

Shannon leaned against the door as she continued talking to her estranged parent.

"I never knew why you abandoned me. Granny and Big Daddy never said not one negative thing about you. Even when I had questions, they just said you were young and had your priorities wrong.", Shannon admitted.

"They are good folks that way, I guess. Your granny is so proud of you. She talked about your career and that you are getting married.", Bernadette disclosed.

"Sounds like to me that you did come here for money!", Shannon blurted.

"No! I'm just saying that things turned out good for you. You know you're better off that I left you with my parents. I tried to raise your brother …", Bernadette expressed.

"A brother …", Shannon choked.

"He's gone. Your father was furious that I wouldn't drop him off too. He beat my baby so badly; your brother just couldn't survive it. I vowed to never let myself get pregnant again after that.", confessed Bernadette.

Shannon could hear the tears in her mother's voice and the shock of it all caused Shannon to nearly collapse against the door.

"I'll be honest with you. I did come here hoping to cash in … do my thang … but I see that I would just mess things up for you. I don't really want that. You're the only good thing I have to show for my life and I can't even take credit … Bye doll.", confessed Bernadette as she touched the door.

Shannon released the tears that had been buried within a child's heart for so long. She hesitantly opened the door to see the woman, her mother, gone. Nicole had been listening on the app and heard the entire conversation; she rushed down the stairs to find her mother in tears.

"Mommy, don't cry!", Nicole wept as she hugged Shannon, "It'll be okay."

"Yes, baby, it will. That was your grandmother at the door.", Shannon informed.

"I know, I heard everything on the app.", confessed Nicole.

Shannon inhaled deeply as she reflected.

"My God. I cried so many years over that woman; a woman I didn't know anything about. Now, I know that my mother was an addict and that the best thing, she could have ever done was leave me with my grandparents.", sighed Shannon.

Shannon held onto Nicole for dear life and for the first time she realized that love can be shown in so many different ways and sometimes it can even mean leaving a child behind to protect what's most precious. For the first time, she was thankful for what her mother had done. She no longer saw it as abandonment but as an act of love.

"Mommy, do you still want to meet Ray's folks tonight? Do you think you can deal with that?", Nicole worried.

"Yes, my sweet baby girl. I am convinced that I'm more ready than I ever was before.", Shannon reassured.

The Washington-Brown manor was in frantic preparation for Shannon's debut. The waitstaff was meticulous with every plate setting and the décor. Lawrence had practically bought out the florist; the dining room and great room were filled to the hilt with bouquets and flower arrangements. Even Eleanor was lucid and instructed staff where to place the flowers. Raymond was astonished at the level of excitement his grandmother displayed. Had he known the effect meeting Shannon would have on his grandmother, he would have arranged it months ago. But just as much as his grandmother was excited his parents were disinterested; they felt proposals should come with the prospect of the family securing more money or a business, neither of which Shannon offered. Raymond stood in the dining room admiring the decorations when his baby sister tickled him from behind.

"Let's hope you go through with *this* wedding.", teased Crystal.

"Thanks, little sis for the pep talk.", laughed Raymond.

"No problem.", giggled Crystal, "You look good."

"Thanks, little one.", offered Raymond.

Raymond didn't want to overdress, but he wanted the dinner to be special. So, he decided to wear a simple Gucci brown signature sports blazer with light brown slim-fit slacks and Gucci signature loafers.

"Is she pretty?", asked Crystal.

"Stunning!", Raymond boasted.

"Well, I just hope she's as nice as she is pretty. You've dated some pretty bitches over the years. That last one was a *real* bitch!", laughed Crystal.

"Tell me about it. But the funny thing is Mother loved her.", chuckled Raymond.

"Well birds of a feather …", laughed Crystal, "I love Mother, but she is an acquired taste for sure."

"That's for damn sure, but there's a lid for every jar and Father is that lid.", joked Raymond.

"Yass! He loves him some Angela.", giggled Crystal.

"They're dysfunctional together, but if it works for them …", laughed Raymond.

"So, tell me, does Shannon have a daughter my age? Do you think we will get along?", inquired Crystal.

"Yes, Shannon does; her daughter's name is Nicole. I do think you two will like each other. You're both adorable and she'll be a good influence on you.", teased Raymond.

"Hey!", laughed Crystal.

"I just mean, she knows exactly what she wants to study and in what profession she wants to work. She wants to be a lawyer.", informed Raymond.

"Oh, thank God; someone to take over the family business one day. I have absolutely no interest in law.", laughed Crystal.

"That's a thought, but I'm sure Shannon and I will have at least one child.", confirmed Raymond.

"Are you two going to keep standing in the way or help?", inquired Lawrence as he winked at Crystal.

"Oh gosh no! That's why we have you and this wonderful staff; the best in town!", teased Crystal as she fluttered her hand.

"That's what I thought. Off with the two of you.", Lawrence fussed.

"Thanks, Lawrence. Everything looks perfect. Now we wait for the true 'la piece de resistance'.", expressed Raymond.

"Indeed, sir.", smiled Lawrence.

Shannon had never been to Franklin Village before; it was a gem hidden in plain sight she thought. Butterflies began to flutter and her nerves almost got the best of her.

"Why are you nervous?", she whispered to herself.

She knew that Raymond would not allow anyone to make her feel uncomfortable or inadequate so she shouldn't let her imagination run wild. If he could survive her grandparents, she could tough it out with his family, she thought. She believed she had seen the most gorgeous manor when she saw the Barrington Estate, but this rivaled its beauty. It was a grand two-story English Tudor manor with a circular brick paved drive with a fountain as the focal point. The home was the standard color of most Tudor homes with shades of dark brown and tan. The great chimney had five stacks and she could only imagine that the fireplace must be massive.

Shannon parked her small SUV in front of the massive home next to Raymond's Bentley and exited her car as she inhaled deeply. She felt so nervous she was light-headed. The Browns were the first family of a boyfriend to whom she would be introduced. She had only met Joe's folks because she was friends with Vivian; otherwise, she doubted she would have ever met them. Okay girlie, she thought as she approached the massive solid wood door and rang the bell. She could hear the ring as it seemed to echo the halls of the home. Crystal heard the doorbell ring; she squealed as she began to run off to answer it.

"Hold it! I should be the first to welcome, the future lady of the house.", insisted Lawrence.

"Awe ...", whined Crystal as she stopped abruptly.

Raymond smiled at his easily excitable little sister and wrapped his arm around her shoulders. The two of them followed behind Lawrence to ensure that his parents wouldn't be next to greet her. He didn't want them to say anything rude that would frighten her off the moment she entered the mansion.

Lawrence opened the massive door and was astonished by the beauty that stood before him. Her smooth dark brown skin was flawless as if an illusion. He had never seen a woman whose beauty was so natural and effortless.

"Madam ...", uttered a speechless Lawrence.

Crystal stood dumbfounded as well. She had assumed that her brother was exaggerating as people in love often do, but the woman who presented herself at the door was uniquely bewitching, no wonder he called her Pixie.

"Please forgive Lawrence and my wide-mouthed sister. Come on in.", laughed Raymond, "I told you she was stunning."

"Hello, Lawrence. Crystal, sweetie, I've heard so much about you.", Shannon greeted the girl with a hug.

"Hi, I thought he was lying about how pretty you are.", Crystal blurted.

Crystal was still shocked by Shannon's looks. She forgot all of her debutant training and eyed her from head to toe as Lawrence looked upon her like a proud future father-in-law. Raymond decided since everyone else had forgotten themselves, he might as well indulge and allow his eyes to lust over her beautiful frame. Vivian and Nicole had insisted on picking something out when Shannon indicated the attire was semi-formal; they refused to trust the evening to whatever Shannon fancied as acceptable.

The ladies had selected a red cold shoulder short-sleeved jumpsuit with a halter neckline and a tie around the neck. Her bare shoulders glistened as if oiled by the gods or perhaps it was pixie dust to enchant him, thought Raymond. The bodice fit snugly revealing just a peek of her cleavage; just enough to make him or any man go wild. The jumpsuit fit tightly around her waist which highlighted her full hips and buttocks; it sported a mock wrap at the waist that revealed the ankle of one leg. Shannon put her silver heels with the embellished bow on repeat and matched it with her designer rhinestone embellished clutch. She wore oversized cubic zirconia hoops which accentuated her pixie curls. She had decided to apply a light dusting of her loose powder along with her eyelash extensions and wore the brightest red lipstick she had.

"Pixie, baby, you look incredible!", Raymond gushed as he kissed her hands.

"Come, Ms. Shannon. Follow me.", Lawrence instructed as he shooed Raymond away from her.

Just as Lawrence and Crystal were stunned by her appearance, Shannon was speechless as she gazed upon the beauty of the massive foyer. There was rich detailed woodwork as would be expected; however, the senior Mrs. Washington-Brown had the ceiling woodwork painted white to soften the entry and make it appear brighter. The expansive staircase was to the left near what she guessed was the study since she noticed an enormous display of books. The chandelier was a graceful centerpiece of the foyer; it was a massive traditional one with candelabras and draping crystal beads from the base to each candelabra. The crystal on it, sparkled like blinding diamonds as the remaining sunlight glistened and bounced from one to the other. There was expensive artwork sprinkled here and there on the walls; everything was tastefully done with pieces Shannon assumed had been owned for generations.

Lawrence strutted like a proud rooster as he led the three to the great room. He couldn't wait to introduce the beauty to the family. He was already imagining a dimple brown bundle of pure joy crying in the nursery. Angela was getting agitated as if Shannon was late; she assumed she would be as she started complaining early. Eleanor stared her daughter-in-law into silence; Angela's pale face became even more so. That evening Eleanor was every bit of the woman that Angela had feared over the years. Lawrence led the trio into the great room just in time to avoid Angela's negative comments.

Just as Shannon had suspected, the fireplace of the great room was as striking as it was large. The white French limestone soared from floor to ceiling with a unique pitched mantel with a triangular point. The surround soared past the mantel to the ceiling with soft filigree detailing the mantel and the edge of the surround. Just as the ceiling in the foyer had been lightened, so had the woodwork in the great room. The walls were painted a soft white and the ceiling beams had been grey-washed to present a contrast. Raymond's parents were sitting on a soft grey French country tufted sofa with silver nail-head trim along the inversed sloped tracked arms of the frame and washed oak legs. An identical one sat parallel to it; the soft grey velvet sofas were elegant and comfortable and there were two oversized grey tufted ottomans in between.

Whereas, at the head of it all, in front of the fireplace, the lady of the manor sat on a French cottage Toile settee covered with a patterned fabric of a perched bird in a shade of navy blue and a white background with washed oak trimming with the matching chair on the opposite end. Eleanor looked every bit the lady and matriarch of the manor in her beautiful navy full-length shirt dress with an up-turned collar and a Gucci gold belt to show off her neat waistline. She wore large pearl studs and a matching pearl necklace. She was regal and it was plainly obvious how beautiful she had once been.

Richard looked dapper in his cream linen suit, tan ascot and tan leather loafers with his bride by his side. Angela wore a dusty rose A-line dress with a white bodice, a high deep V-neck collar and short sleeves with a soft grey thin waistband. She paired her dress with a small strand of pearls, small pearl studs and silver 4-inch heel pumps. It was apparent that the couple was intimidated by a coherent Eleanor.

"Everyone, I'd like to proudly introduce Master Raymond's betrothed, Ms. Shannon Washington. The future and second Mrs. Washington-Brown of the manor.", beamed Lawrence.

"Oh, my word! I thought no one on earth could have skin as smooth, dark and beautiful as your grandfather's, but here she is. Absolutely gorgeous!", confirmed the original Mrs. Washington-Brown, Eleanor, to Raymond.

Angela and Richard were just as stunned as Lawrence and Crystal had been. Her picture did not do her any justice; it paled in comparison to reality. Angela had prepared herself to have something negative to say slyly about her, but to do so would prove her to be a liar as there was nothing negative to be said about the angel before them. For years, Richard had listened to the voice of his maternal grandfather who touted that fair-skinned was more

214

attractive and that he should marry light. Had his grandfather seen Shannon, he would have known that those statements were all lies and that the darkest of skin could be drenched in beauty.

"Shannon, this is my grandmother, my heart, Eleanor.", Raymond introduced.

Eleanor stood so quickly that no one would have suspected she was 90. She beamed and was almost in tears as she eyed Shannon then held her hands.

"My dear. I am so pleased to meet you and I am so proud to welcome you to the family.", Eleanor affirmed.

"Hello, ma'am and thank you. It's nice to meet you too; Ray talks about you all the time.", Shannon greeted.

Raymond inhaled deeply as he turned his attention to his parents who were still stunned.

"Pixie, these are my parents, Angela and Richard.", Raymond introduced awkwardly.

"Nice to meet you both.", Shannon lied.

The pair was the last people on earth that she looked forward to meeting after hearing some of Raymond's accounts. However, she knew it was a necessity and from the look on Raymond's face, he concurred. She couldn't help but smile at him and then kiss him; she blushed as she eyed the expressions of his parents.

"I see you adore Raymond as much as I adore Richard. I never thought I would find a man that truly understood me.", Angela admitted.

"I feel the same. I've waited all my life for a man to *really see* me and appreciate me.", confessed Shannon as she blushed.

Raymond and Crystal were shocked that their mother admitted what everyone else already knew. Richard had been quiet as if waiting for a cue from Angela that he could speak. He stood to greet Shannon.

"Welcome to the family. Looks like you might usher in a change.", indicated Richard.

"Thank you.", uttered Shannon as her eyes questioned Raymond.

Raymond didn't know what his father meant by that and could only hope he meant something positive.   But he was determined to keep things positive and tapped Shannon on her butt as reassurance not to read anything into the comment.

"We haven't had this much excitement in years.", beamed Eleanor then clapped to direct them, "Shall we?"

Eleanor pointed to the hall as she took Shannon by the hand then walked arm-in-arm as they exited the room. Everyone followed suit behind them. Raymond walked with Crystal arm-in-arm instead of his fiancée as Crystal and he watched their grandmother come alive.

"Oh darling, I pray I have enough life in me to see the little one you and my baby boy will have.", confessed Eleanor.

Shannon blushed as she too had been doing a lot of daydreaming about a baby. She had always wanted another, but Joe was done and he had made that known long before the vasectomy. In hindsight, that was a blessing straight from God above, thought Shannon.

"I'm looking forward to it as well. Another child … and a husband are something that I have wanted for a very long time.", admitted Shannon.

"Well, my little Raymond, as I used to call him, is the perfect family man. He will provide for you, honor you and give you your heart's desire. Just like his marvelous grandfather.", reminisced Eleanor.

Just then they passed a painted portrait of Eleanor and the elder Raymond; they looked every bit the part of the power couple that they had been. He was confident and handsome with the stunning Eleanor sitting next to his tall frame while his hand rested possessively on her shoulder.

"He was quite the catch in *so* many ways. I'll commission a painting of you and Raymond before your engagement party.", informed Eleanor.

"Engagement party?", Shannon questioned as she turned her head in search of Raymond.

Raymond smiled and shrugged his shoulders as he knew there was no way of changing his grandmother's mind. At that point, he'd do anything out of excitement about his beautiful bride-to-be and a clear-headed Eleanor.

"Yes, my dear. Did you hear that, Lawrence? I want you to plan an elegant soiree at our favorite venue and put it in the announcements. I want it to be the event of the year.", instructed Eleanor.

"Yes, Madame.", Lawrence reassured.

Lawrence and Raymond had already created a night to remember with what was supposed to be an intimate dinner. Shannon couldn't imagine anything done up more than what she saw in front of her. The enormous formal dining room was filled with beautiful flower arrangements; there was no spot left without adornment. When she finally could pull her sight away from the flowers, she was astonished at the delicious food that was presented on the expansive rectangular table that could easily seat twelve. The luxurious French-style marble table was elegant with a chrome base with grey trim. The parson chairs were covered in the softest cream leather with grey wooden legs.

Above the table hung a contemporary rectangular chrome chandelier with crystals draping down over the expansive table.

There was one centerpiece of white roses and the finest of silverware. The family's finest China was set atop the most delicate silver floral-shaped chargers, she had ever seen. Shannon felt all of it was too beautiful to even eat on. In her Granny's house that would have been removed before anyone could think of placing food on it, she thought.

Eleanor dropped Shannon's arm so that Raymond could take over and escort her to the table as the gentleman she had raised him to be. Raymond took Shannon's hand and planted a kiss upon it then smiled.

"And your grandmother wants to do it bigger than this?", questioned Shannon in a whisper.

"You haven't seen nothing yet!", laughed Raymond.

Raymond held the chair for Shannon to sit down as she gazed at the delightful display of cuisines; she wondered if they tasted as good as they looked. Eleanor had suggested that the staff serve each course plated for them, but Raymond wanted everything to be served family style to be more inviting for Shannon. He felt that it made the atmosphere more comfortable and family-oriented. Hence, the appetizers, soup, entrée and dessert were displayed on serving dishes on the marble table.

Shannon was thankful that they didn't eat like birds or fitness enthusiasts. The cook had prepared spinach and artichoke stuff mushrooms, French onion soup, Port braised short ribs and a chocolate expresso torte. She couldn't wait to taste it all. She was about to dive in and eat her appetizer when she noticed how slowly everyone was slicing their mushrooms. So, she took note and decided to talk and then she could nibble as her questions were being answered. Just then Angela fumbled the dish and dribbled some of the soup broth on the table.

"Henderson, please I can't do this!", insisted Angela to Lawrence's number two in command.

"I can help you.", announced Shannon.

She felt so sorry for the poor thing and attempted to stand when Raymond touched her hand to stop her.

"Let's watch this play out.", smirked Raymond in her ear.

Crystal giggled at her brother who wasn't great at whispering when he was being devilish. Henderson rushed over to assist Angela as she clumsily handed the dish to him for assistance.

"Let me, Madame.", offered Henderson.

"You act like you didn't grow up serving yourself.", contested Eleanor.

Shannon was shocked and looked from Raymond to Angela for answers. Angela felt obliged to explain to Shannon.

"Shannon dear, I grew up wealthy, but my father was a self-made man and extremely frugal; in fact, he came from an impoverished family. He wanted his children to experience doing things for themselves. Unfortunately for me, my parents only had one child; so, I had to help with *everything*.", sighed Angela, "I absolutely hated it. All my high school girlfriends talked about having servants and we didn't have anything but a housekeeper."

Angela sliced her mushroom into small pieces as she shared the details of her childhood with Shannon as Eleanor and Richard sat annoyed by the story that they had heard countless times. Raymond and Crystal on the other hand were amused by the dramatic flair with which Angela told the tale.

"My mother insisted we had at least that or she vowed to divorce him. Such dreadful days …", complained Angela.

"Indeed, Mother it's a wonder that you survived.", chuckled Raymond.

"God rest my father's soul. He at least did right by me when he left his entire fortune and estate to me. And trust me, I enjoy every last cent. The one perk of being the only child.", declared Angela.

"I suppose.", Richard uttered then cleared his throat.

Shannon noted the uncomfortable expressions of Richard and Angela and guessed another family secret was about to reveal itself. Raymond noticed Shannon's peaked interests and decided to lean close and enlighten her.

"My grandfather left his entire estate to me along with all his businesses, shares and assets. My grandfather did, however, establish a trust fund for Crystal for when she comes of age. My father, on the other hand, lives off his trust fund and my mother's inheritance.", Raymond whispered.

Shannon was shocked and had a clearer picture of the dynamic that might exist between father and son as a result. She along with the rest eventually moved passed the awkwardness on to a much happier topic, the wedding. Eleanor was so full of life as she questioned Shannon about her plans.

"My dear have you started planning for the big day?", inquired Eleanor.

"Actually no, we…", Shannon began.

Shannon was embarrassed about the reason why and didn't want to air her and Raymond's dirty relationship drama.

"No need to fret. I'll assist you. I'm sure your friend Vivian will be anxious to be a part of the planning.", insisted Eleanor.

"Yes, she's been bugging me to start.", laughed Shannon.

Shannon's expression turned to panic as she thought of the daunting task and expectations of his family; however, Raymond was quick to reassure her. He did not want a runaway bride on his hands.

"Just breathe and everything will fall into place.", reassured Raymond.

"With my luck, it'll be a domino effect.", joked Shannon.

"With my grandmother and Vivian on the job, there's no way anything will be lacking.", chuckled Raymond.

Crystal giggled and bounced with excitement at the thought of the event.

"I hope I can be a part of the planning.", suggested Crystal.

"Of course, you can. My daughter, Nicole, will be right there with you, I'm sure.", laughed Shannon.

As the evening came to a close, Shannon was so thankful that it hadn't been a disaster. She had been so needlessly nervous that his family wouldn't accept her. Nicole had been right all along, she thought, as she and Raymond said their goodbyes to his family. It was turning out to be the perfect weekend and she couldn't wait to get to his place. She was eager to plant kisses all over his body and feel his muscled frame. Despite her joy, she still felt it all was dreamlike and feared that one day she would awake to find that she was all alone.

Chapter 13

In the weeks that followed the family introduction, Raymond and Shannon were in full engagement party and wedding planning mode and almost everything took a back seat to it; all but one. Raymond stared at his computer monitor as he reviewed some of the décor ideas suggested by the party planner. Although Shannon was involved, he wanted to design a surprise with the party planner that would take Shannon's breath away. Despite that excitement, he couldn't take his mind off Joe Johnston. He had been waiting for what seemed forever to receive an update from Spivey; he thought it should be easy to find evidence to incriminate Joe. It wasn't like the guy was a mastermind, thought Raymond when finally, he received the much-awaited call.

"Boss, sorry for the delay. I wanted to make sure I had my ducks lined up. So, I've got great news!", informed Spivey.

"What did you find?", Raymond eagerly blurted.

"Looks like our guy has been busy. He's been linked to numerous local pharmacy robberies. He's been everything from the getaway driver to setting up the mark. I can have everything ready for you today.", summarized Spivey.

"Cool! I need it ASAP. I can swing by now to get it.", suggested Raymond.

"Sounds good Chief. I'll be here.", reassured Spivey.

"See you soon.", Raymond informed then dialed Gio.

"My man! It's been a minute. What's up?", questioned Gio.

"My private eye has the update I've been waiting on. Can we meet in person?", Raymond requested.

"Sure. I'm at home if you want to come by now.", Gio informed.

"Great, I'll come right after I meet with him. I'm headed there now.", Raymond reassured.

"Cool. See you soon.", Gio stated.

Raymond ended the call so quickly that he barely heard Gio's words.

"Roberta!", shouted Raymond.

"Yes, sir.", breathed Roberta after jogging to his door.

"I'm going to run out and take care of some errands. I'm not sure that I'll be back today. If I do, it'll be after hours.", informed Raymond.

"No problem, sir. You have a clear schedule.", she reassured.

"Thanks. You are the best!", Raymond complimented.

Raymond gathered his cell phone and keys and then left his office. He was relieved to have the goods on Joe. He needed to get rid of him and using the legal system was the best way to do so. He didn't want a guilty conscience hovering over his marriage to Shannon. He wasn't as tough-skinned as Gio and John or even as Vincent, Raymond chuckled at the thought.

Raymond cruised to Spivey's office; the roads were relatively clear of traffic and he seemed to miss every single light. It was as if God moved everyone and any obstacle out of his path like the Red Sea. He took it as a sign that he was doing the right thing and that everyone would finally be rid of Joe Johnston. Ray pulled quickly into the parking lot and jogged to the entrance of Spivey's office. He gathered his composure and adjusted his blazer to ensure he had the look of power and confidence as he entered.

"Chief! It's all here.", boasted Spivey, "Let me know if you need anything else. You know I'm the one to get it done."

"Sure thing.", Raymond indicated as he pulled a roll of cash from his pocket, "For your hard work."

"Always a pleasure!", salivated Spivey as he counted the bills.

"You have no idea how much pleasure *I'm* going to get out of this!", laughed Raymond

At that moment, Raymond felt powerful and invincible; he would stop at almost nothing to remove the obstacle known as Joe from his and Shannon's life. And if that didn't work, he thought, he might have to go Bianchi style on Joe's ass. As he drove out of the city, Raymond laughed at the thought of Gio overhearing his thoughts; he could picture a wicked gleam in Gio's eyes as he plotted a devilish scheme. He continued to laugh as he drove up the driveway of the stately Gross Pointe Shores mansion. He figured Gio's guards might have thought he had gone mad; so, he quickly resumed a normal expression. He didn't want any of the guards to get trigger-happy and shoot up his car fearing that the mighty Giovanni Bianchi would fall from power by his hand.

Just as Raymond figured, one of Giovanni's guards must have told him that he was approaching the house when he noticed Gio standing at the entrance. Good, no chance of being shot, thought Raymond as he exited the car.

"My man! Love looks good on you!", complimented Gio.

"Yeah, *Shannon* does look good on me.", chuckled Raymond.

"What? So, she's really got it like that!", laughed Gio, "Are you sure you don't want me to blast Joe's ass?"

"I'll pass, remember you fucked that up the last time.", Raymond teased, "Seriously though, I have enough evidence on Joe to put him away for a very long time."

"Come on inside and let me see what you've got.", insisted Gio.

Gio led Raymond through the grand foyer to his home office. Gio displayed a huge oil painting of his father above his desk as if Ricky was anointing him to complete the work he had started so long ago.

"Have a seat.", Gio instructed as he pointed to the chair in front of his desk.

"Bro, that punk has been robbing pharmacies. I need him caught up. Can I trust you to ensure that charges get drawn up?", asked Raymond.

"Of course, Bro. Anything.", confirmed Gio.

"I need this to go to trial quickly. I don't want this sitting a year on a judge's docket.", Raymond instructed.

"Count on it. I'll make sure it gets into the right hands. I have a connection on the force and a judge I can count on.", Gio insisted.

"Thanks a million.", Raymond sighed.

"I may need to collect.", laughed Gio.

"Whatever it takes, dude.", laughed Raymond.

Raymond took on a more serious tone.

"Speaking of a dramatic love life ... what's the deal with you and Markita?", Raymond snooped.

"Me and Markita fell off a minute ago.", Gio advised.

"What else is new.", laughed Raymond.

"Naw, Bro, this might be it for us. I don't see us getting back together this time.", confessed Giovani.

"Sorry to hear that Bro, but you're a SIMP so you'll get another one soon. You, players, always bounce back.", Raymond encouraged.

"True, what woman doesn't want all her needs met?", laughed Gio, "But enough about me. Once we get Joe's coffin nailed, you'll be set."

"Coffin nailed?", questioned Raymond.

"Don't worry. I'll keep you updated. Just go and focus on your girl.", reassured Giovanni.

Giovanni then tapped his palm on the desk to signify that the conversation had concluded.

"I've got a lot of work on my plate … a new venture I'm looking into.", informed Giovanni.

"I feel you. I'll let you get to it. I'll see myself out.", Raymond replied.

Giovanni's instant silence was a sure indication that his mind had moved on to different matters. As Raymond left the study, he decided he wouldn't speculate on what Giovanni really meant by coffin nailed; it could have been some old mafia term for finishing the deal. He refused to allow his mind to wander; all his free time and thoughts needed to be devoted to planning the wedding and the engagement party. He would allow Giovanni to handle his part of the bargain.

As he walked toward the exit, he reminded himself that he had enough to consume his time and focus because despite hiring a wedding and a party planner, he and Shannon were hyper-focused on all the details. There wasn't a detail they didn't know of or hadn't provided input on. In fact, he realized he needed to call Shannon about a substitute dish for one of the entrée dinners.

His steps hastened to his car so that he could talk to her as he drove.

"Hey, Bae! I was just thinking of you.", admitted Shannon., "You're on speakerphone."

Shannon heard Nicole laughing; Nicole giggled at her mother's use of the slang term of endearment. Nicole noticed that her mother had become more fun to be around. Shannon smiled and then tossed a handful of soapy bubbles from the dishpan at Nicole.

"Mommy!", giggled Nicole.

"Hi, Nicole.", Raymond greeted.

"Did you hear your soon-to-be-stepdaddy saying hello.", laughed Shannon.

"Stepdaddy?", laughed Raymond, "You know we haven't discussed what she'll call me."

"Definitely not stepdaddy. Daddy could work... Mommy and Daddy.", giggled Nicole, "I wonder what Crystal would have to say about that."

"She would probably puke.", joked Raymond.

"Bye Ray, I'm leaving out the kitchen before you two start that love talk.", teased Nicole.

"Bye, see you soon Nickie.", Raymond doted.

"It's such a blessing that the girls get along. Even though they won't be step-sisters, it's important.", Shannon confessed.

"True. I would hate to imagine Crystal being a little tyrant of an auntie.", laughed Raymond.

"That's right Crystal will be Nicole's aunt!", squealed Shannon, "Too funny!"

"Before I completely forget … one of the seafood cuisines needs to be changed; it's not available due to shipping constraints.", informed Raymond.

"Oh no!", Shannon cried.

"No worries. Remember you wanted to try the Dover Sole fish?", reminded Raymond, "We can order that and it will arrive in time for the engagement party."

"Ok, that'll work.", sighed Shannon, "Leave it to *my man* to save the day!"

"You know I've got you.", Raymond whispered seductively, "Speaking of having things covered. Per Crystal's request, I'm sending the driver to pick up Nicole this Saturday to take the girls shopping for the engagement party."

"I'll let her know; she'll be thrilled if Crystal hasn't already told her.", laughed Shannon.

"Yeah, they do speak the same language … shopping.", chuckled Raymond.

"I'm so glad she's spending more time at home on the weekends this semester. Even though most of her free time is spent with her new bestie, Crystal, I feel we're able to bond more too.", confessed Shannon.

"Same here.", Raymond concurred.

While the two love birds were downstairs laughing, Nicole was sitting on her bed dreading the upcoming engagement party. As she sat looking at her homework, she couldn't focus on it; the closer the date of the engagement party the more nervous she became. She didn't have anything nearly as nice as what she imagined the Brown family and their friends would be wearing. If as on cue, Crystal called her using the video call feature of their cellphones.

"Crystal! What's up?", asked Nicole.

"Raymond is sending the driver to pick you up this Saturday so we can go shopping for the engagement party!", squealed Crystal.

"To be honest, I don't have the money to shop where you buy your dresses.", confessed Nicole.

Crystal was oblivious to Nicole's facial expression or the concerns in which her words were drenched. Subsequently, Crystal didn't skip a beat.

"Don't worry about it. We'll both get credit cards from our dads.", informed Crystal.

"I ..", Nicole attempted to explain.

"Yeah, I'll get a credit card from Dad and you'll get one from Raymond. Easy-peasy.", laughed Crystal, "I'm sorry I was so excited that I cut you off. What were you about to say?"

"I was just going to ask where are we shopping.", beamed Nicole as she fibbed.

Time was moving so fast with all the excitement about the engagement party and the wedding would be upon them before long. Gio did not want anything or anyone around to interfere with the festivities. So, he decided that he needed to meet up with his contact that night. He wasn't holding on to the file for another minute; it was time that Joe was out of the picture for good. He promised Raymond that he would take a step back and do things Raymond's way, but if he ever saw an opportunity to take the reins again, he would.

Giovanni had sent a text message to the Chief from his burner phone advising that they would meet after dark and the location. Schemes like that were best done in the shadows. Giovanni pulled up alongside the unmarked car that was parked in the overrun and unlit parking lot in a less populated area of Detroit.

He scanned the area before getting out of his vintage Lincoln Continental that once belonged to his father. The Chief of Police scanned the area also then joined Giovanni.

"Bianchi.", greeted the chief.

"Bronson. This is legitimate evidence to convict a piece of shit for his crimes. I want these charges to stick. I don't give a fuck how. I just want it done.", ordered Gio.

"No problem, that will make it easier.", reassured the police chief as he took the file folder.

"Isn't your birthday coming soon?", smiled Bianchi.

"Yes sir, same time every damn year!", chuckled Bronson.

"Expect a nice gift from me this year.", smirked Giovanni.

Chapter 14

    As the party season was gearing up for the Fall holidays, the Browns and Washingtons were the major talk of the socialite scene. Most couples prefer Spring or Summer weddings, so this upcoming event was one of the few to discuss and therefore, garnered a lot of attention. Raymond and Eleanor had spared no expense; Eleanor spoiled Shannon as if Shannon was one of her own. Shannon was overwhelmed and overjoyed at the acceptance Eleanor extended. She never expected to be so loved by anyone other than her own grandparents, but she felt every bit of the love that Eleanor had for Raymond was also showered upon her.

    The Browns felt an affair of that magnitude could not be held anywhere other than The Detroit Club. The club welcomed its long-time members and guests to its Presidential Ballroom; it was a picture of wealth and elegance. The floor-to-ceiling drapes and ornate woodwork framing the entrance and ceiling and fireplace were grandiose at the least. The warmth of the room was enhanced by the tongue and groove woodwork of the ceiling; its deep rich and dark coloring was a contrast to the bright floral centerpieces. The peach and ivory centerpieces were striking and were the wedding colors of the couple. The arrangements consisted of orange and white roses, auburn Boston fern leaves, black baby's breath and roses hand-crafted from fall leaves. For the final touch and surprise, Raymond had pulled every string and connection he had in the city to book Shannon's favorite local female saxophonist for the event.

    Raymond was pleased with how everything turned out; it was picture-perfect. Shannon had been so relaxed and excited throughout the planning but Raymond could not help but feel a nagging fear that the floor would drop. He hadn't seen her at all that evening, although his heart had reassured him several times that she was just making herself perfect for the evening; but his mind feared she would sabotage it all. He stepped by the room that was set aside for Shannon and her bridal party; he wanted to make sure she wasn't nervous about being presented to society. He was about to knock on the door when he heard Shannon's melodic laughter along with her girls, Gloria and Vivian. Then he heard the giggles of Nicole and Crystal and knew there was nothing to fear and he could go back to laughing and joking with his fellas at the Uralli Cigar Bar. The bar was on the same floor as the ballroom; the planner had sent him and the guys there to wait for the guests to arrive. Relieved, Raymond returned to the bar to find that his friends were anxiously awaiting him.

"What took so long?", asked Vincent.

Raymond was embarrassed to admit that he had checked in on Shannon.

"Please don't tell us you were snooping on the girls.", fussed Giovanni.

Giovanni puffed on his cigar and then blew smoke in Raymond's face to irritate his friend.

"Well ... can you blame me? She did run off and leave me at the cabin.", explained Raymond.

"Damn Bro, she got you like that!", teased Giovanni.

"I guess so. I finally understand why my grandfather was on pins and needles about my grandmother. He never thought he was worthy of a woman as incredible.", disclosed Raymond, "I can relate. I can't imagine life without my Pixie now."

"Well, you won't have to. You took care of the issue the right way. It's just a matter of time ...", reassured Vincent.

"Can we smoke and drink or what? I want to get my buzz on, the fuck.", Giovanni complained.

"Fuck yeah!", Raymond affirmed.

232

The men toasted to an evening of victory and celebration. Vincent and Giovanni were not going to allow Raymond to waste any more time doubting that everything was coming together. As much as Raymond was nervous, Shannon was confident about her future.

"Shannon, sweetie, you look heavenly!", complimented Gloria.

"Absolutely perfect!", agreed Evelyn as she dabbed her eyes.

"Yes!", agreed Vivian as she snapped her fingers, "Yes!"

"Thank you.", blushed Shannon.

Shannon took all their compliments and stares in as she stood breathlessly speechless and eyed her reflection in the mirror; never had she imagined that day could ever have been possible. She barely recognized the beautiful, confident and joyous woman that stood before her. Her dress was as enchanting as her fairy tale romance with Raymond had been; it was a majestic peach tulle A-line dress with a deep V-neck with hand-stitched peach flowers on the bodice and shoulder that cascaded down one side of the skirt of the dress and on the opposite side was a slit reaching her mid-thigh. She kept her jewelry to a minimum and only wore huge peach morganite stud earrings and her pixie curls wrapped gently around the back of her ears. Her shoes were 4-inch sandals with a peach leather ankle strap and a thin clear strap across her foot to give the appearance of being barefoot. The nails of her slender fingers and toes were painted with the softest shades of peach as if they had been kissed with the color. Evelyn stood behind her and stared at her sophisticated elegance.

"My precious cupcake …", cried Evelyn, "You've battled so many demons to get to this day!"

"Oh Granny, don't cry. I finally decided I won't let anything tear me away from my sweet Raymond.", reassured Shannon.

"Yeah, not even her mother!", blurted Nicole.

Nicole immediately regretted that she had blurted that apparent secret out.

"What? How?", questioned Evelyn.

Shannon was somewhat annoyed that Nicole let that skunk out of the bag. She immediately walked to her grandmother, who was visibly shaken by the news. Vivian and Gloria were stunned that Shannon hadn't said one word about the encounter.

"Bernadette stopped by that morning before I met Ray's family. I was stunned that she even knew where I lived.", Shannon explained.

"Exactly! How did she find out?", Vivian demanded.

"Well when she visited Granny, she saw my address on some boxes I had sent there ...", Shannon provided.

"Oh, no ... Cupcake. Please forgive me ... I didn't know.", pleaded Evelyn.

"It's okay, really. I think it was the closure that I needed. For the first time, I realized my ... mother ... loved me in the best way she could and that was to give me to the two most dependable and loving people she knew.", confessed Shannon.

"Oh, thank you Jesus!", shouted Gloria.

"Amen to that!", Evelyn asserted.

"Yes, your romance has seen enough obstacles. We don't need Bernadette causing any more problems.", fussed Vivian.

"You don't have to worry. She promised she wouldn't return and she hasn't. She definitely won't know where I live after the wedding.", insisted Shannon.

"Sorry Mommy.", whispered Nicole.

"Oh, sweetie it's okay. You didn't do anything wrong. Ironically, that day has been one of the best days of my life.", reassured Shannon as she hugged her daughter.

The planner tapped on the door before she opened it to deliver the news.

"Ladies, the guests have arrived. I've already summoned the men to the Presidential Ballroom and now it's time to present the wedding party; most importantly the future Mrs. Washington-Brown.

Shannon, Vivian, Nicole and Crystal bounced and giggled like four teenage girls. Gloria and Evelyn stood proudly like the mother hens they were; they were so proud and thankful that all their encouragement and prayers over the years were not in vain.

"Ladies, shall we?", the planner guided.

As Shannon neared the ballroom, she heard the live music of the band and when she neared, she saw her all-time favorite saxophonist on the stage. Raymond had hinted at a surprise, but she never would have imagined that he would do something so thoughtful. Never in a million years would she have dreamt that she would have a world-renowned artist play for her, just a simple West-side girl by way of Southwest Detroit, thought Shannon.

Raymond strolled toward her with outstretched hands to present her to friends, family and the local media elite who were honored guests.

"Pixie … damn woman. When I think you can't get any more beautiful, here you come …", Raymond gushed and then swirled her around like a princess at the ball.

The planner handed Raymond the mic so that he could say a few words, but before he could Eleanor approached the couple.

"May I?", asked Eleanor as she reached for the mic.

Raymond gladly passed the mic to his grandmother who was in excellent spirits and whose mind was sharp as a tack that day.

"It is with great honor that I introduce you all to the beautiful, graceful, intelligent and accomplished woman who has accepted my grandson's proposal. But most importantly above any accolades that I could bestow, the most important thing is that she makes my Raymond light up. She means the *world* to him; so, she means *everything* to me. I proudly introduce to you, Shannon Washington, the future Mrs. Shannon Washington-Brown.", beamed Eleanor.

Chapter 15

In the weeks following Shannon's introduction to high society at her engagement party, Joe's world was becoming the opposite of Shannon's; everything was off course or perhaps the problem was it was back on its usual course. He was caught up in his on-and-off-again dysfunctional relationship with Rita and trying to figure out where he would lay his head that night. Additionally, Joe was nearing the last dregs of the money he had received from Vincent and he was plotting how to demand more. He was even debating selling his sports car until he could secure the bag; otherwise, he would have to crash back at his mother's house or that of a random chick. Perhaps, he would take a chance and sleep at his place despite being evicted; hell, why not he thought since the landlord hadn't changed the locks yet. He knew his normal fallback, Shannon, was a completely closed door.

Unknown to him, finding a place to lay his head was the least of his problems as a mysterious pile of evidence had been presented to the police and his name had found its way on the lips of the task force assigned to find him and haul him to booking. As Joe turned the key to his apartment, he knew it would be the last time; however, he had no clue it would be the last time he would be on *that* side of a locked door.

"Joe Johnston.", greeted the officer.

"Who's asking?", Joe demanded as he turned to face the voice.

"You're under arrest for armed robbery and murder.", informed the officer.

The officer and his partner aggressively pushed Joe against the wall and cuffed him; they wouldn't take any chances since they were advised he was armed and dangerous.

"I don't know what you're talking about!", insisted Joe.

"Save the lies for your attorney.", ordered the officer.

The officer began to inform Joe of his rights. Rights, he would barely be able to take advantage of as he didn't have money for a good defense attorney and would have to rely on a public defender.

"Fuck!", screamed Joe.

Joe struggled to get free much to the pleasure of the cops who were itching to deliver a good beat down and a good beat down they did. Each officer took turns punching Joe in the face until the pain silenced him and caused his body to go limp.

"They say he's a tricky one so we need to be extra careful. Make sure he doesn't have a weapon.", instructed the senior officer.

Joe woke up dazed, confused and uncomfortable as he awoke lying on a hard bench. The night's events were confusing to him as he hadn't heard any word on the street that the cops were even on to who committed the dozen pharmacy robberies, he had done months, some even years ago. He wasn't even the mastermind of the job, he thought, so why would his name come up and no one else's? The clearer his head got, he realized that he'd better not snitch; he'd rather do a few months in jail or prison versus being killed.

"Let's get this party started!", shouted Giovanni.

Giovanni entered Vincent's game room with bottles in hand; he and Vincent didn't understand why Raymond wanted to have his bachelor party at Vincent's instead of going out.

"I hear that! I'll have another reason to celebrate once you give me some good news.", Raymond indicated.

"Everything is in motion. I should receive a call any day now.", Giovanni supplied.

"Let's not focus on that. Let's pop some bottles and have a good time.", suggested Vincent.

Vincent took the two bottles from Giovanni and sat them on the bar out of sight. He selected a bottle he had reserved to celebrate the wedding of one of his two best friends; he had no idea that Raymond would be the first to get engaged being that he was so picky.

"I still don't get why you wanted to have your bachelor party here.", nagged Giovanni.

"I just really wanted to be low-key and spend it with just my brothers.", confessed Raymond, "I don't have to pretend with you two. You know what I've gone through to get to this day."

"I feel you … so enough serious talk. Let's play some poker and fill these glasses.", laughed Vincent.

"Hell yeah!", agreed Raymond.

Giovanni was about to chime in when he received a ding on his burner phone.

"Pop the fucking bottles, baby! That piece of shit has been arrested.", shouted Giovanni.

"Fuck yeah! That's what's up!", cheered Raymond.

Vincent joined their laughter as he poured Eagle Rare Bourbon from his aged collection of top-shelf bourbons and whiskeys.

"This is the shit right here!", Giovanni exclaimed as he raised his glass.

"Dudes, you two are the best friends a man could ever have. Much love!", affirmed Raymond.

"Yeah, I'd better love you to break the seal on a $1300 bottle of bourbon!", laughed Vincent.

As they continued to laugh and play cards, Raymond became serious.

"Vincent, of the three of us, you've evolved the most in the past few years. What advice do you have for me as a soon-to-be-married man?", inquired Raymond.

"Just show up for Shannon. Never let her down! Don't give her a chance to recreate the dysfunction she's grown accustomed to.", advised Vincent.

"That's deep … I don't think she really knows she's worthy of being cherished.", Raymond informed.

"Vincent, did you get a psychology degree when you ghosted us back in the day?", teased Giovanni.

"Not hardly … I'm just a better version of Vincent. I'm Vincent 2.0", laughed Vincent.

"Cheers to that!", laughed Raymond.

"Cheers!", seconded the guys.

Shannon and Raymond had discussed their plans for their respective parties and both had agreed that the most important thing for them was to celebrate with their close-knit group; the people who really loved them and applauded their happiness. Since Vincent was hosting the party for Raymond, Shannon convinced her friends to allow her to host her own bachelorette party.

"Come on in Vivian. Everyone's been waiting for *you* so we can get started. They're in the kitchen.", Shannon fussed playfully.

"Hey, girlie, sorry. The baker was a little behind schedule with the cake.", informed Vivian.

"No problem.", Shannon said then kissed her on the cheek.

Shannon and Vivian walked down the narrow hall to the kitchen to join the ladies sitting around the island.

"About time!", teased Gloria.

"Well had we gone to see male strippers, I would have been on time.", teased Vivian.

"Well, I wouldn't have been at *that* party.", informed Evelyn.

"Exactly!", agreed Gloria.

"Yuck, I would hope *not* Granny!", laughed Nicole.

"And you wouldn't be either Ms. Nineteen.", chuckled Evelyn.

"Well if Danny's were still open in Canada, she could have. Nineteen is the legal drinking age there. I miss Danny's. The men used to strip *all the way down* to their birthday suits.", giggled Vivian.

"Thank God, it's closed.", sighed Gloria.

Gloria and Evelyn looked disgusted as they shook their heads in disapproval. Nicole was all smiles as she imagined the fun she could have had.

"Babydoll, don't you get any ideas.", fussed Evelyn.

Nicole's smile turned into laughter which made Evelyn reach over and pinch her.

"I ain't playing!", insisted Evelyn.

"No worries. I'm not in a rush to drink hard liquor, anyway. Besides, I've already tasted wine before and that's enough for me.", reassured Nicole.

241

"Why didn't you want to see strippers? I could have hired some *private* dancers.", Vivian quizzed.

"Girl, after being with Raymond, a small dick just wouldn't do it for me.", laughed Shannon.

"Okay!", laughed Vivian.

"Girl!", giggled Shannon

"I don't want to hear this …", frowned Nicole.

"Oh, Lord! Maybe I should have stayed home.", laughed Evelyn, "I don't want to hear that type of talk about my soon-to-be grandson-in-law."

Gloria laughed and fanned her hand at Evelyn.

"I get it Nicole and Evelyn if you don't want to hear about Ray's penis. That's a bit much for me too!", laughed Gloria, "But believe it or not, Nicole; it's nothing wrong with you participating in a candid discussion with older women about sex. We can teach you some things.", confirmed Gloria.

"Well, that's true. It's not just my cooking that gets their Big Daddy going. Ha, okay!", laughed Evelyn.

Gloria and Evelyn high-fived one another and then leaned on each other in laughter.

"Yuck!", laughed Shannon.

"Gross! I'm *really* not trying to hear all that!", laughed Nicole.

"Well, at least it's not Shannon telling me gross details about her and Joe.", laughed Vivian.

Gloria, Evelyn and Nicole looked as if Vivian had spoken a curse; Joe's name was the last name they wanted to be in anyone's mouth. They all looked nervously at Shannon to gauge her response.

"Sorry, I broke my own rule and mentioned the one that shall not be named.", Vivian apologized.

"Girl, please. It's okay. He's in the past and I haven't heard a peep from him since he dropped off that pitiful bouquet.", Shannon disclosed.

"And you won't since he's been arrested.", murmured Nicole.

"What?", questioned Vivian, "Joe is in jail? No one told *me*."

"Maybe because he was denied bail; so, there was no need for him or his family to contact you for money.", divulged Nicole.

"Did you know cupcake?", asked Evelyn.

Vivian and Gloria speculated as well and gave a nervous side-eye to Shannon as they awaited her response.

"No. I don't keep up with Joe anymore. I have better things to do!", Shannon affirmed.

Evelyn wasn't confident that Shannon really didn't know; Shannon had been known to lie in the past when it came to Joe.

"How did you find out Nicole?", asked Vivian.

"I called my grandmother since we hadn't heard from him in so long … I guess I wanted to see if he was dead or something.", Nicole blurted.

Nicole said it so matter-of-factly and without emotion as she grabbed an appetizer. Evelyn reached for Nicole's hand to reassure her everything would be fine, but Nicole's emotions were so detached from Joe, there really wasn't a need. Evelyn was just so thankful that Raymond had stepped wholeheartedly into a father-figure role; he was just what both her Babydoll and Cupcake needed, stability.

"Well, none of us should be surprised. He no doubt has been involved in criminal activities for decades.", Gloria reminded.

"True. So enough about the one that shall not be named!", Shannon insisted. She lifted her drink and decided to toast to her own special night, "To happiness and the next grand chapters in my life."

"Yes, I'll drink to that!", cheered Gloria.

"Oh, yes!", Evelyn added.

"To my dearest friend, who is like a sister to me. I love you and cheers to your beautiful love story as it unfolds.", marveled Vivian.

Chapter 16

Vivian turned over to grab her cell from the nightstand; the persistent caller would not let her get a few extra winks. Only God knew why she would even want to sleep when she had been having nightmares that something or someone would prevent Shannon from marrying Raymond. Vivian looked at her phone and saw that her mother was the persistent caller. What now, she thought.

"Vivian, why haven't you returned my text messages? I sent messages all day yesterday.", yelled Peggy.

Vivian instantly regretted answering the call.

"Sorry, but I saw it was about Joe and I didn't want to be bothered.", informed Vivian.

"Really Vivian? Your brother really needs you right now; he's been in prison for two months and I can't help but think that he was railroaded. None of my friends have ever seen anybody prosecuted that quickly.", fussed Peggy, "You need to ask Vincent to do something about this!"

"It's sad your friends have experience with this.", joked Vivian.

"Are you going to help him or what?", demanded Peggy.

"No, we are not helping him out. It's time for him to get what he deserves. He's been committing crimes since he was twelve.", Vivian declared.

Peggy was annoyed and fed up; she decided to hang up on Vivian, but as she did, she contemplated the truth behind Vivian's dismissal. She had spent more time and energy on protecting her son and coming to his defense than she had for her girls. Perhaps Vivian was right, it was time to allow the rooster to come home to roost.

Vivian decided that she wouldn't tell Shannon about the call; although Shannon vowed that Joe was a thing of the past, she couldn't chance it. She didn't want Shannon trying to come to Joe's rescue. Vivian would not allow Joe to interfere with Shannon and Raymond's upcoming wedding; even if she had to step in to get rid of Joe, herself. Shannon's and Ray's happy ending was too perfect to be subject to her loser brother.

Larry was not sleeping well either as the days inched closer to the wedding date; Evelyn was a nervous wreck and her tossing and turning disrupted his sleep. The wedding was only three days away and Evelyn was having nightmares about someone or something disrupting the wedding. She had acquiesced and bought an over-the-counter sleep aid, but it was not working well. Larry had insisted she needed it so she would look well-rested and radiant at the wedding, but she knew the real reason was that her tossing was getting on his nerves.

"Honey, I'm going to spend the day with Shannon.", Evelyn informed.

"You said you were cooking my favorite meal today and needed to pick up some things from the grocery store.", reminded Larry, "Are you only doing that because of your nightmares?"

"Don't be silly or selfish. I just want to make sure she doesn't have any last-minute needs.", advised Evelyn.

"That's what Raymond is paying the wedding planner for.", fussed Larry, "Don't be over there making her nervous!"

"Oh, hush. I won't!", snapped Evelyn. "In fact, let me call her right now."

"Good morning, Granny.", greeted Shannon.

"Good morning, Cupcake. I was thinking that I could spend the day with you and take care of anything you might need. I can't believe the wedding is this weekend."

"Funny, Vivian and Gloria suggested the same. I just got off three-way with them.", Shannon pondered.

"Don't be suspicious! We're all just so excited.", explained Evelyn.

"Really?", laughed Shannon, "Okay, well ... see you soon."

"Excellent Cupcake!", giggled Evelyn.

Larry gave Evelyn a stern look when she ended the call.

"Don't call me while you're gone. I'll be in bed.", fussed Larry.

"Oh, so now you're okay with me going over there? A trip!", fussed Evelyn as she hit him with her pillow.

Larry laughed, "No, but I might as well get the sleep you won't let me get at night."

Evelyn leaned over to kiss him before getting ready.

"Okay, big baby.", teased Evelyn.

"That's right, *your* baby; don't you forget it.", laughed Larry.

Shannon had no doubt that they were jittery with fear that she would abandon Raymond at the altar. She did not blame them for their fear, but she had hoped that she had done a decent job at reassuring them; she prayed that Raymond wasn't just as nervous.

The closer the wedding drew near; Vivian and Evelyn were not the only ones who were protective of Raymond and Shannon. Months ago, Vincent had decided to step back after Raymond blew up about his interference, but he was certain that Giovanni might not be as cooperative. Giovanni had invited him over to smoke some of his treasured Cuban cigars; he decided he'd go and make sure Giovanni was in check. When Vincent arrived, the staff informed him that Giovanni was waiting in his office.

"Bro, glad you pulled yourself away from your work.", smiled Giovanni, "Come on in and have a seat."

"Bro, what can I say ... I love what I do.", laughed Vincent.

"The same, but I play just as hard as I work!", joked Giovanni.

Vincent sat on the high-back burgundy leather chair; it looked like it was a remnant from the days of Giovanni's father.

"Can you believe the wedding is in three days? Do you have a date lined up?", inquired Vincent.

"Bro right; it's coming up fast ... Surprisingly, I've decided to go stag.", Giovanni admitted.

"That's a first! Don't tell me the great Giovanni Bianchi can't find a date.", laughed Vincent.

"Never! The fuck!", informed Giovanni, "I'm just keeping my head clear. I have some big moves I'm working on."

"Moves? Like what?", questioned Vincent.

Giovanni ignored Vincent's questions and maintained control of the direction of the conversation.

"Well speaking of moves, Raymond's plan worked out well and things are coming together ... Joe was sentenced to life in prison.", Giovanni informed.

"Damn, that was fast!", exclaimed Vincent.

"I pulled some strings to make it happen, but that's not enough. We need to get rid of his ass, the fuck!", Giovanni exploded.

"Stick to the plan. You know Raymond likes to do things by the book.", insisted Vincent to his hot-headed friend.

"Well sometimes you got to write a new chapter in that bitch!", Giovanni interjected.

Vincent threw his hands up; he knew there was absolutely nothing he could do when Giovanni had his mind set on something. With that statement, Giovanni pulled his burner phone from his pocket. Vincent just hoped that whatever Giovanni did, it wouldn't blow up in Raymond's face, as their past gestures had.

"Hey, boss.", greeted Giovanni's contact.

"We need to meet.", ordered Giovanni.

Vincent knew that was his cue to leave; the less he knew the better. Vincent stood and waved at his friend then left Giovanni's office.

"When?", asked the hired man.

"Give me an hour and we can meet at the funeral home.", instructed Giovanni.

"Cool.", replied the hired hand.

Giovanni disconnected the call. He hoped this final act would be the answer to all the prayers Shannon's loved ones had ever prayed over the years. It was the least he could do for a friend who had been more of a brother to him since childhood.

Shannon placed a call to Raymond; they had decided not to see one another the week of their wedding. It was torture, but at least they had agreed to speak on the phone. She couldn't imagine not hearing his comforting voice if she couldn't see his gorgeous face.

"Hey baby!", purred Shannon.

"Good morning, Pixie! What's up with you today?", Raymond inquired.

"Waiting for my girls and Granny to come over. I just hope they don't get on my nerves.", laughed Shannon.

"That's one of the reasons I decided to go in to work all week. That prevents my friends from monopolizing my time.", chuckled Raymond, "They're so unnerved you'd think they were about to tie the knot."

"Exactly! Lord, help me!", cried Shannon, "I know *everyone* has good reason, but … that's the past. I know I have a *good* man!"

"About time you recognize!", joked Raymond, "But seriously … you are *everything* to me."

"Ray …", purred Shannon.

It was times like that, she wished he was there naked in her arms. Her body was starting to react in ways that could not be quenched properly.

"Look, if I don't get off this phone now, I'll need to blow the dust off one of my old dildos.", laughed Shannon.

"Be strong my Pixie … I don't want you to experience that without my tongue being on the job.", whispered Raymond.

Raymond's seductive tone was all she needed to peak all on her own and her quivering breath revealed that she couldn't wait. Raymond reveled in delight as he heard the effect of his voice and his love on her body. There was no greater boost to his ego than knowing the impact of his mere words on his Pixie. It was enough to motivate his willpower to wait for their wedding night before he touched her again.

Mike, Giovanni's contact, nervously entered the funeral home to meet with Giovanni; the atmosphere was ominous, to say the least. He had heard so many gruesome tales committed by the deadly Bianchi family; although the family now focused the majority of its attention on the legitimate sector, he doubted they all strayed far from their roots.

"Is Gio Bianchi available?", Mike murmured.

"Mr. Bianchi is in the rear viewing room.", directed Carrol.

"Thanks.", replied Mike.

Mike gingerly walked to the rear viewing room; he found it eerie to walk the halls. He figured one false move and he'd be thrown into the crematorium. If he felt nervous beforehand, it did not compare to when he entered the room and saw Giovanni surrounded by his men. Giovanni dismissed the men with a wave of his hand and at that moment he saw the fearlessness for which the Bianchis were known.

"Sir.", gulped Mike.

"I need Joe Johnston six feet under. He's a prisoner in Jackson prison.", informed Giovanni.

Giovanni passed Joe's mugshot with his prisoner number on it to Mike so that no one made any mistakes.

"I have a man inside …", began Mike.

"Save the details. Just make it happen. Here's the money … make it stretch between the two of you.", ordered Giovanni as he lifted the envelope of cash from the table.

Giovanni handed the envelope to Mike for his inspection.

"This is more than enough, Chief! Always a pleasure!", confirmed Mike.

Giovanni dismissed Mike with a smirk; he was thrilled that his plan was in motion and Joe would be sent to hell and would no longer be able to put Shannon through it.

The day that once seemed so elusive was finally upon Shannon and her loved ones. The sky was the bluest it had been in weeks and puffy clouds filled the sky as if they rejoiced with her. The church bells echoed along the street as it announced the celebratory occasion to the Greektown businesses, patrons and wedding guests. It felt like all the angels in heaven were also celebrating the glorious event that was the culmination of Evelyn's and Gloria's prayers.

"My God!", cried Evelyn, "Honey, I never thought I would see this day!"

"Yes …", paused Larry.

Larry vigorously wiped his eyes as he parked the car; he was not able to say much about the wedding without choking up. The couple had decided to marry at Raymond's family church, Old St. Mary's Catholic Church, which was also the family church of the Bianchis. They agreed that they would have Shannon's pastor and Raymond's priest officiate the ceremony; her pastor was from a neighboring church in Greektown, Second Baptist Church of Detroit. It was the oldest African American church in Detroit and her family had attended for generations.

"I don't know what's wrong with me …", sniffled Larry.

"Oh Sweetie, it's okay. You don't have to be strong today.", advised Evelyn.

"Oh yes, I do. I need to be clear-headed in case, she decides to do something stupid!", affirmed Larry.

"I think our girl finally has it together. We are going to be positive and push out all negative thoughts! Understood?", insisted Evelyn.

"Yes, dear.", confirmed Larry.

The two entered the magnificent structure; the cathedral ceiling was breathtaking with colors of gold, green and red perfectly detailing the architectural design of the interior. The pillars stood strong as elements of support and beauty. The Brown family definitely had not spared any expense as they approved the wedding planner to select the prettiest and most delicate of flowers. The pews along the aisle were lined with peach and ivory roses, peonies, white baby's breath and draping green and red ferns.

"Why don't you check in with the wedding planner or her assistant? I need to find Shannon.", suggested Evelyn.

A hesitant Larry nodded in response; he would have much rather preferred to have laid his eyes on his granddaughter. He took a deep breath and remembered the pillar of strength he wanted to be as he walked toward Raymond and his groomsmen. Raymond looked almost as nervous as Larry felt. Raymond was dressed impeccably in his Ivory and gold floral fabric Mandani collar tuxedo; it was a single-breasted Italian-designed blazer with gold buttons and cuff links. A solid ivory satin ascot and ivory red-bottom patent leather shoes polished off his look. The best man and groomsman wore identical suits in black.

"You did it Ray! Shannon's going to be your bride!", Larry reassured as he squeezed Raymond's shoulder.

"I look that nervous, huh?", laughed Raymond.

"You really do.", laughed Larry, "But if it makes you feel any better, I think we're all on pins and needles."

"Not us!", reassured Giovanni as he pointed to Vincent and himself.

"Yeah, we've been keeping our man together!", Vincent laughed.

The priest and the pastor approached the men as everyone was filtering inside to await the ceremony. The priest eyed the nervous groom and decided to add what he hoped would be humor.

"Do we have a runaway groom here?", teased Father Aldo.

Giovanni leaned over to the father.

"Maybe a runaway bride.", whispered Giovanni

Father Aldo sympathized with Raymond and patted him on the back as reassurance.

"God has reassured me that today will be a joyous day!", prophesied Father Aldo.

"Amen! Thank you, God!", chimed Pastor Sutton.

"Thank you, Pastor Sutton. I really appreciate your willingness to co-officiate my wedding.", Raymond offered.

"It's my pleasure and thank you for allowing my wife to play the organ. She was trained on this type of organ and gets so excited whenever she has an opportunity to play one.", Pastor Sutton informed.

Raymond leaned over to Larry for privacy.

"Where is Ms. Evelyn?", whispered Raymond.

"She's checking on Cupcake.", whispered Larry.

Evelyn was thankful that the room designated for the bride was near the entrance and she didn't have to tire herself in search of it. At that moment, she was glad that Larry had insisted that she carry her cane and not give in to vanity and be in pain during the entire event. She entered the room to find everyone hovering close to ensure there would be no mishaps.

"You all look so beautiful! But no one can touch my Cupcake! Oh, my God!", cried Evelyn.

Shannon blushed at the compliment, but she did not say anything. In fact, she had been uncharacteristically quiet and her actions were robotic. No one realized that she was trying to keep her mind distant from the fact of the event otherwise she did not trust herself to keep it together. She would be a blubbering fool if she thought about how blessed she was.

"My matron and maid of honor are perfect. They really chose beautiful dresses.", Shannon complimented.

Vivian and Gloria had selected a dress that could be worn six different ways and no one would be the wiser that it was the same dress. It was a peach sheath column satin dress with an empire waist and an asymmetrical train; Vivian wore her gown with a crisscross bodice secured around her neck and twisted down to her waistband to reveal her slender shoulders and her back. Vivian wore embellished muted gold glitter chain mesh 4-inch platform sandals with a single buckled strapped ankle. Unlike Vivian, Gloria chose to wear her dress modestly as a short-sleeved version with a discrete V-neck that completely covered her back pairing her dress with 2-inch kitten heel sandals with a crisscross muted gold glitter chain mesh with a buckled fastener at the ankle.

The show stopper was indeed Shannon as she should have been. She was as elegant as she was beautiful in her handcrafted masterpiece that hugged all the curves of her frame. She wanted to bare her soul to Raymond and her family; she did not want a veil to hide her face. She placed a simple rhinestone clip in her hair to pin back one side of her pixie curls. She wore an ivory column sheath dress designed with satin with a ruched sleeveless bodice as well as a sweetheart neckline revealing just a slight view of her cleavage. It gave the appearance of a mock bow as she was indeed a gift to Raymond from God above, thought Evelyn. Shannon's brush train was simple yet grand and the dress had a front slit that soared to the top of her thigh to reveal her smooth chocolate leg that was sure to drive Raymond absolutely wild. She wore a muted gold glittered nobble tapered 4-inch heel with a bow.

The ladies noticed that Shannon was constantly inhaling deeply and looked as if she was doing everything in her power not to flee. Evelyn decided she would leave the room and hunt down the wedding coordinator to get the show on the road.

As wonderful and blossoming as everything was for Shannon, it was the converse for Joe in lockup. Yet, he was thankful that he had made a friend in lock up so fast; one that knew the ropes and could look out for him. Prison could be even more deadly than the outside world without the right connections and since he was doing life, he made it a point to connect with the right one. In fact, that friend had helped him get on the cleaning detail of the dining hall. He felt lucky as he mopped the floor and then he looked up and noticed his buddy entering the hall; he was surprised since his friend wasn't scheduled that day.

"Tim, what's up brother?", greeted Joe.

"I just thought I'd sneak in and tell you some great news. I'm about to come into a lot of money.", whispered Tim.

"For real? What are you getting into? Any room for one more?", chuckled Joe hoping to get a few coins.

"Come over here ...", Tim advised.

Tim lured Joe into the blind spot of the one camera in the area and then he scanned their surroundings to be sure they were alone.

"I don't want anyone hearing this.", confessed Tim.

"Sure brother.", Joe reassured as he moved closer to his new friend.

"See this guy is going to give me a shit load of money. I just got to do one thing.", laughed Tim.

"Okay, what's that? Don't be holding out on me.", teased Joe.

"You got it, brother.", whispered Tim.

With those whispered words, Tim overpowered Joe and shanked him several times in the abdomen and then his back. Blood was oozing everywhere from the dozen or so stab wounds he inflicted upon Joe. Then Tim decided he would not take any chances so he covered Joe's mouth and slit his throat. Tim would only get paid if Joe died and he was not going to miss out on that payday.

"Excuse me! We need to start the ceremony now.", begged Evelyn.

"Of course, we are ready to start on time.", reassured the planner.

The planner signaled the party and the organist so that she would begin playing one of the songs on the playlist. Raymond and the men of God took their places to begin the ceremony. Giovanni, Vincent, Larry and Evelyn followed the wedding planner to the hallway to await the ladies to meet them.

"It's time.", announced the planner as she opened the door.

"Ready, Shannon?", asked Vivian.

"Yes.", smiled Shannon, "I'll be out in a minute."

The girls followed Vivian and Gloria to the hallway and then headed to their seats to await the march. Everyone nervously took their places and said silent prayers that nothing would go wrong. The organist stopped playing traditional hymns and the sound engineer began playing the prerecorded instrumental music just as the wedding party stood at the entrance to the sanctuary. The planner directed Vincent and Vivian to begin their march down the aisle then Giovanni and Gloria followed course leaving Larry and Evelyn nervously eyeing the door where Shannon remained. Shannon stood nervously in front of her image.

"Well, girlie! This is it. A new life begins.", whispered Shannon as she continued to inhale deeply.

Eleanor beamed as she witnessed the bridal party approach Raymond. She was overjoyed for her precious boy and

Raymond felt blessed that her mental capacities were very keen that day. The day truly was positioned to be perfect.

The engineer switched the music to a melodic romantic instrumental song for the bride to enter. Raymond and Shannon's folks didn't know if Shannon was really delayed or if their fears made it feel so. Raymond felt his heart begin to sink when he felt Vincent's strong grip on his arm. Vincent's eyes reassured him that there was nothing to fear. Similarly, Larry looked nervously at Evelyn as they stood waiting for Shannon in the vestibule; his eyes suggested he check on Shannon.

"She'll be out momentarily. Our Cupcake has truly grown. She won't let herself down anymore let alone Raymond.", Evelyn reassured.

Larry's eyes said that he was not sure, but his heart would not allow him to move. Then he released a sigh of relief.

"I'm ready.", whispered Shannon as she approached her grandparents.

Evelyn had been holding back her tears all morning long, but she released them like a flood. Once that happened Larry couldn't contain his joy and relief; his tears began to flow as Shannon smiled at them both.

"It's time I marry that incredible guy waiting for me.", smiled Shannon as a single tear ran down her cheek.

The engineer put the song on a loop so it would start over once he saw the doors open to reveal Raymond's Pixie. Shannon's beauty snatched Raymond's breath away from his body when he eyed her.

"Pixie ...", uttered Raymond as he fought back tears.

Raymond inhaled deeply as he watched the most beautiful woman in the world being led to him by the two people who had poured their love into her so that he could bast in the magnificence they had fostered. He felt as if he were the luckiest and most blessed man on the planet. He knew at that moment that nothing would stop their happiness. Larry and Evelyn handed their most prized possession over to Raymond.

"Cherish her, always.", instructed Larry as he placed Shannon's hand in Raymond's.

Larry guided Evelyn to their seats and kissed his own bride on the lips as they sat and directed their attention to the pastor and priest.

"Beloved children of the most high, God. We gather here today to witness the union of this couple who are cherished by You and their families.", announced Pastor Sutton with outstretched arms.

"We stand proudly, as we are bestowed by God with this great honor of wedding Raymond Jefferson Brown II and Shannon Denise Washington.", proclaimed Father Aldo.

"Marriage is one of the greatest joys, honors and duties that God established and should not be entered into lightly.", informed Pastor Sutton.

"Raymond, do you take this precious woman as your wife and promise to honor and cherish her all the days of your life?", questioned Father Aldo.

"I do and I will.", vowed Raymond.

"Shannon, do you take this man given by God to be your husband and do you promise to honor him and cherish him?", asked Pastor Sutton.

"I do and I will.", promised Shannon.

"Raymond, you would like to share some words with your bride, families and the congregation.", announced Father Aldo.

"Thank you, Father.", smiled Raymond then he vowed, "Never in a million years would I have guessed that I would be blessed to know and love a woman as beautiful and selfless as you, Shannon. I vow before God, our families, friends and you that I will always cherish you, defend you and fight to keep our love alive and strong. I would even die for you Shannon. I love you, Pixie."

It took every ounce of strength for Shannon to remain upright, but Raymond was there to steady her as he held her arm for support. His eyes reassured her that he always would.

"With the power vested in me by the great state of Michigan and God, I now pronounce you husband and wife!", proclaimed Father Aldo.

"You may now kiss your bride!", instructed Pastor Sutton.

Raymond unapologetically grabbed Shannon around her hips and pulled her in for a passionate kiss as if the world consisted only of the two of them. The church was filled with shouts of joy from Shannon's family and the more reserved Brown family was not used to such outbursts in church. But the emotions of the occasion had their way with Eleanor and she began shouting and dancing with Evelyn who threw her head back in praise as the organist played a song of celebration.

"Thank you! Thank you, Jesus!", shouted Evelyn.

Distant relatives of the Brown family were certain that Eleanor was indeed suffering from Alzheimer's because there was no way that the refined matriarch would behave as Shannon's middle-class relatives were; shouting and dancing in the church was not becoming so they thought. However, joy can be contagious and it was spreading from loved one to loved one who genuinely supported the couple.

"Yeah!", shouted Vincent.

Giovanni was about to join in with a celebratory shout when he received a text message. He discreetly took out his burner phone and read the text message which indicated the coffin was nailed.

"Hallelujah!", shouted Giovanni.

Raymond and Vincent were surprised by his choice of words to express his excitement but just assumed Giovanni was being funny. Father Aldo, however, saw Giovanni check his phone and knew there had to be more to it; Father Aldo leaned in to whisper.

"Will you need the confessional later?", inquired Father Aldo.

"Oh, yeah, I'm going to need that.", laughed Giovanni, "Hallelujah!"

In all her life, Shannon had never felt so loved and to think it took meeting the sexy, successful, kind, not to forget rich Raymond Brown II for her to feel loved, she thought, he embodied all her hopes and dreams.

"I don't feel worthy of you and the life you plan to give me.", confessed Shannon.

"Neither do I. So, we'll work on feeling worthy together.", Raymond said and then kissed his bride all over again.

Discover the world of the Reflections Series written by
Natasha Hughes Smith

Natasha is a native Detroiter and loves everything about her home state of Michigan. She has loved the art of storytelling and writing since childhood, but only recently decided to tap into that love and gift professionally. Her first novel, Reflections was inspired by a dream she had; she loved the concept so much that she decided it had to be put on paper.

As she finished the story, she realized that she didn't want to leave the family. So, she started thinking of what past actions could have affected the lives of the characters. That's when the prequel, Wealth of Lies, was birthed. Readers will find historical nuggets about Michigan woven throughout the series. Now that the 4th novel of the series is complete, she will start on a stand-alone story. However, readers and fans have requested that she write additional stories to fill in the gap years between each story in the series. So, who knows what the future might hold!

Social Media Connections

https://www.facebook.com/Author-Natasha-Hughes-Smith-100342758595594/

HTTPS://www.Instagram.com/author_Natasha_Hughes_Smith
https://podcasts.apple.com/us/podcast/talking-stories-with-natasha/id1582696146

https://linktr.ee/AuthorNatasha
https://www.tiktok.com/@authornatashahughessmith?_t=8WX9dH
HO130&_r=1

The Reflections Series:

Reflections

What price is too great to pay for the one you love? Is it worth losing your identity to be who they want or need you to be? Vincent, a billionaire playboy, Jeff Woods, a struggling attorney and Vivian Johnston, a corporate executive, are faced with this very question. All that they know will change in an instant.

When the paths of Vincent and Jeff cross, it's a battle for Vivian's love.   It's a story of intensity, money, power, sex, drugs, love, betrayal and revelation with the Motor City as the backdrop; it adds flare to this non-traditional love triangle in this suspenseful romantic thriller.

Wealth of Lies

Wealth of Lies is the prequel to the Reflections series, a suspenseful romance thriller series. John Barrington (Reflections) told Jeff (Reflections) that the history and wealth of his family were built on a foundation of lies. Some secrets went to the grave of John's father, Bernard. During John's childhood, Bernard Barrington was distant and he never knew why. Even finding the love of his life, Josephine, couldn't prevent the path that lay before Bernard. In this novel, you find out what lies laid the foundation of the family and how those lies rippled across time to affect the lives of the Barrington clan.

Boxed in, trapped and caged were all of the ways Josephine, a seamstress, felt her mother wanted to keep her. Josephine Epstein would not live the life her mother wanted her to, nor would she allow anyone to deny her the love of her life, Bernard Barrington. He came from a world of privilege and wealth. Josephine came from a world of hard work and deception. Little did they know that both of their lives had been shaped by their family secrets. But neither would be bound by them.

As Josephine navigated the world of her former high school peers, she saw, all too well, what her mother was denied. But she was not her mother; she wouldn't be denied. Wealth, prestige, respect and Bernard would all be hers. But at what cost?

This story merges the worlds of the working class, the wealthy and the mob to provide a suspenseful story of romance, suspense and thrills. Just like in Reflections, you are in for a shock!

Bianchi

It's 1970s Detroit, and Ricky Bianchi (Wealth of Lies) is the confirmed bachelor that every woman wants and every man wants to be. However, he has grown weary of the parties, wild times and the endless stream of women. His best friend, Bernard Barrington (Wealth of Lies) wants him to settle down like the rest of his friends. However, no acceptable woman captures his heart until Vittoria enters his world.

Vittoria Rossi is tall, striking and undeniably the most beautiful woman that Ricky has ever seen, but elusive. She's the daughter of a meat market owner from a middle-class family in the Woodbridge Community far from the wealthy, sophisticated and elite world to which Ricky aspires.

Can she trust her heart and body with this mobster or is he too worldly and carnal for a simple girl like her? Ricky sees beyond the surface of what Vittoria reveals to everyone else and wants to discover more about her. He wants nothing more than to win her heart and give her the world and she wants it too, but fear cripples her. Something dark lurks beneath the surface in both of their worlds that threatens everything they want.

Discover the world of the Reflections Series; it's a suspenseful romance thriller ride that will leave you speechless and wanting more.

Books can be purchased online from Amazon and other major book retailers online.

www.ingramcontent.com/pod-product-compliance
Lightning Source LLC
Chambersburg PA
CBHW071132260626
47162CB00003B/759